CloudWorld At War

Also by David Cunningham:
Cloud World, *Faber and Faber, 2006*

David Cunningham

CloudWorld
At War

Kennedy & Boyd

Kennedy & Boyd
an imprint of
Zeticula
57 St Vincent Crescent
Glasgow
G3 8NQ
Scotland

http://www.kennedyandboyd.co.uk
admin@kennedyandboyd.co.uk

ISBN-13 978 1 904999 90 4
ISBN-10   1 904999 90 5

"Look at the stars! look, look up at the skies!
O look at all the fire-folk sitting in the air!
The bright boroughs, the circle-citadels there!"

The Starlight Night
Gerard Manley Hopkins

What Has Been...

On a planet entirely covered in a thick cloud layer, mountain peaks – thousands of miles apart – rise up from the restlessly shifting, vaporous ocean. Some of these peaks have citadels standing on them. Each of the citadels is built in layers. The layers narrow as they rise and are encircled by fortified walls, the topmost layer crowned by a marble palace. The true nature of the cloud depths is an abiding mystery to all the citadels' inhabitants – some believe it to be the domain of the god Omnium, who created their world.

Travel and trade between the citadels is by aëro:cruisers: huge airships with open decks and tubular, hand-operated engines called impellers that run the length of their hulls. Over several centuries the different citadels in the northern hemisphere have engaged in conflicts with one another for control of the best trading currents: streams of cold air that can carry aëro:cruisers and their cargo to their destinations more quickly. These battles culminated in the Hemispheric Wars, which, though long since ended, have left unresolved tensions between different regimes.

The King of one of the citadels – Heliopolis – is returning from a diplomatic mission when his aëro:cruiser gets into trouble and plunges into the clouds. His son, Marcus, who lives an isolated life in the palace, insists that a mission be staged to search for him, in spite of the onset of autumn and the many storms – called tumults – that are brewing all over the cloudscape. Two aëro:cruisers, well crewed and equipped with all manner of ordnance, embark on this mission, with Marcus aboard one of them. He soon discovers, however, that danger lies closer to home. Seeking absolute power, General Titus, leader of the citadel's armed forces, attacks his aëro:cruiser.

Marcus and the aëro:cruiser's crew – called Cloudfarers – are plunged into a terrifying new world beneath the clouds. Called Daldriadh, it is a freezing, snow-clad, permanently overcast place. Among the survivors of the stricken vessel are the young female first officer, Rhea, the pilot, Theus, the navigator, Nestor, and an ordinary Cloudfarer called Magnis. Using what few resources they have at their disposal, the survivors fashion an ice yacht out of the wreckage of their aëro:cruiser and set off in search of some link between this world and their own. On the way they are ambushed by the Nullmaurs – squat creatures, who speak a fragmented version of the cloud dwellers' own language and make up for their abbreviated height by being tirelessly brutal.

These creatures command a basic technology of weapons and flying machines, salvaged from the wreckage that has fallen through the clouds over many centuries. Using these, they persecute a neighbouring race, the Eihlans. Peaceable – if somewhat passive – the Eihlans are farmers, who have also salvaged wreckage from the skies but created a whole religion around it.

The Nullmaurs capture Marcus and the Cloudfarers and hope to further oppress the Eihlans by displaying their 'sky gods' in chains. They transport the captives to the Eihlan village in heavekairts – wooden contraptions borne by beasts called Grashiels. On the way, however, the imprisoned Cloudfarers escape by seizing their captors' weapons and firing them at the overhanging branches of trees to bring down a hail of needle sharp icicles. Reaching the Eihlan village, they take the chance to rest a while in its semi-subterranean lodges (called 'holms'.)

Guilty at the way in which centuries of aeronautical conflict across the cloudscape have supplied the Nullmaurs with the means to persecute their neighbours, the Cloudfarers help the Eihlans to reinforce their defences and train them in the art of combat. Marcus also forms a close friendship with Breah – the daughter of one of the Eihlan elders, Aònghas – and discovers in her company a warmth and ease he has never experienced before with anyone his own age.

Before long, however, the Nullmaurs launch a concerted attack on the village. Fighting side by side, the Eihlans and

Cloudfarers manage to repulse them, albeit with the loss of several lives. In the aftermath, a number of Cloudfarers swear an oath to remain in Daldriadh for the time being and continue to protect the Eihlans. Meanwhile, Marcus, Rhea, Theus, Magnis and Nestor set off towards the base of the vast mountain – called the Ins'lberg by the Eihlans – upon which Heliopolis sits, many miles above.

The ascent of the Ins'lberg is long and arduous. Marcus and the others traverse buttresses and inch up flutings of ice, braving crevasses and avalanches. They are sustained in part by the strength of their lungs, accustomed to thin, dry air. They also tether themselves to canvas balloons filled with a special gas called proleyne. Devised by Magnis, the balloons lend them extra buoyancy on the later stages of their climb. In spite of this, one of their number – the navigator, Nestor – perishes, plucked from the rock face by carnivorous flying creatures which remain unseen amid the thick mist of the cloud layer.

Though deeply distressed by the loss of Nestor, the others have no choice but to push on. Soon after, they emerge from the clouds and see Heliopolis in the distance once again – its contours majestic against the great span of blue sky that frames it. Edging towards the shelter of an orchard at the fringes of the mountain peak, Marcus prepares himself for all that still lies ahead. He must not only find a way of fomenting revolution among the oppressed citizens of Heliopolis, but also confront the man who betrayed him and his father…

Prologue

Out over the cloudscape...

Icy and wind scoured, it stretches away to the far horizon.

In certain places it is raked into undulating ridges, some straight, some curved. Occasionally, these ridges merge up to form patterns of great complexity.

Between the ridges rise plateaus of creamy featurelessness, with undecided borders. In other places the air currents sculpt the cloud into craggy, tapering peaks.

It is a lonely, trackless region...

And yet...

In the far distance, three aëro:cruisers emerge from behind the swollen peak of a cumulus cloud. Two of them are lashed together and revolving slowly counter-clockwise. The third – a trading vessel called a Mercanteer, with a blunter prow and more girth amidships – hovers slightly apart...

The two lashed-together aëro:cruisers fire repeatedly upon one another. The arcing cannon shells glow white hot, like an exchange of shooting stars. Their trails of smoke weave a frail web around both vessels. Some of the stray shells vault the deck of the Mercanteer and even glance against its hull. It moves further off, still observing...

One of the aëro:cruisers begins to sink. Heeled over at a sharp angle, the other is dragged inexorably down with it. Soon they vanish, leaving not the faintest blemish on the face of the cloudscape. All is still again, the only sound the moaning of the wind. After some time, the Mercanteer ejects two wooden gliders. Their hinged wings flapping, they gain height and bank eastward. The Mercanteer itself continues to patrol the arches and twisting columns of cloud...

More than an hour later, the surviving aëro:cruiser breaks the surface of the cloudscape again, miles from where it vanished. Scorch marks streak its hull and it trails severed cables. After drifting for a while, it points its prow westward and departs…

Concealed in an ever-shifting canyon, the Mercanteer follows at a discreet distance, unobserved…

.

CloudWorld At War

I.

Return to Heliopolis

Marcus, Rhea, Theus and Magnis emerged from the cloudscape where it met the edge of the mountaintop. The cloud was banked up, like the foaming crest of a wave that constantly threatened to break but never quite did. Bruised, cut, begrimed and utterly exhausted by league after league of struggle on the ascent from Daldriadh, they edged forward and gazed up at the view that gradually solidified before them out of the receding cloud.

Just a few yards away were the fringes of the orchard. Windfall fruit that had dropped from branches and rolled away before it could be picked sat rotting at their feet. Tendrils of cloud snaked upwards, curling between the tree trunks. Beyond the orchard lay the gentle slope of the fields – ploughed into fresh, glistening furrows after the harvest – then the first of the citadel's walls. Called the 'Great Wall,' it was dotted with sentinels. Their heads and torsos protruding above it, they patrolled its whole circumference, moving restlessly back and forth. Above them, the rest of Heliopolis looked magnificent, the contours of its different layers sharply defined in the high, clean air.

Concealed by the brimming ground mist, as long as they crouched, Marcus and the others continued to edge forward. Crouching was agony, since for hours already they had bowed their heads beneath the air sacs and tethered proleyne stoves to which they had been harnessed during the final stages of the ascent. But as soon as they entered the orchard they were able to drop their packs and straighten up. Every muscle Marcus possessed was aching. No matter which way he moved or which posture he assumed there was a symphony of protest from different parts of his body. There were weals on the skin under his arms too, where the straps of the harness had dug into it. The only slight respite from discomfort was provided by a breeze blowing off the cloudscape, which cooled the damp back of his tunic.

They paused again at the very edge of the orchard. By now they had definitely left the clouds behind. But, beyond the treetops, the upward slope of the fields was less clear than it had been a few moments before. A thickening haze encroached upon it. Marcus frowned questioningly at Magnis.

"More ground mist?" he asked.

Magnis shook his head.

"Too late in the day – it would have cleared up there already. No, they're burning stubble now that the harvest is over. Then they'll till the soil and re-seed it."

"Of course."

He lowered his gaze to the orchard once again. It was thickly planted and filled with webs of shadow. None the less, the sun stole in thin shafts between the branches and laid glowing coins of light on the ground.

"It's weird isn't it," he observed. "The trees got sparser and sparser then vanished altogether when we began to climb the Ins'lberg; yet here, so many miles above, there are orchards and pines and crops growing."

"Perhaps the moisture that the sun burns off the cloudscape gives them the nutrients they need," offered Rhea.

Marcus nodded.

"Perhaps."

As he continued to peer into the orchard, he saw several figures moving between the trees. They were so dark and indistinct that they seemed to merge with the trunks when they passed behind them. He and the others moved forward into the orchard, eyes adjusting to the diminished light. None of the figures looked like a guard – none had the rigid posture or muscular outline lent by body armour; nor did any of them wield a sword. Instead they all had packs slung over their shoulders and were carrying wicker baskets. Every now and then they crouched close to the ground, bending carefully at the knee so as not to spill any of the baskets' contents. They were collecting the last of the season's fruit, before it rotted where it had fallen.

Marcus watched them a little longer. As he did so he felt another surge of tiredness crest within him, bringing dizziness in its wake. It was so powerful it made him rock slightly on his heels. Shaking it off, he took a deep breath and said, "Well, this is it."

"How exactly do we introduce ourselves?" asked Theus.

"Very politely," replied Rhea. "Take off your swords. We don't want to alarm them."

They unclipped their sword belts and lay them down in the long, tousled grass. Then they stepped forward.

"Hello," said Marcus softly.

The Farmers spun round, fruit flying from their over-laden baskets. They clutched at one another and began to retreat up the slope. Though their eyes were wide with surprise as they all stared at him, Marcus detected no flicker of recognition.

"We don't want to harm you," he told them. "I know it seems impossible. But I am…"

"Magnis?"

One of the Farmers – taller than the others and broad-shouldered, with fair hair and a plain, open face – squinted past Marcus.

Magnis stepped forward, beaming, arms outstretched.

"Brebix!" he cried.

Magnis and Brebix embraced one another. Everyone else stood around, slightly at a loss. The other Farmers continued to eye Marcus, Rhea and Theus with suspicion.

Turning to Marcus, Magnis wiped his shining eyes and said, "My second cousin."

Marcus smiled at Brebix with genuine relief. This, hopefully, would at least make the first stage of the task before them a little easier.

"Pleased to meet you," he said.

Brebix nodded vaguely at him then stepped back from Magnis and looked him up and down, eyes settling on his bandaged hands.

"You look terrible," he said. "The last we were told you had been assigned to the mission to search for the King. When we heard nothing more we assumed you were dead: lost in the cloud depths. How do come to be here?"

"We've uh... we've just arrived back," replied Magnis.

Brebix looked past him, to where the mountaintop slipped away into the brimming cloud.

"Back? From *where*?" he asked, bewildered.

Magnis sighed.

"I... I could tell you Brebix, but I'm not sure you'd believe me right now," he replied. "We were betrayed, but we survived and fought our way back by relying on one another... We've seen things you can't imagine. We've discovered that our world is vaster and deeper than anyone could have believed."

He paused, as if uncertain how much more to disclose and glanced at Rhea. Gesturing at Marcus, she said, "This is King Antior's son."

Brebix peered at Marcus, rubbing his face.

"Really?" he said. "I'm sorry, I didn't recognise you. We did have a portrait of you in our home. But it was a copy of a copy of a copy. It didn't look like you – it didn't look much like anyone really."

"It's okay," replied Marcus, holding up his hands. "I didn't expect a hero's welcome."

Though Brebix blinked slightly at this, he said nothing.

"Please," said Rhea, in as gentle a tone as possible. "It's crucial that we know everything that's happened since the aëro:cruisers left to search for the King. Can you tell us?"

Brebix glanced uncertainly at Magnis, who nodded and said, "We can't put anything right until we know."

"All right...all right," Brebix replied, sighing heavily, as if weighed down by the dismalness of what he was about to tell them. "A few days after we saw the aëro:cruisers leave, a large detachment of guards came down to our layer. We didn't recognise any of them. They were third or fourth generation Cloudfarers, very superior all round, in their tone and bearing. They said that martial law would be imposed, just temporarily, to keep order until the King returned. They said signals received just before it went down suggested that the *Regulus* had been the victim of an unprovoked attack by a warship from one of the Northern Citadels. They said that the economy would have to be militarised to confront any further imperialistic aggression that might arise. We had no idea what they were talking about at first. But it turned out to mean that we'd all have to work a lot harder on a lot less food and rest. Every spare effort would go into building new aëro:cruisers. Henceforth, only men would work in the fields – and work much longer shifts. Women would stay inside the Laborium, sewing canvases for air sacs and suchlike."

Rhea snorted at this but Brebix offered only a listless shrug in response.

"Children too young to work would be kept out of the way in the Juvenum, instead of playing in the fields under the watch of their parents, like before" he continued. "And only pure-bred Cloudfarers – that's what they called themselves…I remember because they looked at us all with such contempt when they said it – would be guards and sentinels in the lower reaches of the citadel. Those Cloudfarers who came from Farming or Artisanal layers would not be allowed to descend and visit their families for the time being. They said that all this had been agreed upon by the Ministers in the Executive; that it had to be, for the security of the 'Polis and everyone in it."

"And you believed them?" asked Theus, unable to keep note of dismay from creeping into his voice.

Brebix looked at him, unmoved by his tone.

"We are taught from birth to accept what we are told from above," he replied flatly. "If these changes had been assented to on high and were for the good of the citizenry at large, who were we to question them?"

He paused. At last his impassive expression faltered.

"But we soon realised that things had changed far more than we thought. We were used to long shifts, but these new ones were inhuman: twelve, fourteen hours without a break. If anyone in the fields flagged or made a mistake they were beaten mercilessly by the guards. The women in the Laborium weren't allowed to say a word to one another unless it was about work. There was a strict curfew too – no one allowed out of their dwellings after nightfall, unless they were going on shift. I mean life under the King was…"

He trailed off and glanced at Marcus.

"It's all right. Tell us whatever you want," Marcus urged him. "After all we've been through you're not going to tread on my sensibilities, believe me. And it's important that we know everything."

Brebix nodded and offered a grudging smile.

"Life… *before* wasn't so wonderful," he continued. "It was mainly routine and drudgery and knowing your place. But it wasn't cruel; it wasn't violent. This was something different altogether."

"Has anyone tried to resist?" asked Rhea.

"There were a few skirmishes at first, when the guards tried to beat the older, slower workers in the fields," said Brebix. "But they were quickly put down. Like I said before, we're used to accepting the will of those above. And we have our children's safety to think of. These 'pure breds'… they're pitiless: the kind of people who douse the smallest flame of disobedience with a deluge of cruelty."

"What's happened since this new regime started?" asked Marcus.

"About a week after both aëro:cruisers left, only one came limping back," Brebix told him. "One of its impeller casings was partly smashed – you could see the twisted blades glistening inside it. It was trailing severed lanyards and some of its air sacs had collapsed. We were told that Scythian warships, lurking on the fringes of the eastward trading currents, had attacked it and the other in a new ambush. The King was dead: lost in the cloud depths – and now the Prince too. Heliopolis had been…how did they put it? 'Forced into war by unprovoked aggression.' Martial law would be maintained. The next evening we were corralled onto the walls at sword-point. General Titus appeared on one of the Palace balconies far above. We were told that the Prime Minister and other members of the Executive had agreed that he should continue to lead us and assume a new title: Imperator. But we didn't see the Prime Minister on the balcony. The Kabal sentinels prodded us with their swords and we cheered him. Then we went straight back to our dwellings to observe the curfew"

"And there was no rebellion against Titus?" asked Rhea.

"By then our layer was infested with Kabal guards watching our every move. It all seemed very suspicious, of course, but we didn't know what to believe. The problem now is that we're barely allowed to talk to one another, as I told you, so no news gets around except Kabal propaganda and directives. There may be small cells of people planning some kind of disobedience, but I haven't heard of anything."

As he said this, Brebix glanced back towards the smoke-wreathed fields.

"What is it?" asked Magnis.

"If we're out of sight too long the guards will come looking for us," said Brebix. "We'll have to get back soon."

"Can you get us into the citadel?" asked Marcus urgently. "Hide us in your dwelling for a while?"

Brebix looked away, shaking his head. The other Farmers shifted from foot to foot, as if even by considering this he was imperilling them too.

"I know it's a lot to ask," said Magnis. "But we can't stay out here. The Kabal would find us sooner or later. We have nowhere else to go."

"And if I do help you... then what?" asked Brebix.

Fighting another onslaught of tiredness, Marcus said, "We all desperately need rest." He nodded towards Magnis's bandaged hands. "And some time to heal and regain our strength. Then..."

He glanced at Rhea, who shook her head imperceptibly. She was right: now was not the time to share with Brebix all his plans for an uprising and idealistic vision of a new, people's republic. In the current situation they would sound ridiculous, even insane.

"Then we'll see what we can do…" he finished lamely.

Brebix still looked uncertain.

"I will be placing my family in mortal danger," he murmured, as much to himself as to the others.

"I…" began Marcus.

Magnis stepped closer to Brebix.

"You can trust him Brebix," Magnis said. "I swear it. I'd never met him until just before we left aboard the *Noble Quest*. I expected a pampered little brat – spoiled and self-centred. True enough, he was a bit awkward at first and didn't seem to have much of a clue about life outside the Palace. But right from the start he treated us all with respect and was eager to help whenever he could. And since we fell into that other world I've seen him do things I wouldn't ever have thought possible from someone his age. He doesn't see any of us as being beneath him. He means what he says."

Marcus ducked his head and stared down at his feet, abashed in spite of his tiredness at so earnest an endorsement. Brebix still seemed unconvinced. But before he could reply they were all startled by an overarching rumble that was so deep it seemed to acquire a physical force and pressed down upon them, flattening the tops of the trees. Everyone looked up, but could only glimpse fragments of sky, glinting like shards of sapphire between the restless leaves. So Farmers and fugitives alike hastened wordlessly down the slope, back towards the fringes of the orchard and the lapping cloud. As soon as they emerged from the trees they raised their eyes towards the citadel.

At first there was nothing to see – and indeed the rumbling sound had started to diminish. But just a few moments later a dark, bulbous shape began to emerge around the rightmost edge of the Cloudfarers' layer. Dazzled by the sun, Marcus thought it had to be the brawny shoulder of a storm cloud on the horizon – after all, sharply changeable weather was far from unknown at this time of year. Shielding his eyes, he took a closer look.

No – it wasn't a distant storm cloud at all; it lay much closer. It was, in fact, a mass of black smoke, swelling and spreading. But where could it be coming from?

The answer was soon provided. Another shape emerged from the edge of the Cloudfarers' layer, framed by the smoke. It was paler, with more mass, more solidity. Marcus's eyes quickly identified it. This was a Mercanteer – its somewhat graceless outline and immense girth amidships were unmistakable. But was it the *same* Mercanteer from Selenopolis that had become embroiled in Titus's attack on the *Noble Quest*? It bore all the signs of having done so: splintered gunwales, streaked scorch marks on the hull. But these injuries could have been sustained in the last few minutes' conflict, which Marcus and the others had heard but not witnessed. None the less, he felt sure it was the same vessel. And as it moved ponderously into full view he saw the reason for the smoke.

The Mercanteer was in trouble – graver trouble than he'd first imagined. Its hull was breached. Not only that, it was on fire.

II.

The Mercanteer

The noise had died away completely now. But there was some indefinable quality to the ensuing silence that told Marcus and the others it signified a pause in hostilities rather than the aftermath. The smoke had thinned slightly too. It remained thick only where it clung to the underside of the hull, like a black cushion that was straining to bear the vessel up. The Cloudfarers aboard had presumably managed to fight their way to the source of the fire in the hold and get it under control. Marcus could easily imagine them edging along companionways in a crouch, eyes screwed up, damp rags pressed to their noses and mouths.

The Mercanteer now lay about fifty yards off from the citadel and was edging sideways with its prow pointed at an oblique angle towards the largest of the landing stages.

As it continued to drift diagonally, Marcus hissed to Rhea, "Is it the same one that saw Titus attacking us do you think?"

"I suppose it must be," she replied. "But what I can't understand is how it has taken so long to follow the *Valorous Mission* back from the Soriana Abyssal."

Theus shook his head wonderingly.

"Maybe they had to stop first and make repairs," he said. She nodded and continued to gaze upwards.

"They could have been here for some time, concealed in the cloud banks a few miles out from the citadel," offered Magnis. "Maybe they've been observing it through their telescopes, searching for signs of upheaval."

Before they could speculate any further the tiny, frail looking figure of a lookout advanced irresolutely onto the narrow platform that jutted from the Mercanteer's bridge. Marcus couldn't help but sympathise with the lookout's reluctance to be so exposed. Pausing at the end of the platform, clutching two brightly coloured flags, the man launched into a complex series of gestures.

"Can anyone make out what he's saying?" Marcus asked.

Shading his eyes, Theus squinted upwards.

"Barely," he conceded. "We need Lucis here – he has much sharper eyes than the rest of us... Let's see."

They all continued to peer up at the Cloudfarer as his gestures became more urgent – presumably in response to whichever message was being transmitted by his opposite number in Heliopolis.

"He's saying that the Mercanteer observed an attack by one Heliopolitan vessel upon another near the Soriana Abyssal... He's saying that both vessels foundered in the cloud depths but that only one emerged...He's saying that the surviving vessel also fired on the Mercanteer..."

"But why would they..." began Magnis.

"*Wait*...This is important," interrupted Theus, still struggling to see. "He's saying that the Mercanteer launched two ornithopters – special ones, equipped for long range journeys – to report back to Selenopolis about a perfidious attack by one Heliopolitan vessel upon another."

Marcus and Rhea exchanged a guardedly hopeful look. This at least meant that news – however indirect – of Titus's treachery had spread elsewhere in the hemisphere.

"He's saying that confederates of General Titus Grath have been detained in Selenopolis and charged with complicity in regicide by planting a bomb aboard the Heliopolitan vessel *Regulus*... He demands an explanation, on behalf of the Republican Government of Selenopolis, of the acts he has described and the conduct of whichever interim regime currently governs Heliopolis."

"Good for him," muttered Rhea.

Lowering his arms, the lookout gripped the railings of the platform and awaited a reaction from Heliopolis.

Standing in the narrow, shifting territory between the trees on one side and the banked cloud on the other, the fugitives waited too. There was no sound of activity from the fields – no slap of earth being turned or rasp of a plough being dragged. All the Farmers had paused in their labours, heedless of chastisement, to stare at the scene developing above. So had the sentinels ranged along the fortified walls.

As Marcus strained his eyes upwards, the drifting hull of the Mercanteer passed in front of the sun. It immediately became easier to see, with the upper reaches of the citadel snapping into clearer focus too. A few seconds later another figure appeared at the edge of the main landing stage. Only visible from the waist up, it paused then began to pace back and forth.

The figure paced only a short distance each time, before turning round again and retracing its steps. Its torso was twisted slightly towards the floating Mercanteer, in a posture of keen vigilance, while its scarlet cloak streamed behind it in the wind. This whole display conveyed an impression of churning aggression, which only constant movement could prevent from boiling over. At one point it turned to signal and shout orders to subordinates, who remained out of sight, further back on the landing stage. There was something about its confident body language that delivered a thud of recognition to the centre of Marcus's chest. He felt certain that it was Titus.

Titus – the repository of all his hatred, still living and breathing. Titus – the man who had assassinated his father and tried to kill him; who had grimly dismantled, piece by piece, all the certainties upon which his life had been founded. Titus – the man who had been a surrogate father, the one to whom he had looked for guidance during the King's long absences. Titus – whose vainglory had inaugurated all the grievous events of the past few months. As he continued to gaze up at the restlessly pacing figure, he felt loathing writhe within him, painfully entwined with grief and desire for revenge. His heart seemed to be labouring to pump the blood around his body, as if rage had thickened it.

No sooner had these thoughts and emotions overwhelmed him than the sun flared out again from behind the starboard side of the Mercanteer's drifting hull. Marcus threw his hand back up, shielding his eyes just in time to see Titus turn smartly from the edge of the landing stage, cloak snapping around his torso, and raise his arm in a new signal. As fleeting and distant as this gesture was, it drenched Marcus in a chill sense of panic and foreboding.

"No...no, he can't...he musn't," said Rhea in a hoarse, fractured tone, clearly prey to the same dread as he.

The next few seconds seemed stretched out to unbearable length. Then it happened... A dense barrage of shells erupted from the serried rows of cannons on either side of the landing stage and pummelled the Mercanteer. The sound of cannon fire rolled around the landing stage itself like caged thunder. The Mercanteer convulsed, the lanyards that connected the hull to the air sacs straining, some even snapping. Two of the air sacs deflated almost instantly, the others collapsing inwards to fill the void created. There was an explosion on the underside of the hull, amidships. Several flailing, burning bodies fell from it. The speed at which they fell meant that the flame that smothered them was elongated until it looked like a reddish orange teardrop. Only a few seconds later they vanished into the tree tops of the orchard, further round the mountainside from where Marcus stood. Columns of smoke rose to mark the places they had landed. Other falling chunks of debris gouged blackened craters out of the fields, scattering the watching farmers.

The lookout on the Mercanteer now hung from the shattered railing of his platform by one hand, clawing at it with the other, legs swinging wildly. The hull was breached in several places too, revealing the horizontal divisions of the decks within. More gouts of black smoke issued from the breaches. Marcus guessed that some produce in the hold – a vat of tallow, perhaps – had caught fire.

With an effortful groan that rose in pitch and volume, the Mercanteer's already damaged impellers ground into motion as its commander tried to move it, stern first, out of the cannons' range. At the same time those members of its crew who had managed to fight their way through smoke and flames and reach its own cannons loosed a few token shells back towards the citadel. A couple found their target, creating avalanches of broken masonry, which tumbled down the sloping sides of the Cloudfarers' layer and smashed across the fortified walls below amid a commotion of fleeing sentinels.

But this sparse volley was nothing compared to the next onslaught from the citadel. It sheared off Mercanteer's starboard impeller casing like the rind peeled from a piece of fruit. The shells also bent back the exposed blades of the impellers themselves as easily as a strong breath passing over strands of hair. The aft castle, containing the crew's quarters, was reduced to a blizzard of spinning charred wood. More of the air sacs puckered, sagged and deflated. Crewmembers slid across the sharply tilted deck and fell to their doom, the sundered gunwales unable to stop them.

The Mercanteer continued to sink, stern first, towards the clouds. The sound of its still labouring impellers was like the lamentation of a wounded beast. Marcus and the others edged back down the incline to gain a clearer view of its inexorable descent.

A few moments later the stern had vanished, devoured by the foaming edge of the cloudscape. The rest of the vessel rapidly followed, vanishing all the way up to the foredeck. But the prow – the only part still visible – seemed to pause. Wracked by a single shudder, it remained upright for a few more seconds before tilting inward towards the mountainside. Then, with a resounding crash that transmitted itself across the intervening rock and up through the fugitives' already trembling legs, the Mercanteer landed.

"The stern must have lodged against something further down, out of sight," said Rhea. "Maybe in a crevice or against an outcrop of rock."

Theus nodded.

"Something substantial enough to stop its fall anyway," he added.

"But for how long?" asked Marcus.

They were all aware that the Mercanteer might linger in its current position only very briefly. But they remained rooted to the spot by the sense of awe mingled with fear that the spectacle of its foundering had induced in them. These emotions were dispelled a few seconds later, however, when a small number of figures staggered out of the banked cloud and collapsed onto the air sacs.

"Survivors!" exclaimed Magnis.

Before anyone could stop him, he picked up his discarded sword belt, refastened it and set off at considerable speed around the curve of the mountainside, keeping close to the fringes of the orchards, lest he be spied from the Great Wall. It occurred to Marcus that becoming embroiled in the aftermath of the attack they had just witnessed didn't exactly fit in with their goal of remaining concealed from the Kabal at all costs. Then again, it might be possible to learn more from the Selenopolitans about whether or not their citadel had already dispatched further aëro:cruisers to challenge Titus's regime. With this thought uppermost in his mind, he retrieved his sword and followed close on Magnis's heels, paying silent tribute to his comrade's courage. Rhea and Theus paused for only a fraction of a second before doing likewise.

Nearing where the survivors lay, Marcus exchanged the grassy terrain for the more treacherous, moisture-soaked surface of the canvas air sacs – collapsed upon themselves and overlaid with tangled webs of severed rigging. Twice he felt his feet sliding out from under him and nearly fell before regaining his balance. Approaching the nearest Selenopolitan, he crouched beside him. The man had managed to raise himself onto his knees and was coughing fiercely between deep draughts of air.

"Can you speak?" Marcus asked, placing a hand on his shoulder.

The man looked up. His eyes were wide with fear and astonishment, the areas around the pupils gleaming an intense white compared to the rest of his smoke blackened features.

"Will your citadel be sending reinforcements?" Marcus persisted, guilty at interrogating someone in so parlous a condition. "It's crucial that we know."

The man bowed his head, struggling to control his coughing. Then, with a grimace, he began to speak, barely audible.

"Didn'…"

But he had barely begun the second syllable before sounds of commotion in the orchard claimed both his and Marcus's attention. Looking round, Marcus could just about make out something glinting here and there in the thin beams of light that filtered down between the branches. Soon the glints converged and resolved themselves into a detachment of Kabal guards.

In most respects, they looked just like the guards Marcus had been accustomed to watching from the Palace balcony every day of his life. Only the fact that each one was wearing a black armband identified them as Kabal. Rivalling the trunks of the trees in their girth and rigid, upright bearing, they paused for a few seconds, peering into the curtain of mingled cloud and smoke that reared up before them. Then, detecting movement amidst it, they drew their swords and set off at a run down the incline, heading towards the fugitives.

III.

Titus Ascendant

Even as he rose and drew his own sword, Marcus felt his arms and legs aching almost unbearably. Though a burst of adrenalin had dispelled the exhaustion that clogged his mind, he could still sense it on the fringes, held at bay but ready to return at any moment. Close by, Rhea, Theus and Magnis also prepared themselves to confront the guards. He could tell, from the heaviness of their movements that they too were summoning every last particle of strength they possessed.

Very soon the guards were upon them. Lent extra momentum by the downward slope, they approached shoulder to shoulder, like an inundation – albeit one endowed with thought and purpose. One of them peeled off towards Marcus.

Gripping his sword with both hands, Marcus raised it above his head and prepared to repel a blow, which would surely have colossal strength behind it. No matter how tightly he held the sword, he knew that his chances of surviving the onslaught were slim. Yet in the very last second before the guard was upon him, he felt his clenched knuckles enfolded by another, larger pair of hands, which lent instant extra strength to his stance.

The blades clashed, beads of moisture spraying from both. But Marcus managed to stand his ground. Brought to an abrupt halt, the guard slewed sideways and went sprawling. None the less, being well trained to react swiftly to such unexpected developments, he rolled over just once then sprang back to his feet.

During the few moments that the guard was sprawled on the ground, Marcus glanced over his shoulder. Doing so, he saw that the Selenopolitan had indeed reached up with the little strength he still possessed to help him hold the sword. They exchanged the briefest of smiles before the light dimmed in the injured man's eyes and he slumped down again, passed out. Resisting the urge to help him in some way, Marcus prepared instead to re-engage their opponent. A split second later, he was defending himself once more.

All around him, on the strangely rumpled, uneven field of conflict formed by the deflated air sacs, his comrades were also deeply involved in fighting off the Kabal guards (who struggled to discern their true identities through the misty air.) Even Brebix and the other Farmers had, after a brief hesitation, entered the fray – though only to attend as best they could to the Selenopolitans, most of whom lay ominously motionless and insensible where they had fallen. The one saving grace in the whole dismal scenario was the absence of any Kabal reinforcements; it was clearly assumed that the small number of troops already dispatched would be equal to the task of eliminating any survivors from the Mercanteer.

The few glances Marcus was able to steal around him when not fully occupied with defending himself showed that the Kabal were gaining the advantage. Controlling the slightly higher ground, they were pushing Rhea and the others further down the incline. Their taller stature with respect to their victims meant that they were able to assail them with broad, horizontal strokes – as if they were harvesting corn – that cost them little effort. They also had the advantage of not being utterly drained after a long and arduous climb. Yet none of them seemed to have noticed that while they bore down upon the fugitives they were growing more entangled with the webs of rigging that lay across the canvas. Struggling backwards, their victims' heels only nudged against the coiled ropes, but the toes of the guards' boots insinuated themselves between them more and more thoroughly the further they advanced.

As the sword strokes of his own looming foe became even more vicious and frequent, Marcus grew blind to anything else going on around him. Yet preoccupied as he was, he couldn't help but notice a new noise, rising above the grunts of effort and clash of iron upon iron that accompanied the fighting. Within a few seconds his brain registered that it was coming from the Mercanteer. The vessel was resuming – albeit in more subdued tones – the same sound it had emitted during its fall; except that this time it was doing so because the ledge of rock its stern had settled against further down the mountaintop was beginning to crumble.

The implication of this new development didn't register with Marcus straight away; he was still too busy trying to avoid dismemberment at the hands of the guard. But as the groan of the buckling thwart planks and straining bulkheads grew louder, his mind began to race through the possible consequences of what was going to happen next. He also noticed that the acreage of canvas on which he and everyone else was standing had started to slide down the incline – tugged at by the hull of the Mercanteer, as it rolled over towards its plunge into oblivion.

Struggling to stand their ground, none of the fugitives could afford the distraction of calling warnings to one another about this new development; apart from anything else, doing so would also have warned the Kabal troops. But some common instinct, perhaps developed by all the perils they had shared on the journey up from Daldriadh, told them what to do next. And so, just as the downward movement of the air sacs began to accelerate – the edges bunching into pleats and folds in the process – Marcus and Rhea hurled themselves sideways onto the bare ground. Theus and Magnis did likewise, shouting at Brebix and the other Farmers to follow them.

Suddenly awake to the imminent prospect of perishing, the Kabal guards attempted to escape as well. But only now did they notice the lengths of rope wound so many times around their ankles and entwined in turn with one another. Casting aside their swords, they reached down to free themselves. But as soon as they did so, the last barrier of rock that prevented the Mercanteer from plummeting disintegrated and the canvas was abruptly wrenched from beneath their feet. Unable to free themselves – and too astonished to scream – they and the vessel's still unconscious survivors vanished in an instant, swept away with the remains of the air sac into the swirling cloud.

After a few moments, the only sign of the Mercanteer's existence was a black smear, created by the oily smoke that had continued to pour from the recesses of its hold. But soon even this dispersed – spread more and more thinly and diluted into paler shades of grey by the ever-shifting contours of the clouds. Silence prevailed: a far more emphatic silence than the previous one.

Marcus and the others sat where they had fallen on the shale-littered incline for some time. Avoiding one another's eyes, they listened to the Mercanteer breaking apart far below. Each sundering of the hull became more substantial the further it fell, so for a long time the sounds of disintegration didn't seem to diminish in volume at all. Marcus felt himself twitch with horror at every one of them. Then, mercifully, they faded into nothingness.

After a while, Brebix, his gaze still fixed on the rising opacity of cloud in front of him, said, "We did all we could. All the survivors were so badly injured, I don't think any of them would have survived, even with proper attention."

"But now we'll never know for sure, will we?" said Marcus.

"The only saving grace is that the guards were dragged down with them," observed Theus. "So still the Kabal don't know we're back."

"They might just guess if they stumble upon us all sitting around out here in the open," Rhea pointed out dryly.

Unable to ignore the truth of this, they all rose with a succession of groans and hobbled back towards the shelter of the orchard. Looking up as they did so, they saw that on the distant citadel walls and in the fields, Kabal and Farmers alike had been stunned into immobility by the awful spectacle of the Mercanteer's destruction. Indeed the only sign of motion in the whole citadel came from the flags that bore the Heliopolitan crest shivering against their poles.

After a few more moments, the distant figures began to stir, albeit uncertainly at first. The Sentinels gathered in certain places to examine the masonry that had tumbled down from the Cloudfarers' layer and assess the damage it had caused, all the time glancing up in case more was dislodged. In the fields, Guards and Farmers mingled in disarray at first, as if they had momentarily forgotten their respective roles as oppressor and oppressed. Then the Guards began to assume more vigilant postures again, drawing themselves up to full height, shoulders back. With emphatic, threatening gestures – swords in hand – they corralled the Farmers into groups and ordered them to fill in the craters and clear the still smoking debris. Others headed towards the place where the Mercanteer had originally fallen, in order to discover why the comrades already dispatched there had not yet re-emerged from the mist.

Concealed once again by the shade of the trees further round the mountain top, the fugitives and Farmers paused to take stock. Perhaps because of all the struggles they had endured over the past month, it took Marcus, Rhea, Theus and Magnis a relatively short time to recover from what they had just experienced. Brebix and the other Farmers seemed far more shaken, still gazing back with disbelief at the abbreviated hillocks of cloud where the Mercanteer had sunk.

Though his sense of outrage refused to be quelled, Marcus kept his tone as gentle as possible and summoned up all his dimly remembered rhetorical skills when he began speaking to them.

"You see? Titus is pitiless. More so even than he has revealed to you already. This won't stop. The stroke you've just seen is decisive. You heard what the Selenopolitan lookout said. When the Mercanteer fails to return they'll dispatch warships to find out why. Titus is precipitating war. That's what he wants. The peril you and your family face if you help us is nothing compared to how grievously they'll be endangered when the Selenopolitans launch a full-scale assault on the citadel to avenge the loss of their comrades."

Brebix sighed and nodded. His shoulders sagged, as if he were accepting the burden of a truth he could no longer evade. He glanced back at the other Farmers, who returned similar looks of resigned acceptance, still tinged, none the less, with fear at taking so great a risk.

"We can't deny the truth of what he says Brebix," said one of them, gesturing out at the cloudscape. "Given evidence as stark as this."

"I know, Armath," Brebix replied.

He thought a little longer then nodded reluctantly.

"All right," he said. He glanced over his shoulder again. "We are at least in luck – if you can call it that. There's still stubble being burnt, so there will be enough smoke to conceal us as we cross the fields, at least partially. And the other men and I are about to finish our shift anyway. We have been working since long before dawn: scalding, plucking and gutting fowl in the Laborium, then salting the carcasses and hanging them out to dry. Our final task is to carry the remaining fruit inside and stack it for collection in the atrium, just beyond the walls. Take the baskets from the others. Hoist them up on your shoulders to conceal your faces. I will lead you inside."

"What about our packs?" asked Theus. "We can't just leave them at the edge of the orchard – the Kabal guards might discover them."

"That's true," said Rhea. She pondered for a few moments, looking at Brebix and the other Farmers.

"What do you have in *your* packs?" she asked.

"Not much," Brebix replied. "Some food to sustain us during our shift and a few implements we might need."

"Okay, so we can hang onto our own packs without arousing too much suspicion. We'll keep in them what we most need and conceal the rest of our equipment in the fringes of the clouds."

So the fugitives hurried back down the incline. Enveloped by the cloud vapour once more, they stuffed their discarded possessions into one of the canvas balloons that had supported them on their climb and buried them beneath a small pile of stones. The only items they retained in their packs were a couple of adzes, a few ice picks – and the bombs they had salvaged after the Nullmaurs' attack on the Eihlan village. Rhea suggested to the others that it might not be a good idea to tell Brebix that they were smuggling ordnance into his dwelling.

"It'll only make him more nervous," she said.

"Agreed," replied Marcus.

Their swords they slid down the inside of their trouser legs to conceal them. When they returned to the orchard, the other Farmers, at Brebix's renewed prompting, reluctantly handed over their baskets. These were kidney-shaped, curving round either side of the head and resting on the shoulders. The Farmer who handed his to Marcus looked far too old to still be toiling in the fields. He smiled, revealing a sparse collection of teeth.

"Good luck," he whispered.

"What will you and the others do?" Marcus asked him.

"We will wait until a thick cloud of smoke drifts by then slip into the fields again and look busy. Hopefully the guards won't notice anything amiss."

Marcus, Rhea, Theus and Magnis shouldered their baskets. Then, closely following Brebix, they stepped from the speckled shadows of the orchard into the haze that drifted across the fields. They pursued a meandering course up towards the citadel's walls, seeking the places where the smoke was thickest. Often they had to stop and wait for it to grow denser somewhere ahead, hoping that the patch in which they stood wouldn't disperse around them in the meantime. Every now and then the silhouette of a guard loomed some way off and they edged, as discreetly as possible, away from it while trying to stay concealed.

At last the curving, battlemented wall loomed up in front of them. A series of narrow gaps ran along the top of it, offering space through which the sentinels could fire their cross-shots. Wider gaps were crammed with the snub-nosed barrels of cannons, angled upward to fire at attacking aëro:cruisers. Still others, just as wide, contained large, curved horns resting on plinths. Blown in unison, all round the wall, these horns marked the end of each shift in the fields.

Fighting a strong inclination to stare up in wonder, Marcus stepped through the great archway, following Rhea, Theus, Magnis and Brebix. They had assembled themselves two abreast and shifted their baskets round to opposing shoulders, so that their faces would be concealed from the guards on either side.

Passing the guards, Marcus saw just enough to note that they wore expressions unlike any he had ever seen during his Palace childhood: a mixture of boredom and contempt, as if they were searching in a desultory fashion for the slightest excuse to victimise one of the toiling Farmers.

Stepping through the immensely thick, ribbed archway, Marcus found himself in a more open space. It wasn't much like any atrium he'd been in before. Its dirt- covered floor was uneven and the walls stood at so many different angles to one another that they created a kind of warped semicircle. The only similarity was that it had an open roof, though this one was covered not by glass but by a stretched white canopy, much patched and repaired, and translucent in the glow of the sun. The canopy was there to offer some shade to the baskets of fruit and vegetables stacked up everywhere, awaiting collection. In spite of this, the smell of organic matter poised on the verge of rotting was intense. Flies and wasps buzzed in and out of the gaps around the edge of the canopy, where unfiltered the sun stole in – a waterfall of light streaming down the walls. Here too were the salted and trussed carcasses of the fowl that Brebix had mentioned, hung out to dry.

Ramshackle dwellings, with tiny windows and moss-furred walls, were banked steeply up above the far side of the atrium. The shutters that hadn't fallen off the windows were unpainted and the plaster on the walls looked friable, as if it were steadily dissolving in the overripe air. There wasn't a right angle anywhere to be seen. To Marcus, accustomed to the clean lines of Palace architecture, all the disorder was hard to comprehend at first glance.

Narrow cobbled alleys ran up between the stacked dwellings, piled with rubbish on either side, like clogged arteries leading from the heart of the layer. Brebix stopped next to the entrance of one of these lanes. He knelt on the floor, leaned forward, then slipped the curved basket over his head with practised ease and lay it down. The others did likewise, careful the whole time to keep their backs turned to the archway and the sentinels.

"The Kabal remain constantly on duty in the Laborium and in the fields – but they don't often move between, unless there's a change of shift," Brebix assured them. "If we take care, we should be able to reach my dwelling without being seen."

Divested of their burden, but with their heads still discreetly lowered in case they encountered any more guards, the others followed Brebix into the tall, shaded alleys. Taking a deep breath, Marcus plunged into a world even more unfamiliar to him than the dizzying leagues of the cloud depths or the oppressive landscapes of Daldriadh.

IV.

The Farmers' Layer

It took a few moments for Marcus's eyes to adjust to the diminished light, after the diffuse glow beneath the canopy of the atrium. But he sensed an immediate change in the smells percolating around him. They were the kind of smells with which he had only recently become familiar and they identified themselves readily to his nostrils: blocked drains, stale sweat, old cooking and too many people crammed into too small a space.

While he was still straining to make out the walls of the alley curving up ahead, something damp slapped him in the face. Seized by the kind of disorientation that renders you hopelessly clumsy, he clawed at it until he felt a hand touch his arm.

"It's all right," Brebix whispered. "It's just sheets. We hang them out to air them."

Peeling it from his face, Marcus looked up. Sure enough, ropes stretched at intervals across the lane, sagging in the middle where bed linen hung from them. Slightly further ahead, Magnis was also plucking one from his shoulder. Grateful not to be the only person who had grown entangled, Marcus smiled ruefully then lowered his head and carried on. Though he said nothing to Brebix, he did wonder how fresh the linen could possibly become in such enclosed air.

They all continued to zigzag up the main alley. Then they turned onto others that led off it. These were even narrower, but thankfully free of mouldering laundry. None the less, as they followed the twisting, turning route, Marcus's acute sense of exposure meant that their journey seemed to take forever. At one point, a group of children, too young even for Titus to conscript ran past, shouting and laughing. Marcus envied them their heedlessness, their disregard for the changed world they now lived in.

Eventually, without any warning, Brebix darted to the right up a set of worn, irregular steps, set into the wall.

"This way," he hissed.

As he ascended the steps, Marcus noticed that not one of them was the same width and depth as any of the others. Eventually he found himself exchanging the cramped, dingy alley for an equally cramped, dingy room with a flagstone floor. The low ceiling was made lower still by the thick beams that stretched across it at seemingly random angles. The plaster of the ceiling also bulged in the centre, as if the dwelling directly above were going to collapse into this one at any moment.

Marcus moved beneath the beams with relative ease. But the Cloudfarers were unable to walk even a few paces without bumping their heads. Brebix, nearly as tall as they, but well used to the inconveniences of his living arrangements, bustled about with an odd, swooping gait, ducking his head instinctively every few seconds.

Low beams aside, the room was dominated by a rickety looking, roughly circular wooden table with spindly low chairs grouped round it. In one corner squatted a blackened stove. Next to the stove there was a granite work surface and a deep, wide sink with a hand pump fixed to the wall above it. A brown stain bloomed at the bottom of it where the pump had dripped. There was also a wide, discoloured pipe hugging the wall and running from floor to ceiling.

In an alcove, partially concealed by a frayed curtain, there was also a bathtub. Its base was iron (mined from ferrous seams in the core of the mountain top) and its sides carved from cedar wood – the graceful curves were testimony to the Artisans' dexterity, but it had long since seen better days. It sat on stubby legs and a fire lay beneath it, enclosed in a grate. Between the grate and the underside of the bath was a layer of hollow clay bricks, called tubuli, which conducted the heat and ensured that it was as evenly spread as possible. A network of flues at the rear of the alcove conducted the smoke from the fire up a narrow chimney.

A doorway, also curtained, led to the rest of the dwelling – comprising only one other room, Marcus guessed. A pair of ill-fitting shutters in the opposite wall glowed fiercely round the edges. Brebix threw them open, letting in some welcome sunlight and fresh air. The latter carried with it a musty, agrarian tinge from the continued activity in the fields below.

It occurred to Marcus with a considerable sense of shame that this dwelling would, just a few weeks before, have struck him as mean and pitiful. Now, having writhed in discomfort on a wind-scoured beach, a basalt tower, the juddering floor of a heavekairt – not to mention a succession of narrow mountain outcrops – he found it blissfully welcoming.

Out of the corner of his eye he saw the curtain twitch and he heard low, urgent whispering. Two small faces insinuated themselves round either side of it. One, belonging to a boy of six, hovered about a foot above the other, which belonged to a girl of four. Both had clear, long-lashed gazes. The boy's head was topped off with an abundance of fair hair so springy that it looked rather like a cap; the girl's thick brown hair had been twisted up at the crown, but flopped over on all sides. Both had small features, slightly crowded in the centre of their faces and a scattering of freckles – traits inherited from their father. They continued to look apprehensive until they spotted Magnis. Then they hurled themselves at him with delighted cries and clasped themselves firmly to each leg. Beaming, he hugged them, introducing them to the others as Imlac and Nekayah.

Magnis crouched before the children and responded to their barrage of questions by embarking on a whispered prologue to his recent adventures. Marcus, Rhea and Theus couldn't help but smile at the sight of a man whom they had seen wrestle beasts under control and slay foes with implacable courage slip so naturally back into the role of favoured uncle. It was incongruous, verging on the surreal, yet cheering at the same time.

"Well, you'll be ready to clean up and get some food and rest," said Brebix. "As for everything else, I'd rather wait for my wife to return from the Laborium before we discuss any of it."

"Is she working late?" asked Rhea.

Brebix nodded.

"From midday until midnight. We call it a back shift."

Nekayah tugged at his sleeve. He leaned down and she whispered in his ear, a cupped hand pressed conspiratorially against the side of his tilted head. When she had finished he straightened up and surveyed the hollow-eyed, partially stooped, wholly exhausted fugitives.

"Yes," he said with a sigh. "She will be surprised, won't she."

First the fugitives removed the outer garments that had insulated them during the climb as they had struggled upwards into air that was colder and thinner, yet still remote from any compensating sunlight. With groans of relief, they shrugged out of cloaks, unwound scarves, slipped off gloves and unbuttoned tunics. They already knew that Magnis's bandaged hands – cut by sharp edges of rock during the climb –would require more attention. Yet when Theus tried to remove his gloves he emitted an anguished groan, and they couldn't help but notice the spasm of pain that distorted his features, in spite of the fact that he had turned slightly away from them to conceal it.

"What is it?" Marcus asked.

"I think…I think I may have a touch of frost bite," said Theus.

"Here, sit down and let us look at it," Rhea told him.

Theus sat obediently at the table and Rhea and Marcus eased off his gloves. The skin on his fingers was discoloured – it had acquired a yellowy grey tinge – and the fingers themselves were rigid. When Magnis, kneeling in front of him, gently squeezed them, Theus winced again, even more deeply.

"The skin is unyielding to the touch", said Magnis. "It's definitely frostbite. It's still unthawed but I don't think it's too serious. If it were, the tissue would be white and rock hard. I have seen this before, years ago. One of my comrades got it when we went ice-climbing on a lay-over at Scythium."

"What should we do?" asked Marcus.

"We don't want to thaw the fingers too quickly – that could permanently damage the tissue." He looked up at Theus, still gently holding his hands. "Whatever we do, I am afraid it's going to hurt quite a bit."

Theus smiled mordantly, perhaps recalling all the discomfort they had endured over the past month.

"I'll be brave," he said.

"The best thing to do", continued Magnis. "Is probably to soak your hands in warm water for a while."

"I'll heat a saucepan," said Brebix.

He rose and set to work at the stove. Magnis continued to kneel in front of Theus, talking soothingly to him as the pulses of pain in the elder man's reawakening nerves transmitted themselves to his drawn features. Marcus and Rhea stood on either side of him, looking on worriedly.

"Do you have clean bandages?" Magnis asked Brebix. "We'll need to wrap them around the fingers to keep them separate."

"Um… yes, somewhere," said Brebix. "I'll look for them in the other room if someone can watch the saucepan and make sure it doesn't overheat."

So Rhea replaced Brebix at the stove, while he went off to retrieve the bandages and tear them into narrower strips. Once the water was ready, they placed the saucepan on the table and Theus immersed his now trembling hands in it. Finally, the discomfort became too much for him. Brebix and Magnis had to hold his arms rigid to stop him removing his fingers from the water while he screwed his eyes up tight and bowed his head, as if in humble acknowledgement of the pain's mastery over him. Brebix glanced over at the sundial, which sat on the ledge of the window.

"We'll take them out after twenty minutes and see if you can move more than a bit," he said. "We'll have to put them back in after, but the pain will lessen gradually, I promise."

Theus nodded, eyes still closed. Magnis continued talking, as much to distract him as to describe the next stage in detail.

"We'll wrap your fingers loosely in the bandages. You should use them as little as possible at first, but we can help you with things like eating. A few hours after thawing, the tissue will swell and over the next couple of days you'll probably get blisters forming. We'll have to be careful not to break them. They should settle during the week. Eventually, the shell of the blisters – it's called the carapace – will come away and there should be healthy new pink skin underneath."

After two more immersions, Theus was able to flex his fingers very gingerly and the pain seemed to have abated. While he rested, his hands swaddled in bandages, Brebix suggested that the others might appreciate the chance to bathe.

As soon as he said this, Marcus, Rhea and Magnis stirred, lent a final burst of energy by the blissful prospect of immersing themselves in hot water and eating some food. Wrestling the hand pump into creaking motion, Brebix filled several buckets. He transferred these to the bath then let lit the fire beneath it. The resinous wood hissed and spat behind the ill-fitting grate, but soon heat was radiating up into the water. In the meantime Marcus, Rhea and Theus were deputised by Brebix to help make dinner – a vegetable stew whose carefully hoarded ingredients would now have to stretch a lot further than originally intended.

Marcus had never cooked before – the fact striking him with renewed mortification – and Theus had been eating Cloudfaring Corps rations for years. Rhea had too, but she at least possessed some knowledge, gleaned from helping her mother in the kitchen when she was a girl. As a result, she did the actual cooking – frying onions, turnips and carrots with crushed aromatic seedpods – while Marcus and Theus washed and chopped. Crowded together, the three of them jostled elbows almost constantly. Rhea and Theus, instead of banging their heads against the beams, now banged them against the pots hanging down over the stove and the sink.

During the few moments when all the pots weren't clanging together, the air was filled with the sound of Magnis recounting to the children the story of Titus's attack on the *Noble Quest*. His narrative was punctuated and enhanced by a rich selection of piercing sound effects. While the children listened avidly to him, Rhea added stock, scalded tomatoes and rinsed lentils to the stew then covered it to simmer.

Once the bath water was hot, they took it in turns to bathe. They were all nervous about polluting the water with days of accumulated grime. But it proved, on closer inspection, to be so discoloured after its journey through the layer's ancient pluming system that there was little need for self-consciousness.

When Marcus's turn came, he gripped the warped sides of the bathtub and sank into the water, feeling the warmth not only envelop his body, but invade his pores like a powerful anaesthetic, somehow rendering his limbs weightless and ponderous at the same time. He slid down until the surface was a fraction of an inch beneath his nostrils. His breathing sent tiny ripples across it.

He felt as if he could sleep for a month, preferably without the inconvenience of having to get out of the water again. His calves ached and when he raised his elbows to plant them on either side of the tub, bands of pain seemed to radiate up from his armpits and settle on his shoulders. He closed his eyes, lulled by Magnis's resumed repertoire of pursed-lip cannon fire and growling explosions, all accompanied by the children's gasps.

As he sank deeper still into the water, head tilted back, he found all sorts of recollections he'd tried so long to suppress brimming up inside him. It was as if the warm liquid in which he was immersed was dissolving the barriers he had created against thoughts of people in his life whom he had lost, or left behind, or whose fate was still undecided.

He thought of Asperia, his tutor. He remembered her upright, inflexible bearing; her clear, sceptical gaze. He remembered, too, the way she constantly importuned him to do better, work harder, adopt a more noble posture. All these things had frustrated him when he was young. Now, though, he realised that restrictions were also comforting; that the very things he'd chafed against had also protected him. She had been part of the solid, unalterable world that had surrounded him. And her strictness with him had been a form of love, which he had sensed on some deeper level, even if he'd never been fully aware of it at the time. To put it more simply, she would never have pushed him so hard if she hadn't cared for him so much.

Now, though, he worried about her. He knew only too well how forthright she was: how unwilling to curb her tongue when faced with a situation she thought false or unacceptable in even the smallest respect. Given this characteristic, would she already have provoked punishment, perhaps even death, at the hands of a regime, which, he felt sure, would tolerate not a whisper of dissent? There was no way of knowing, but he feared the worst.

He turned his thoughts instead to his comrades, still marooned in the sun-starved depths of Daldriadh. The face of each man came to him, one after the other: Jarrid, Denihr, Amik, Lucis, Tafril and Persis. He wondered if they too were still alive. Perhaps they had already perished in a fresh Nullmaur onslaught, alongside the Eihlans they had sworn to assist.

Reflecting on these things brought Breah to the forefront of his mind: her fortitude, her impulsiveness, her disquieting maturity and acceptance of her people's circumstances. He thought too of the warmth and empathy that lay beneath these qualities of hers, like the thin rays of sunlight that occasionally shot through a gap in the clouds. The time that they had shared had been brief and beset on all sides by danger or the threat of danger. Yet she had offered him the first experience in his life of contact with someone close to his own age that wasn't either pinched with formality or crippled by awkwardness. Though her eyes had never beheld the unclouded sun, there was a lustre in her gaze that made him feel as if she understood him fully and awakened an ease in him that he'd never felt before.

Breah seemed to realise also that the somewhat grave cautiousness which tempered his moments with her was the legacy of his upbringing rather than a reflection of his true character. Already her untutored openness had melted some of it and he knew she could help him rid himself of it completely, if only he was able to spend more time with her. Yet for them to be together he would, in all likelihood, have to live in Daldriadh, which for a large part of the year lay rain-soaked and freezing in the impoverished light. Then again, perhaps they could move closer to the equator: away from the predations of the Nullmaurs and towards the southern uplands he had heard Breah's father mention, where there was more light and a warmer climate? As soon as this thought had occurred to him, however, he knew that it was probably wishful thinking.

The idea of living in exile – cut off from the life-giving sun; cut off from the beauty of the cloudscape – was almost too much to contemplate. None the less, its beauty and familiarity aside, what was there in this world that could nourish his soul or offer him any consolation for the loss of his father? Even if he were to defeat Titus – a mammoth task in itself, riddled with all kinds of uncertainties – he would be alone. He would have the friendship of Rhea, Theus and Magnis certainly: a friendship forged in adversity, which had erased the gap in age between him and them. But he would still be deprived of the tender, becalmed feeling, lit with the promise of an even greater closeness, that he seemed to share with Breah.

He closed his eyes. They stung not only with tiredness, but also with all the intense emotions released by this first moment of repose in what seemed like an eternity. Sighing, he slid right down and ran his fingers through his swaying submerged hair, while the displaced water lapped the edges of the tub.

Only guilt at continuing to deny Theus his turn to bathe prised him from the water. Limbs deadened, he clambered out with even less ease than he'd clambered in. He towelled himself down and dressed again. Then, casting one guilty glance back at the ring around the tub, which already looked as if it was going to become pretty much indelible, he pulled the curtain aside and rejoined the others.

Rhea and Theus were standing over the pot, periodically removing its lid and peering into its steaming interior, as if it contained some volatile science experiment, which, if not constantly monitored, might explode at any moment. Passing by, Brebix glanced into it and pronounced dinner almost ready. While Theus bathed, he fed the children first then told them to go and play in the other room. Still keen to hear more of Magnis's stories, they fought a lengthy rear guard action of pleading and protesting, but eventually allowed themselves to be ushered out, still casting wistful looks back at their uncle.

Once Theus had reappeared, he, Marcus, Rhea and Magnis assembled around the table. The warm water had practically induced a coma in all of them; only hunger kept them alert. There weren't enough chairs for everyone, so Marcus and Rhea – the lightest – had to perch on children's stools retrieved from the other room. Magnis and Theus's chairs received their broad frames with a plaintive creak.

Brebix set out some spoons and chipped bowls and Theus served the food. The table's legs were all slightly different lengths. Every time Theus ladled stew into one of the bowls, which became heavier, the table top tilted and the other bowls slid across it. Everyone ended up with a different bowl from the one that had originally been set down in front of them, but they were far too tired to say anything.

The stew was fairly insipid, its ingredients stretched further than they should have been. But it was the first hot meal Marcus had eaten since the Eihlan village, so it tasted incredibly strong, flooding his mouth with an intensity out of all proportion to its actual flavour. He chewed each sparse mouthful as often as he could, trying to get as much nutrition out of it as possible.

"Now," said Brebix, clearly relieved to be able to ask the question that had plagued him since the orchard. "Tell me...What *happened*? Where have you been all this time?"

Magnis glanced at Marcus, who nodded wearily. He felt that the account of their adventures and the revelation of a world beneath the clouds would seem less shocking if it came from someone Brebix knew well. So, sitting up, summoning his last reserves of wakefulness, Magnis described to Brebix the attack on the *Noble Quest*, the plunge into the frozen landscapes of Daldriadh, their encounters with the Nullmaurs and the Eihlans, the ascent of the Ins'lberg and Nestor's death. Brebix listened with alternating expressions of wonder, pity and fear. When Magnis finished, he stared at him in silence for a while, mouth forming different shapes, as if he were unable to frame an appropriate response.

"And now that you've returned... What happens next?" he said at last.

Marcus hesitated. What Magnis had just described had happened in stages for him and the others: they'd had time to adjust to each act of perfidy or the unfolding of each new vista before the next was upon them. But Brebix had had to absorb it all in condensed form and, for the moment at least, looked stunned. To start bombarding him with ideas of revolution and democracy seemed unfair. Then again, he sensed that the Farmer was too shrewd, in his own understated way, to believe that, having fought their way back, they were just going to accept the new regime and surrender themselves to the Kabal.

"Well…you *did* say yourself that things are much worse now than they ever were before," he began hesitantly. "Maybe if we work together we can find a way to… help you improve your lives. To rid you of the Kabal regime."

Brebix sighed.

"That is something that would affect my whole family," he replied. "So I think we should wait until Ampliata returns before discussing any of it. It'll still be hours before she is back from the Laborium. Until then I suggest you all get some sleep." He waved his hand towards the other room. "We don't exactly have guest quarters, as you might have realised. But there is some spare bedding that I can lay down to make the floor in here a bit more comfortable… or less uncomfortable, at any rate. And I'll gag the children for a few hours to give you peace."

Marcus smiled.

"Thank you."

He and the others could barely keep their eyes open now. But somehow they managed to stumble over to the sink and rinse out their bowls. Theus and Magnis no longer even frowned when their brows connected with a low ceiling beam. Then they all sank down on the coarse brown bed linen that Brebix had spread thinly across the floor next to the table. He apologised, somewhat distractedly, for the absence of pillows. But they simply rolled up their cloaks and rested their heads on them, as they had done so many times in the past month. They were asleep within seconds.

Only a few seconds after that, or so it seemed, Marcus was shaken awake. Propping himself up on an elbow, he felt finger points of pain knead every part of his torso. Through eyes filmed with drowsiness, he saw a slightly stout woman – still young, but careworn – standing motionless at the doorway, surveying the four bodies huddled together on the floor.

With the same amiable, vaguely apologetic smile he had offered Brebix in the orchard, Marcus said, "Hello."

She frowned at him with a flicker of recognition. Far from reassuring her, the fact that he looked vaguely familiar seemed to only trouble her even more. She shot Brebix a searching look. Even Marcus, with his slender experience of family life, saw that it was tinged with the "What have you done now?" exasperation of the long-suffering spouse.

"It's King Antior's son, Marcus Hyperios," said Brebix, only a faint quaver of defensiveness in his voice.

"I can *see* that," replied Ampliata. "What is he doing on our kitchen floor?"

"He survived the attack on the *Noble Quest*," said Brebix. "Along with some of the crew. And look… look who's with them."

Without taking his eyes off Ampliata, he stepped sideways and kicked Magnis's slumbering form, albeit as lightly as possible. Magnis responded with a groan and sat up blinking. As soon as Ampliata recognised him she melted. While Marcus, Rhea and Theus looked on, yawning, she sank to her knees and hugged him. Having slept only a few hours, Marcus felt at most semi-rested, his brain still clogged with fatigue. The spectacle of Ampliata surrendering her grip on Magnis, holding him at arm's length and plying him with questions had the surreal tincture of a dream about it.

"But where have you… how did you…" began Ampliata.

With simple answers, delivered in as soothing a tone as possible, Magnis staunched her flow of questions, heading off each one before it was fully formed. Then, once she was calm, he and the others hauled themselves to their feet and congregated around the table again.

While Brebix busied himself with heating some of the stew he had left out for Ampliata, Magnis once again described, in considerable detail, all that had happened to them. Watching him do so, Marcus, Rhea and Theus sat slumped in their places, chins cupped in upturned palms.

Ampliata listened with the same range of expressions as Brebix had, scarcely taking her eyes off Magnis as she ate.

But when he had finished, she showed no sign of struggling to respond. Instead she stared at the table in silence for at least a minute. Then she got up, took her bowl over to the sink and rinsed it, keeping her back to the others for several more minutes. When she did turn round, she picked up a frayed dishcloth and began folding and refolding it, eyes still lowered.

Looking up at last, she said to Brebix, "Did you tell them we would help them against the Kabal... against Titus?"

"No, I wanted to discuss it with you first," he replied.

This drew a smile from her. For all their brusqueness and plain speaking, Marcus sensed that they had once been a much more playful, light hearted couple, before the grind of their daily toil had worn away much of their joy in one another.

She looked at Marcus, her smile fading, erased by anxiety.

"For us to help you would be to place ourselves and our children in mortal danger, it's as simple as that," she said. "Why should we risk what is most precious to us to restore *your* family to power? Our lives at present may be painful, but, as I'm sure Brebix has told you, they're not unendurable."

"Not yet," began Theus. "But if the Kabal..."

Marcus placed a hand gently on his arm to silence him. Then he glanced at Rhea. Knowing what he was about to say, she gave him an equivocal look that wasn't discouraging, but wasn't especially positive either. But he felt he had no choice. There was no other way to win over Brebix and Ampliata than to be honest with them – especially if *they* were to somehow win over the other citizens in turn. He leaned across the table.

"Listen to me," he began softly. "I know what I'm about to say might make me sound pompous or as if I'm pretending to be more grown up than I am. But I can't help that, because I've learned things that most people never know at my age – things even my father never found out his entire life."

Brebix and Ampliata looked vaguely perplexed by these words, as if wondering, somewhat warily, what they were a prelude to. But he could see that he had their attention.

"I was born in the Palace," he told them. "As a baby, I was swaddled in silk. Growing up, I was clad in yet more finery. I had a privileged life. But it was also a lonely one. I wandered rooms with ceilings higher than three tiers of this layer, but always on my own. My tutor – Asperia – taught me well about all manner of subjects. But I had no experience of real life. I didn't know how to stand up for myself because I'd never had to. And I knew nothing about how people thought and felt in the rest of the citadel."

As he talked, an unbidden monologue started up inside his head. A wearier, more cynical voice provided a distracting counterpoint to what he was saying. *You were like some kind of municipal symbol*, it told him. *A crown or a jewelled staff. Kept immaculately on display, but all the time out of everyone's reach.*

"Then something awful happened," he went on, trying to ignore it. "Titus happened. He revealed who he really was and he destroyed all the certainties that had been the foundation of my life."

He just emerged his chrysalis, that's all, the voice told him. *He'd been in it for years – straining to liberate himself – but you and your father had been too blind to see. He came out glorious in his way: an incarnation of pure evil."*

"When the *Valorous Mission* attacked the *Noble Quest*, my whole world was turned upside down – literally," he said, forcing the hectoring interior voice to subside. "I fell into an alien land: a land more strange than you could possibly imagine. For the first time in my life I saw everything in a completely different way than I had before. And I realised that my upbringing had taught me nothing about how to survive – either in this new place or the one I was used to.

To begin with I floundered – I'm not ashamed to admit that. I had no idea how to deal with the people I had been marooned alongside. I tried to pretend that I wasn't who

I was, so that they might treat me normally. I was clumsy and I was over-earnest and I was always trying to prove myself... But they were patient with me and we grew close. All the time we struggled to survive down there and find a way back to Heliopolis, I thought about..."

No...'thought about' isn't enough. You did more than think about it.

"I brooded," he corrected himself, aloud. "I brooded on why everything had happened the way it had. And the more I brooded, the more clearly I came to see that Titus couldn't have planned his coup if it wasn't for the way our citadel is built: everyone in their layers, everyone told to accept their lot, people at the highest levels ignorant of everything except their own concerns. It's wrong. It's more than wrong, it's *unjust*. And it can't go on"

He glanced at Rhea, who smiled supportively, emboldening him.

"Getting home took every ounce of strength we possessed," he continued. "It even took the life of one of our closest comrades. We fought every inch of the way from the other world to this. And while we were struggling upwards two things kept me going. One was the thought of revenge, I'll admit that. But the other was to make sure that life in Heliopolis – life for you and your children and your friends and other relations – changed at last. It's time for the citizens to choose their own leaders and for the leaders to live among the citizenry and understand them, instead of being so distant, so cut off, far above them." He gestured round the table at Rhea, Theus and Magnis. "We've sought shelter among people who have none of our technology. They live in dwellings made of wood patched with glazed clay. They collect mud with their bare hands, dry it in the freezing wind, and burn it to keep themselves warm. But they understand how to be fair to each other in a way we never have. It's time for us to learn from them."

Rhea already knew the great change that their adventures had wrought in him, but the others all looked shocked into unwonted wakefulness. Huddled together round the table one moment, they leaned right back from it the next, like the petals of a flower, bursting open in astonishment. Ampliata placed a hand to her brow. Theus and Magnis shifted uncomfortably in their seats, as if seeking an angle from which all this would seem less shocking.

Still profoundly weary, Marcus was drained from delivering so long and carefully phrased a speech. Sensing this, Rhea picked up the thread and completed what he had to say.

"*This* is how we can get the other Farmers and the Artisans to rise up against Titus," she said. "We have to show them that although they might have been made to feel powerless over so many centuries there are far more of them than of the people oppressing them. Think about it: the layers they live in are much bigger and more populous than the ones above. The whole way the citadel is built has always meant that those in the lower layers have the greatest power, it's just that they've never realised it. I know it won't be easy to persuade them; I know the hardest thing of all will be to spread the word under the noses of the Kabal without them being aware of it. But if we can give the people something to believe in, if we can make them see they're fighting for *themselves* – for their own freedom – I think we might just manage it."

"But the Kabal..." began Brebix.

"I know it won't be easy," she persisted. "I know the Kabal are better armed and drilled. But if we all rise up together I'm sure we can overwhelm them." She looked round at the others. "We just need a good plan."

As soon as she had finished there was an inrush of silence. It seemed to fill every dusty crevice of the room to bursting point. Everyone stared at the knots and whorls on the unvarnished surface of the table, at a loss. Slowly, however, they became aware of faint, conspiratorial whisperings behind the doorway to the bedroom. These whisperings were punctuated by slightly louder shushing noises, and by a lot of twitching around the frayed edges of the curtain.

Brebix smiled down at his folded hands then rose, strode over and bundled the children in the curtain's folds. They shrieked with surprise and glee then, after their standard litany of protests, allowed themselves to be ushered off to bed again. Twisted round in her chair, Ampliata offered them a fond, lingering glance then looked back at Marcus and Rhea.

"We need time to think about what you've said," she told them. "It's too much to take in all at once – especially at the end of a long shift."

"I understand," replied Marcus. He gestured to Rhea, Theus and Magnis. "We're pretty tired too."

"We'll talk again tomorrow," said Brebix.

With that, he and Ampliata rose to prepare for bed. The fugitives did the same, merely by sinking from their chairs onto the floor.

"Do the Kabal search your dwellings?" asked Theus, settling down again.

"Rarely," replied Brebix. "But we must exercise caution if you are to stay with us." He gestured around him. "Concealing anything in a home such as this isn't easy."

The fugitives murmured their assent, already drifting back into sleep. Lowering his head onto his folded cloak, Marcus tried to gauge how persuasive he had been with Brebix and Ampliata. He thought he'd detected hints of restiveness – a newly awakened sense of greater possibilities – bobbing to the surface now and then amid their turmoil of anxiety. He would have like to ask Rhea what she thought. But her slow, even breathing told him that she was already asleep. And soon he too, utterly drained, drifted back into unconsciousness.

V.

Breah

In Daldriadh, bending down and digging her slender fingers into the turf-covered peat, Breah struggled to prise loose the rectangular section her father had just cut. He crouched a few feet away, cutting more. All around them, randomly distributed over the peat bog, other Eihlans worked similarly in pairs – collecting extra fuel against the deepening of winter. Above, the grey underbelly of the clouds pressed down upon them with its familiar, imperturbable blankness. The flat, fibrous ground where they worked was enclosed on three sides by a series of low hills, which grew steeper as they receded and were crowned by a dense forest of pines.

Having freed the damp, sagging rectangle, she held it awkwardly in her arms, trying to make sure that no part of it split or crumbled. Though it remained completely inert, doing this reminded her of holding her younger sister, Eithné, when she was a squirming, newborn baby, terrified that she might drop her flushed, precious cargo. With great care, therefore, she transferred the peat to the uncovered cart that stood a few feet away, then prepared to repeat the whole process again. All the time she and the others worked, a freezing wind blew down off the surrounding, snow-clad hills. Hunched over, they tried to keep their backs to it as much as they could.

But the unremittingly barbarous wind was not the only element that made their current situation uncomfortable. While clawing at the earth, they all glanced up every few moments, as if gripped by some collective nervous tic. They had good reason for their vigilance. For some days now, at different times, ornithopters had appeared from the north, the steady beating of their wooden wings a kind of monitory greeting. Swooping low, each one had deposited its cargo of bombs then gained height again, wings clawing the damp air. If everyone was within the stockade that encircled the village when the attack came, they could take swift shelter inside the holms. But anyone out in the fields or peat bogs was far more vulnerable and already there had been deaths.

The ornithopters had made no appearance so far today and already the pallid light – never entirely confident in its banishment of darkness at this time of year – was beginning to fade. So Breah's gaze continued to alternate anxiously between her busy, begrimed hands and the sky during the next hour.

The cart was almost full and she was just beginning to entertain the notion that perhaps night would arrive without an attack when a strange trembling, barely perceptible at first, transmitted itself from the ground to her fingertips and through her entire body. She looked up at the sky, but there was nothing. Then cries and frenzied gestures from the others brought her attention to the nearest hills. Cresting a portion of them was a sight unlike any she had witnessed before.

Planed-down tree trunks, their tips sharpened to lethal points, were hurtling down the slopes. Having already built up speed on the steeper, more distant inclines, they moved terrifyingly fast, with minimal resistance from the compacted snow.

"They're all around!" shouted Aònghas.

She turned her head. Sure enough, the logs were racing down on all sides, converging on her and the other Eihlans. Presumably launched by the Nullmaurs at the edge of the forest far above, they were like an avalanche that had grown innumerable needle-sharp teeth. If she or any of the other Eihlans remained in the peat bog for even another second they were sure to be trapped between them and impaled.

Detained for only a fraction of a second by her amazement at the Nullmaurs' fiendish ingenuity, Breah grabbed her father's hand and started running as fast as possible towards the village. The other Eihlans followed. After a short time, the firm ground gave way to shallow, oily marshland. The surface water here was clad in a metallic sheen, while the mud beneath it sucked tenaciously at their feet. None the less, they splashed and staggered through it with undiminished vigour. All the time Breah kept her eyes fixed on the stockade. As it drew closer, she gave silent thanks, once again, at the mixture of speed and thoroughness with which the Cloudfarers had repaired its defences after the Nullmaurs' most concerted assault. The posts that had been torn completely from it had been replaced, while others, bent outward by the force of explosions, had been pushed upright again and driven back into the ground more firmly than before.

At last they quit the marshes and, scrambling up the incline on the other side, hurled themselves through the entrance of the stockade to safety. Behind them, the peat bog was engulfed in the Nullmaurs' improvised bombardment. Most of the sharpened trunks slid between one another before ploughing to a halt, but enough lodged in the ground for the area where the Eihlans had been working to be left surreally bristling with them. It looked like a petrified forest of branch-less trees, all growing at improbable angles.

Breah and the others turned, wheezing, to contemplate this strange new feature in the landscape.

"They grow ever more inventive," commented Aònghas. "I only wish it were not so."

He spoke in the formal tones of their sacred language – derived, as it had turned out, from Heliopolitan books, the tattered remnants of which had tumbled through the clouds amid the wreckage of aëro:cruisers over so many centuries. Her father, she was aware, had lost faith in the language's sacred origin. But it was known to relatively few of the Eihlans (principally the Elders, of whom he had been one.) So he used it with her in company when he wished his words to remain private – usually because his frank assessments of their plight were apt to disturb the more fretful members of the tribe. Though she grieved for his loss of faith, she felt proud to be deemed worthy of sharing in his lack of delusion.

She nodded.

"How much longer can we resist them?" she asked.

Her father shook his head sorrowfully.

"I don't know," he said. "I don't know."

With the onset of darkness, the Eihlans and Cloudfarers both sought shelter – as was village custom – in the largest, communal holm, where they ate their evening meal together. Life within the stockade, since the departure of Marcus, Rhea, Theus, Magnis and Nestor, had settled into a new routine: one of diligent labour, accompanied by constant, anxious vigilance and interspersed with moments of stark terror. It was, in short, the dismal routine of the besieged. Yet the threat that encroached on everyone had allowed a sense of kinship to develop more rapidly between the Cloudfarers and the Eihlans than it might otherwise have done.

The Cloudfarers were mainly engaged in further strengthening the village's fortifications. But they also assisted with more mundane, everyday tasks, like patching the wattle on the roofs of the holms. And all the time they and the villagers worked together, both parties provided a muted running commentary in their respective languages. The ordinary Eihlans understood only fragments of the Cloudfarers' speech, while the Cloudfarers understood none of the Eihlans'. Yet simply hearing one another's voices – without the effort of comprehending the actual words – proved to be unexpectedly comforting. It somehow allowed them to merge their efforts more efficiently and lent an ease to their movements as they worked side by side.

As for Breah, she found herself more profoundly unsettled than she had expected by the advent of refugees from a battle in the world above the clouds. Unlike her father's, her discomfiture had not much to do with loss of faith. Being younger than him and still more malleable, she found it easier to adapt herself to a new outlook.

No... it wasn't something lost that so affected her; it was something gained – a sense of far greater possibilities than she had ever dreamed of before, but that her current circumstances made it lethal to pursue. She had always prided herself on her inquisitive nature. Her father, too, had encouraged this quality in her, to her mother's frequent dismay and occasional terror. Yet now the range of her curiosity – which until recently had extended just a few hundred miles around the village where she had spent her whole life – seemed pitifully restricted. The world was far greater and more strange than she had ever imagined and this fact haunted her.

Any time she dwelt on this subject, which was almost all the time, her churning thoughts seemed to acquire their only clarity in focusing upon one person: Marcus. Though she had declared herself appalled when he told her about the loneliness of his upbringing, she had felt too shy to admit that his words had so affected her partly because they chimed with her own experience. Her childhood had been far from solitary. The tall stockade that surrounded the village corralled its inhabitants together much of the time. And Eihlan children were further confined to the web of subterranean alleys that stretched between the holms. Yet only after talking to Marcus did she recall how often she had yearned to be alone.

She had always, she now realised, felt different from friends her own age. In particular, she had found it impossible to share their acceptance of – indeed love of – being enclosed: enclosed by earth walls in the alleys, by wood and clay walls in the holms, even by the clouds that so often smothered the land, descending like a dreamless sleep. She'd also told Marcus that the prospect of a limitless, unoccluded sky would terrify her. But her reaction had been prompted only by the initial shock of the idea. The more she considered it, the more the thought of living in a world with far fewer restrictions to chafe against thrilled her.

Having recognized these things inside herself, she felt mortified now to reflect on how incurious she must have seemed to Marcus when they talked of such things; with any hint of restlessness in her nature smothered by the closeness of her family life. But then she sensed that he would be unlikely to judge her. In spite of how exalted – to her – his origins were, he gave little impression of superiority. Indeed his character was full of contradictions. Foremost among them was the way he had displayed so much courage and vigour in resolving to liberate his people, yet tended, when there was no immediate challenge to be overcome, to lapse into a kind of mournful reflectiveness. His face looked so sad in repose! It made her want to always be there, to help lighten his expression. What did that mean, though, in terms of her feelings for him? She thought she knew, given how powerful the emotion was. But since she had nothing in her past to compare it with, she was reluctant to bestow a name on it.

Instead she sought to spend as much time as possible each evening in the Cloudfarers' company. Eating with them in the communal holm, she loved to hear the gruff interplay of their talk, especially when any of it referred to the world above the clouds – that realm of boundless vistas. The other Eihlans no longer feared the Cloudfarers, but they still felt enough awe to attend to them with grave respect and leave them alone whenever they were eating or talking. But because they represented her only link with Marcus, however, Breah was much less inclined to keep her distance from Tafril, Jarrid, Denihr and the others. None the less, their bluff demeanour did make her feel a little shy about being too familiar with them. The only one amongst them who tended always to be a little quieter and whose body language bespoke less daunting confidence was Persis.

The other Cloudfarers no longer displayed any resentment towards him for the fact that he had been one of Titus's erstwhile confederates – albeit against his will. But the bonds of comradeship that connected them so securely were frailer with respect to him. This meant that he often sat ever so slightly apart from them, smiling at their banter but contributing little. At such times, Breah found a discreet place beside him, balancing her bowl of stew carefully as she lowered herself onto the animal skins with which the floor was strewn. When she did so, Persis always put her at ease by greeting her with a murmured salutation.

As they both continued to eat, he said, "I didn't see what happened in the peat bogs, but I heard about it."

She shrugged, affecting an indifference she had felt little of at the time.

"You would think there was a simpler way to try and kill us," she replied.

"I've no wish to belittle what you went through out there. But I suspect that killing you and the others was only incidental to their plan. I think their main purpose was to cut off access to a supply of fuel," Persis pointed out.

"Well, they managed that at least. It'll take ages to clear the logs and bring in the peat we cut."

There was a few moments' silence as Persis considered this, nodding slowly. Privately, Breah congratulated herself on how natural her comment had sounded to her own ears. Having learned Heliopolitan as not only a second language but a sacred one, her command of it had always been scrupulously correct. But gradually, through listening to exchanges between the Cloudfarers, she was learning to speak it in a less formal manner.

"It will," Persis replied. "Always assuming they allow us to venture out of the village at all."

They talked on. As they did so, she steered the conversation towards her perennial topic: Heliopolis and its society. By the time each evening came round she had managed to fully replenish her store of questions about the lives of people there. Persis answered her with infallible patience. And to her silent gratitude, he failed to remark on the fact that so many of her questions related to Marcus. The most he ever did was to avert his face slightly and allow himself a discreet, indulgent smile at her guileless fascination.

VI.

Silent Hours

Marcus woke comparatively early the next morning. Though his sleep had been interrupted for a while by Ampliata's return late at night, he had been more or less unconscious since mid-afternoon the previous day, so he felt well rested at last. He opened his eyes. What was clearly a well-worn domestic scene was taking place before him albeit in a restricted fashion, like a play being performed on a smaller stage than normal. Ampliata bustled about at the stove and the work surface next to it. Though she had her back to him, something about her hunched posture and the slight clumsiness of her movements told him that she was barely awake.

Sure enough, when she turned to set the table her face was pinched with tiredness. As she moved back and forth with plates, bowls and cutlery she kept glancing down to avoid stepping on the slumbering bodies strewn across the floor – as if crossing a series of slippery stones amid fast flowing water.

Sitting up, Marcus shivered. Draughts stole through gaps in the exterior wall and seemed to chase one another about the room. He felt them swirl across his face, prodding it with icy fingers. It was still dark outside, so the only illumination was provided by slightly too few candles, all of which guttered in the restless air, creating an inconstant, flickering light.

In spite of the cold, Brebix was bathing the children in the alcove and washing their hair. Each one sat cross-legged in the tub, eyes screwed shut and bowed heads trembling as their father vigorously massaged their scalps.

Feeling guilty about contributing nothing to the morning's preparations except another obstacle on the floor, Marcus rose and helped Ampliata finish setting the table.

By indulging in a certain amount of not strictly necessary cupboard and drawer slamming they also woke the others, who slowly stirred themselves and greeted the new day with a succession of groans.

Sitting up, Theus, Rhea and Magnis stretched and yawned then reached around their torsos and over their shoulders, searching for the origin of new aches and pains. Rhea's hair was pressed flat on one side of her head, while the other – springy and unkempt – could easily have nested several small birds.

Meanwhile, the shutters rattled now and then – the frail clasp of the latch straining – as if someone on the other side was trying to force them open. The rattling was accompanied by the sound of the wind rising and falling. Strained between the shutters, it sounded like a thin whine, but somewhere behind this there was a deeper, more sonorous note. The winter storms had begun in earnest at last.

To give Brebix, Ampliata and the children space around the table for the first 'breakfast shift', the others withdrew to the fringes of the room. Knees drawn up, they leaned against the walls, with their cloaks folded beneath them and the bed linen bunched behind the small of their backs. Ampliata poured each of them a bowl of kheifra. The customary morning drink throughout the citadel, made from chickpeas brewed with rye, it was thick, slightly gritty and bracingly strong. Then she settled down with her husband and children to eat a simple breakfast of figs and dates, accompanied by bread with a thin scraping of honey on it.

"I looked out earlier," commented Brebix. "The cloudscape has turned turbid at last. I think winter's well and truly here."

Marcus nodded, glancing towards the window.

"Even if Titus wasn't in control, I think a rescue mission to Daldriadh would be out of the question for months now."

"It might be out of the question for a lot longer than that," added Magnis. "After all, we still don't have a safe method of descending, so we?"

"No. But there has to be some kind of solution."

This exchange aside, conversation was infrequent. Marcus and the others seemed to sense that any proper discussion of plans – or decision from Brebix and Ampliata about whether or not to help – would have to wait until evening. Only the children displayed any sign of liveliness, ducking their heads to whisper to one another across the table, immersed in their world of private amusements, but casting excited glances at the fugitives, as if distracted by exotic creatures that might perform some amazing trick at any moment.

Presently, with drawn-out sighs that acknowledged the prospect of another day's toil, Brebix and Ampliata pushed back their chairs, seemingly indifferent to the rasp of the legs on the flagstone floor. They paused for a moment, smiling at one another, exchanging an infusion of mutual support. Then they rose and took their cups and bowls over to the sink. The children dodged between them, untroubled by such concerns, and donned the capes made of flax that they wore over the rest of their clothes. Then they went to the other room to gather the loosely bound scraps of parchment and sparsely feathered quill pens that constituted all their school supplies.

Kneeling down to adjust the children's garments, Ampliata said, "Like all the spaces within our layer, the Juvenum – where the children are taught – has no direct light. We used to warm the air and dry the damp walls in winter with proleyne stoves. But we've been ordered to conserve fuel. Also the children used to spend less time there because Brebix and I worked shorter shifts that didn't overlap so much. Don't worry though – I've told them to say nothing about your presence here." She offered a resigned half-smile. "Mind you, these days their lives are so restricted that it's difficult to threaten them with the withdrawal of any treats or freedoms."

The children stood gazing up solemnly at Marcus while she said this – squirming and scratching themselves where the coarse material chafed against their skins.

"Please, we can wash up," Marcus told Ampliata as she retuned to the sink. "It's the least we can do, given all the inconvenience we're causing you."

"Not to mention the burden we're placing on your larder," added Rhea.

Ampliata smiled at both of them, but didn't disagree with this assessment of the situation.

"Very well," she replied. "But please tread as softly as possible. Our dwelling is in the third tier of the layer. Everyone's roof here is someone else's floor, and vice versa. I'm sure you don't wish to draw attention to your presence – for your own sake as much as ours…"

"And if the Kabal come calling?" asked Theus, adopting as light a tone as possible, but giving voice to the anxiety they all shared.

Brebix shrugged.

"There is guttering above the window and a ledge below", replied Brebix. "I don't know how sturdy they are – already the maintenance of the lowest layers is being neglected while we pour all our efforts and resources into making yet more weapons. But you could climb out there and cling on if you had enough warning. It won't be particularly dignified. But then neither is being disembowelled with the dull edge of a sword."

Theus nodded.

"Indeed," he said, with feeling.

"Perhaps it's best for one of us to station ourselves as a sentry on the stairs at all times," suggested Marcus. "We can take shifts."

"I feel like I've been living my whole life in shifts lately," said Magnis ruefully.

"Well then that's something we've *all* got in common isn't it?" said Marcus, smiling at Brebix and Ampliata.

"Yes…yes it is," said Rhea.

With a brisk nod and a reluctant smile, Ampliata ushered the children down the stairs. Brebix followed, drawing the curtain behind him. As soon as he had gone, in spite of all the peril that attended their current circumstances, Marcus couldn't help but feel a sense of awkwardness ebb from the room. Everyone's posture grew slightly less stiff. It was so strange, he thought, how the prospect of discovery, torture and perhaps even death at the hands of armed Kabal guards could somehow feel less tense, from moment to moment, than being uninvited guests in someone else's already cramped home.

Marcus, Rhea, Theus and Magnis ate an even more meagre breakfast than the family had, then cleared up. This task was accomplished in an exaggeratedly slow and deliberate fashion, partly to make as little sound as possible, partly to use up some of the barren hours that stretched ahead.

While Rhea and Theus dried the dishes they had washed and Magnis put them away, Marcus tiptoed over to the window and opened the shutters just a fraction. Behind them there was another, smaller pair of shutters with angled slats in them that divided the view into horizontal stripes. Peering through these, he saw that the main cloudscape was raked by winds from the north and there was a pewter coloured glaze of altostratus across the whole sky. It was very stormy. The trees in the orchard thrashed and jostled against one another. Leaves spun through the air above their branches. Sometimes the leaves almost seemed to flock like birds – corralled together by a freak gust – then dispersed again. In the fields the farmers were more warmly clad than before and bent closer to the ground as they worked. And on the fortified wall immediately below, the sentinels' cloaks streamed out almost at a right angle from their armour-clad torsos.

Closing the window, Marcus turned back to the others. Having dried everything, Rhea and Theus were standing by the sink, at a loss what to do next. Both stared at their feet, lips slightly pursed: a perfect tableau of uncertainty. Magnis was reaching up to the cupboard to put the last cup away. Just as he was about to place it on the highest shelf, it slipped from his grasp. While the others watched, frozen in horror, he tried to grab it again. It sprang repeatedly from his hands, as if suddenly granted life and determined to make the most of its new-found agility. Every time he failed to get a grip on it, it tumbled slightly closer to the floor. He caught it at last when it was within inches of smashing. There were a few moments' silence, then everyone let out a tremulous sigh of relief.

"I think it's going to be a long day," observed Marcus resignedly.

It was indeed a long day. Forced to be as quiet as possible, they gingerly lifted the four chairs grouped around the table to the window and sat at it in a tight semi-circle. For hours they all peered out at the cloudscape. So static was everything inside the dwelling that every shift in the appearance of the clouds – no matter how small – mesmerised them. The only time anyone moved was to creep over to the staircase and relieve whoever else was on watch. Trips to the toilet were timed to coincide with these changeovers and they all tried to drink as little water as possible to reduce any discomfort during their long vigil. The only other thing they could do was talk, albeit in hushed tones. After some time, while Magnis was on watch, Theus shifted in his seat and glanced at Marcus and Rhea.

"What you said last night to Brebix and Ampliata, about the way the citadel is organised… about a Republic…" he began.

"Yes?" asked Marcus, eager to hear Theus's reaction.

"I…"

Theus hesitated and shifted again. His eyes strayed to the horizon and the wind stirred his grey hair, which had grown increasingly unkempt over the past few weeks.

"It all shocked me a little at first, I must confess. But then I thought more about it. And I realised that…" He sighed, searching for the right words. "I realised that though I always loved the Corps and the opportunities it gave me to see faraway places, some of the things you said *have* occurred to me before. When I used to visit my family in the Artisans' layer I felt guilty about the life I had compared to theirs. It's not that they complained. But from the way they described their daily routine, I could tell it was pretty restricted – their world was confined to the walls they lived and worked within. The view from their gardens was their only hint of something better. They had an air of... I don't know, *resignation* about them. Even the youngest men and women seemed already to have accepted that they would never experience anything better. And when I told them about *my* experiences over the cloudscape and in other citadels I could sense that they feared what they weren't familiar with.

So what worries me, I suppose, is that it's exactly that fear and resignation that'll make it so difficult to persuade them to rise up – especially now that they're labouring under such a harsh regime. And from a purely practical point of view, even if they were willing to revolt – to take that huge gamble with their lives and try to master their own destinies – how would we spread the word to them in the first place? How do you conjure ferment amongst people if you can't even reach them?"

Rhea glanced at Marcus, as if fearful that he might feel dispirited, or even annoyed, by Theus's comments. But he merely inclined his head in thoughtful acknowledgement of them. All the doubts and reservations that Theus expressed had already occurred to him more than once and he was far from immune from them himself.

There was one other factor in their favour: the knowledge that the Mercanteer had sent ornithopters back to Selenopolis. But there was no guarantee that such small gliders would reach home safely so late in the year, with the cloudscape assuming the ferocious unpredictability of its winter state. Even if they did return home, the same likelihood of hibernal storms might prevent the Selenopolitans from dispatching aëro:cruisers to Heliopolis. And even if they were dispatched, they might arrive too late to help in any uprising… It was a long chain of 'ifs' – far too frail to hang any hopes on.

So, instead of mentioning possible intervention by the great citadel to the east – their closest neighbour and sometime ally – Marcus said, "Okay. Well let's take this one stage at a time. Assuming Brebix and Ampliata are willing to help us and the Kabal don't discover us, how do we let the people in only this layer to start with know that we're back and what Titus did to us and my father?"

"There's no other way to do it than through Brebix and Ampliata themselves," replied Rhea. "They're the only ones among us who can move about the layer."

"But they're under the collective eye of the Kabal every moment of the day," countered Theus. "We all saw what it was like in the fields. I'm pretty sure the Laborium will be even worse. How can they spread news if they're not allowed to talk to one another? Even if they wrote things down, the guards would be sure to see the messages they passed…"

Marcus nodded and glanced out between the slats of the window again. Through one of the gaps he saw a row of dark, forbidding storm clouds, stretched like a cliff face along the horizon. They bore the promise of turmoil in their wake. Theus was right of course. One remote hope of salvation aside, the task before them was all but impossible. It was far more challenging even than climbing the Ins'lberg, because just to prepare for it was to risk disclosure and capture. Yet what choice did they have but to attempt it?

They continued to discuss these problems for hours and hours over the next few days. To cheer himself up, Marcus imagined himself approaching them as a sculptor might a huge slab of marble or stone – restlessly circling it, chipping away at the most accessible parts, trying to create something plausible out of the challenge it represented. Yet there were times when they could make no further progress and needed a respite. At such moments, the conversation tended to turn, perhaps inevitably, towards family and friends – not seen for months, parted from calmly, in ignorance of the pain and danger that would intervene before any chance of a reunion.

"It's so strange," said Magnis. "To think that my family lives only a few hundred yards away, in the next quadrant of the tier above."

"How many of them are there?" asked Marcus.

"Five – my parents, my sister, her husband and their baby, all of them in a dwelling not much bigger than this." Magnis smiled wistfully. "In the evenings I can just picture them: my mother standing guard over the stove to stop my father from picking at the food before it's ready; my sister sitting at the table trying to feed the baby; her husband – my brother in law – taking the washing down to stop it smelling of cooking, even though it's not completely dry yet; my father opening the shutters and letting out some of the steam then my sister scolding him and telling him to close it again because the cold air will chill the baby… The more time passes since I last saw them, the more vivid they seem to me."

Marcus listened attentively. After countless solitary childhood hours spent roaming huge rooms beneath ornate ceilings, this description of family life – so cramped and entwined, yet also warm and mutually supportive – still fascinated him. To his ears it sounded as exotic as tales of ancient customs in distant, equatorial citadels might to Brebix and Ampliata.

"And not one of them knows what really happened to me," continued Magnis. "I mean they will have heard Titus's false story about the downing of the *Noble Quest*. But they won't know if I was burnt, or lost limbs, or fell whole. I hope they just imagine me having strayed into the cloudscape and become like a wraith – in a kind of peaceful way."

"They probably struggle not to imagine it at all – they're probably already trying to build a cage for those thoughts in the back of their minds, to stop them from roaming around and causing more pain than they can bear," observed Marcus.

The others smiled feelingly at Marcus. They knew he was describing a means of coping that he was only too familiar with himself.

"Still," Marcus continued. "At least there's hope that your family is not aware of yet. It may be no consolation to them at the moment, but it's enough that it exists."

"Well, that's true," said Magnis. "It just seems odd that they're so close at hand, yet still almost as out of reach as if I was a thousand miles away and leagues deep in Daldriadh."

"I know, I know."

After a brief silence, Theus said, "Only my mother is still alive, in the Artisans' layer. She lives with my brother and sister-in-law. But she's very aged and not really aware of things anymore. I'm afraid I didn't go down to visit her as often as I should in the last few years because she didn't always recognise who I was and it grieved me. You can imagine how guilty that makes me feel now. But then again – maybe it's a blessing for her. I hope the others haven't tried to make her understand that I'm... well, gone."

"I'm sure they won't," said Rhea.

Marcus nodded, but he could just imagine Titus sending an emissary to seek her out and – placing a hand on either side of her head to direct her misted gaze towards his – assure her that her son had died in terror and pain and was lost to her forever.

"I'm from the Artisans' layer too," continued Rhea. "My family live crammed together there – my parents and my brothers, all three of them still at home, none of them showing the slightest desire to get married." She smiled ruefully at the thought then frowned again. "My mother and father didn't want me to go into the Corps. They had a trio of hulking sons, yet I was the one, when I was tested, who showed aptitude for the skills required: geometrics, nephology, meteorology."

In spite of her sorrowful expression, the vaguest hint of pride crept into her tone when she said this.

"My parents didn't know how to react when they heard I was to be recruited. It wasn't that they wanted to deny I was bright and capable; it was just that they felt cloudfaring was too dangerous for a young woman. When I used to visit them and tell them tales of what I'd been doing – my latest voyages; other societies and their customs; freak weather out over the cloudscape – I could tell they were proud and pleased for me, but I could see the worry in their eyes too. I can't imagine how awful it must be for them now, to believe that all their fears have been confirmed."

She ran her fingers through her hair and Marcus noticed that a thin but unmistakable seam of premature grey had opened up at the left side of her temple. Its meandering course seemed a symbol of all the unexpected events and calamities that had befallen her and the rest of them in the past month.

Marcus sighed.

"I know… think we'll all go mad if we think too much about these things," he said. "As for me… well, you all know only too well, I'm sure, that I don't have parents or brothers or sisters to worry about in that way. But there's Asperia, who's like family to me. I've no idea what's happened to her. And… well, as you've probably guessed, there are people back in Daldriadh, people I became close to, whom I think of a lot and whose safety I worry about very much."

Knowing he meant Breah and her family in particular, the others smiled with grave courtesy, but said nothing.

VII.

The Nullmaurs' Gambit

The events in the peat bog kept everyone especially vigilant over the next few days, their usual alertness compounded by uncertainty over what might happen next. The old spectacle of the ornithopters swooping in to disgorge their cargo of bombs seemed almost comforting in retrospect, given how predictable it has been.

They tensed themselves for some strange new form of bombardment, but none came. Instead the clouds pressed down and squeezed the mist inward from the surrounding hills, as if it had itself become a besieging force. This phenomenon lent the landscape beyond the hills an oddly muffled, becalmed feeling, which only served to heighten their anxieties – there was no way of knowing what forces the Nullmaurs might be mustering out there.

Eventually, however, the illusion of peace came to an end, like a villain shedding a not terribly plausible disguise to reveal the true threat that dwelt beneath. It happened early in the morning. Breah was crouched in one of the deep, narrow trenches that had been dug just outside the stockade to offer its outer ring of defenders some protection in the event of another Nullmaur attack. Along with Aònghas and Persis, she was helping with a frame that Aònghas devised to strengthen the trench's forward-facing wall. Called hurdlework, the frame consisted of rods of hazel, woven between one another at right angles. As they worked, Aònghas was explaining to Persis the next stage in its construction.

"We'll brace the hurdlework by covering it in daub. That's a clay mixture strengthened with straw and coarse hair from the pelts of Grashiels," he said.

"Hair? Really?" asked Persis, unable to disguise his puzzlement.

Aònghas nodded.

"It's a special mixture we sometimes use. When it dries it is more…"

He paused with a frown, searching for the right word. Breah had noticed him doing this more and more often recently when speaking the Cloudfarers' language. The shock of lost faith seemed to have brought forgetfulness in its wake, depleting the treasury of words he had once so cherished.

"Resilient?" she suggested.

"Yes, thank you," he replied, smiling at her. "More resilient than clay alone."

They worked a while longer. Other Eihlans brought a wooden pail full of fresh daub then clambered into the trench to help them apply it. Though fairly straightforward, the process was hampered by the limited space available to them all. And it was accompanied by frequent apologies as the occupants trod on one another's toes and elbowed each other in the side of the head.

After nearly an hour of this, Persis, the only one amongst them tall enough to see over the lip of the trench, paused in his labours, his eyes straying across the marshes. Breah noticed him frowning.

"How resilient did you say the daub was?" he asked, the light tone of his voice trying but failing to mask genuine apprehension.

"Why?" asked Aònghas.

Persis nodded towards the hills. Gripping an undaubed portion of the hurdlework, Aònghas and Breah hoisted themselves up and followed his gaze.

All around the brows of the hills, where the steeper incline of trees would have begun, were it visible, they noticed the mist seeming to darken in different places, as if stained by an alien presence. The way it did so was eerily familiar to Breah. It reminded her of ornithopters emerging from it in the past. But this time there was no hint of the swirling agitation that their wings set in motion. The mist just continued to thicken here and there. She guessed that unknowable objects were being stationed at regular intervals along the tree line. But to what purpose?

The purpose became clearer – along with the contours of the objects – when they edged a little further forward. The strange interplay of light and perspective between the village and the distant trees meant that it took a few moments for her to comprehend what she was seeing. Each object consisted of two Grashiels yoked together and supporting a heavekairt, which in turn contained two Nullmaurs. The arrangement was perfectly familiar to her. But there was one addition that made her scowl with a mixture of perplexity and fear. Mounted atop the heavekairt was a weapon far more substantial – and therefore malevolent – in outline than any she had seen before.

"It looks like the same type of smoothbore cannon we use aboard our aëro:cruisers," said Persis. "They must have scavenged them and got them working again... But I wonder why they've never deployed them before."

"Perhaps it has taken them this long to master them," suggested Aònghas.

"Perhaps they feel they need a stronger weapon," added Breah. "Now that our defences are improved."

"Possibly," said Persis. "But I think it's more likely that after encountering us they ventured forth to find the wreckage of the *Noble Quest*. Its hull *did* break apart on the shore. But much of what its hold contained – including plenty of ordnance – would have survived intact."

Aònghas nodded glumly.

"And become visible to them with the retreat of the tide," he said.

"Indeed," replied Persis. He glanced at Breah. "I think without intending to we may yet again have placed power in the hands of your enemy. I'm truly sorry."

"But you have placed yourselves amongst us too," Aònghas pointed out. "We have at least been granted that mercy by..."

His voice faltered. Breah sensed that he had been going to say, out of habit, "by the Gods." He lowered his head briefly, the renewed sense of lost faith apparent in the diminished lustre of his gaze. Then, looking up again, he said, "By fate."

In spite of how tenuous her grip on the hurdlework was, Breah reached over and patted his arm consolingly.

A few moments later, the barrels of all the cannons tilted slowly upwards, as if they were awakening from a profound slumber. Seeing this, Breah and the others finally shook off their own trance of appalled fascination. Scrambling out of the trench, they hastened back inside the compound just as the first salvo of shells carved their scorching trajectories through the damp air, towards the village.

The siege had begun.

VIII.

Brebix and Ampliata Decide

Marcus and the others continued to discuss how they might set an uprising in motion if... *if* Brebix and Ampliata agreed to at least help spread the word. Over successive days, all sorts of ideas were suggested, examined and cast, regretfully, aside.

On the evening of the third day – with shadows pooling in the valleys of the cloudscape – the sound of returning workers filled the streets below the tiered dwellings. But amid the tread of innumerable pairs of ill-shod feet and the rasp of sleeves against the stone walls, there was none of the murmurous chatter or eruptions of mirth you would normally expect to hear, signalling the end of a working day.

Brebix returned exhausted and begrimed as ever, a burlap sack slung over his shoulder. The others rose to greet him, no longer compelled to be still, since the walls and ceiling resounded with the movement of returning workers now also entering their adjacent dwellings. Rhea moved her chair back over to the table for him and he sat down, closing his eyes briefly.

"How was your day?" she asked.

"No one was needlessly beaten for slowness. No one was forced to do a pointless task over and over again for supposed insolence. No-one was dragged down through the orchards and cast over for incompetence. So, all in all, that counts as a passable day." He opened his eyes. "How was yours?"

"Quiet," replied Marcus.

"Hmm. Well, I can't say I'm sorry to hear that, given the alternative."

"Indeed," commented Theus dryly.

"Will Ampliata be finished soon too?" asked Magnis.

Brebix yawned.

"Not for another hour or two. She'll collect the children from the Juvenum. In the meantime I'll prepare dinner. But first I need to bathe."

"Of course," replied Marcus. "Why don't we get things started in the meantime?"

Brebix nodded.

"Thank you. We have some meat tonight too. It's strictly rationed these days. The Kabal only provide it when people start collapsing in the fields from malnourishment."

He rummaged in the sack at his feet and withdrew a piece of twine, to which three birds, each one about the size of a man's hand, were tied by the feet. As he held them up they twisted slightly on the twine, wings agape. Marcus recognised them as squabs – one of the types of fowl most frequently eaten by Heliopolitans.

"You soak them in warm water to make them easier to pluck," Brebix explained. "Then they'll need their gizzards and livers taken out. After that you can wash them, pat them dry and season them. Maybe add some thyme leaves too. Do you think you could do that?"

None of them looked entirely certain, but Magnis, taking the birds from Brebix, smiled at the others and said, "It's all right – I used to help my father gut fowl in the aviaries when I was a boy. I'm sure we'll manage."

"Good."

So Brebix heated a pan full of water to wash himself then returned to the alcove that contained the bath, pulling the curtain closed after him. Meanwhile, the others crowded together in the partitioned kitchen area and set about preparing the ingredients. While Rhea concentrated on the vegetables, Marcus and Theus soaked and plucked the carcasses of the squabs then handed them to Magnis to be gutted. It was inescapably grisly work, but under his supervision they made decent progress.

None the less, a little while later, pausing to gaze down at the pitifully small number of peppers she was coring, Rhea said flatly, "We can't go on like this. Things have to move faster. We can't place such a burden on this household – they'll starve. And the Kabal are sure to discover us before long. A stray footfall or something dropped inopportunely is all it will take."

Ordinarily Marcus felt nothing for Rhea other than affection and respect. But as he listened to her the rising note of urgency in her voice provoked a trace of defensiveness in him.

"Well what would you have us *do* Rhea?" he asked. "Reveal ourselves to the Kabal? If we're captured and executed, how does that help Brebix and Ampliata and all the other families like them, in this layer and the one above? How does it help them to free themselves from drudgery and injustice?"

"Drudgery and injustice won't endanger their lives – not if they're lucky anyway. But if they're found to be sheltering us they'll surely be killed, and maybe even their children too."

"Yes… yes, I do realise that," replied Marcus, his tone softening.

"These are *good* people," she persisted. "They're hard working and respectful of each other and gentle with their children. We have to persuade Brebix and Ampliata to decide whether they're going to help or not. If not, we can't go on endangering them. We must find some other way…"

Marcus sighed and nodded. All these sentiments had occurred to him too. But his thirst for revenge, allied to his desire to see the people wrest control of the citadel from Titus, was so all-consuming that he had tried to ignore them. At the same time, however, he couldn't help but concede that they were living in an impossible situation. He noticed Theus and Magnis glancing at one another; he could tell that they agreed with her too.

"Okay, we'll talk about it tonight for sure."

She smiled.

"Good."

They resumed work. Once Brebix had washed and dressed again, he drew the curtain aside and nodded approval at their preparations. He announced that he would sear the squabs in a skillet and fry the vegetables in another pan. Relieved at having such tasks to absorb them, they set to work.

Some time later Ampliata returned, the children preceding her. They burst into the room with so much momentum and in such disorder you'd think they had just fallen down a flight of steps instead of run up them. Clutching a sheaf of parchments each, they hastened over to Magnis and tugged at his tunic to show him what they had done during the day. Marcus couldn't help but feel admiration for how little enfeebled they seemed by so many hours of strict discipline in the damp air and poor light of the Juvenum.

"Was your day bearable?" Rhea asked Ampliata. Even her short experience of a Farming family's life under the Kabal had taught her not to frame the question in any more positive terms. Ampliata, as exhausted as Brebix, offered a hollow-eyed smile in acknowledgement of Rhea's tact.

"More or less," she replied.

Nodding to the others, she managed to conceal all but the vaguest disquiet at their continued presence in her home. Then she and her husband hugged one another with their usual understated intensity and she went to the other room to change, the children at her heels. While she was away Theus and Rhea returned to the kitchen alcove – he to toss the squab legs, wings and halved breasts in the skillet, while she seasoned the vegetables. Marcus smiled as he watched Magnis lavish the childrens' parchments with praise.

Presently, Ampliata returned with her hair tied up in a scarf. She paused briefly to look into the pot of sweltering vegetables and gave a vaguely approving nod. Then she knelt over the edge of the bath to wash her face and hands with water that Brebix had left in the pan for her. As she did so, Marcus and Rhea set the table with Nekayah's enthusiastic, if slightly haphazard, assistance.

At last everyone settled down to eat. As on previous nights, Brebix, Ampliata and the children sat on the four chairs, the children raised up on a couple of cushions each. Rhea, Theus and Magnis sat on stools. Two of these had been retrieved from the bedroom, while the third was normally stowed under the sink, so that Ampliata could stand on it to reach the top shelf of the cupboard. Marcus sat on a bedside table, also retrieved from the other room. It creaked with a discreet but unmistakable note of complaint every time he shifted his weight.

Squab meat, though dark, had a distinctively delicate taste. But given that Marcus – as on previous days – had eaten nothing since breakfast, it was, once again, blissfully flavoursome. The others seemed to feel the same way and everyone ate in silence for some time, chewing each mouthful again and again, to get as much nutrition from it as possible.

After they had finished, Theus and Magnis cleared up, while Brebix made kheifra. Marcus stared at the surface of the table, lost in thought. But then he felt someone nudge his leg. Looking up, he saw Rhea levelling a steady, meaningful look across the table at him. Nodding, he glanced at Ampliata and Brebix. There seemed no way of broaching the topic that didn't sound somewhat stilted.

"Have you...had a chance to think about what we discussed before?" he asked.

"We have thought of little else," replied Brebix.

"We have spoken about it every night," added Ampliata.

"And have you reached any conclusion?" asked Rhea, in as gently inquisitorial a tone as possible.

"What conclusion can we reach... other than that helping foment revolution, in even the most minor way, is to risk placing our heads and those of our children on the executioner's block," Ampliata told her.

Marcus felt a familiar sense of despondency settle upon him and squared his shoulders to receive its weight. But this reaction changed to surprise just a few moments later when Ampliata resumed talking.

"Yet, at the same time, what is our alternative? To continue like this? To submit to a life that is little more than mere existence? To condemn our children to the same? How can I bear to imagine that their whole future will be no better than that?"

She slowly surveyed the fugitives' faces, addressing them all equally.

"I don't want Imlac and Nekaya to live like we did – even before Titus usurped power. I don't want them to spend their days with their heads bowed over their work in the fields or the Laborium, never daring to look up and dream of something better for themselves. I don't want them to live in a place where they have to be vigilant of their neighbours because there isn't enough food to go around and someone might try to steal what little they have… But more than that, more than any of that, they should have choices in their life, the way we never had." At this point her eyes settled on Marcus in particular. "This is what happens when you're poor. You have no choices: your life is constantly about 'or' when it should be 'and'. I want them to have the chance to travel out over the cloudscape; to see life in other citadels, so they can come back with a better view of this one."

As Marcus listened to her, he paid keen attention not only to what she was saying but to the way she said it. Throughout his childhood, he had been told that inhabitants of the Farmers' layer received only a limited education, consistent with their humble position in Heliopolitan society. Yet he was struck – as he had been when listening to Brebix earlier – by the way she expressed herself. Her speech might have been slightly plainer than his own, but it was vivid and concise and it bespoke a strong, down to earth intelligence. Reflecting on this, Marcus suspected that much of what he'd been taught about the lower layers was probably false – or, at any rate, distorted; based more on social prejudice than any kind of reality. He felt ashamed that he had believed it all.

Once she had finished talking, he nodded vigorously.

"I believe all of that too, Ampliata," he said, trying to quell the over-earnest tone that he knew still encroached on his voice when discussing such things. "It's what everything I've been through has taught me. It's why I want us to try and overthrow Titus – so we can make a better fairer life for everyone in the citadel."

Ampliata studied his face, like someone scrutinising a map, as if its features might lead her to a better understanding of his true feelings.

"But where does that leave *you*?" she asked. "Let's say we do prevail; let's say we do free ourselves of the Kabal. You will have given up the role you were born to. It's a noble thing to do, but what will your life be then, with your mother and father already gone?"

Marcus looked down at his folded hands. He knew that Ampliata didn't intend to sound callous. Her harsh experience of life had simply bred an unsentimental outlook, in which realities were bluntly acknowledged – in this regard she reminded him of Breah. None the less, the question still pained him. He had tried hard to keep it at bay within himself, mainly because he didn't know the answer to it and didn't want it to distract him from his purpose. Yet when forced to consider it, he found his thoughts straying from the room and plunging through the cloudscape to seek out the Eihlans, his marooned comrades and Breah herself in particular. Her limber physical presence, her blend of strength and empathy, her delicate yet resolute features: all these things had formed such a deep impression on his mind. He realised that when he allowed himself to imagine the future, in even the vaguest terms, it was dominated by her – in spite of the great, perhaps irreversible decision he would have to make if they were to share a life together. But he didn't want to talk about such things to Ampliata – or even to Rhea – just yet.

"I don't know," he said. "I really don't. But that doesn't matter right now. Just give me my moment with Titus... As for all the rest – I'll work it out later, somehow."

He offered a wry smile.

"Then again, Titus is much larger and stronger than I am, and a far more experienced swordsman too. So if we do face each other, my future might not be something anyone has to worry about, least of all me."

He could tell that Ampliata didn't think this a particularly satisfactory response. But he also sensed that she wouldn't pursue it any further, out of respect for him. She frowned and her hand stole across the table to clasp Brebix's. They stared at one another, impassive, for a while, as if communicating by thought alone. Brebix nodded, his eyes still on her. Then he looked at the others and said, "Very well. We're with you."

There was a palpable easing of tension in the room. Marcus, Rhea, Theus and Magnis all exchanged guardedly optimistic smiles.

"Thank you," said Marcus.

"Thank you both," added Rhea.

But their gratitude drew a characteristic reproof from Ampliata.

"Don't thank us too fulsomely, just yet. We may be willing to help. But we have no idea how to go about overthrowing the Kabal."

"Well then," said Theus. "That's what we have to discuss next, isn't it?"

And so they did, for many hours. At one point, late into the evening, their murmurous talk was interrupted by the shutters bursting open, like someone's arms thrown wide in advance of a sensational announcement. Suitably startled, everyone flinched then emitted a groan of comprehension as the shutters continued to flap back and forth. Marcus rose with a sigh and went over to close them. He reached out to grasp each shutter, but what he saw when glancing up into the night sky gave him pause.

Far, far above, in the remotest reaches of the atmosphere, slender clouds glowed brightly amid the stars – as if illuminated by an upward shining light whose source was nowhere visible.

Joining him as he continued to stare at this phenomenon, Rhea said, "Hmm, noctilucent clouds."

"Of course," replied Marcus. "Asperia taught me about these, but I've never seen them before."

Rhea nodded.

"They're very rare indeed."

"What causes them? Asperia told me once, but I've forgotten exactly."

"No-one really knows. It's thought they're made up of ice crystals in the mesosphere and illuminated by sunlight from below the horizon."

"Maybe they're a good omen," suggested Marcus.

"Maybe," said Rhea, smiling.

They watched the beautiful streaks of light for a little longer, before the encroaching cold forced them to lock the shutters and return to the others.

IX.

The Eihlans Besieged

As soon as the villagers saw Breah, Aònghas, Persis and the rest of their work party burst through the entrance of the stockade and run towards the holms – uttering garbled but unmistakably urgent warnings – their well honed sense of self-preservation prompted them to do the same. Vaulting discarded baskets and trampling bales of straw, each of them headed for the nearest refuge. Some hurled themselves into the widest trench stretching between the holms, while others sought the narrower ones that diverged from it like arteries. As they did so, the first barrage of shells plunged, sizzling, through the damp mist and struck the ground. Everywhere they landed they conjured geysers of dirt, which quickly subsided to leave smouldering craters scattered all across the compound.

Some of the slowest moving villagers, caught between the competing shockwaves of the explosions, lurched this way and that – as if wrenched at by invisible hands – before being slammed to the ground, where they lay motionless. Those who had already reached the partial sanctuary of the trenches crouched in them until the initial bombardment had ceased. Then, pressing themselves against the musty walls, they peered over the edges with such expressions of wonder and fear that they might have been mistaken for subterranean creatures emerging from prolonged hibernation.

Eventually the initial bombardment thinned then ceased. Conscious that it would probably take their enemies – so adept at the craft of warfare – only a short time to reload, several of the Cloudfarers scrambled out of the main trench and ran in a crouch to where the stricken villagers lay. Unable to show much regard for the dignity of each prone body, they grabbed it by the collar and dragged it clear of the ravaged compound as quickly as they could.

The stragglers having been rescued, everyone crouched again in the trenches as the next round of shells swept in like a squall of lethal weather. Huddled against a wall, knees drawn up, Breah felt rivulets of soil trickling down her neck as the ground shivered with each explosion. She had dreaded this moment: the onset of the Nullmaurs' concerted hostility. No longer was there any hint, as there had been during previous attacks, that this might prove to be a temporary assault – brief as it was fierce – leaving behind it, for those who survived, a strange sense of elation. No. This time it would persist as long as even one of them remained alive.

In spite of this, the occupants of the trenches showed little inclination to endure the bombardment in a spirit of despair. Instead, Cloudfarers and Eihlans alike began to edge along, converging on one of the largest holms. In spite of its size, its entrance was half as high as those of the other dwellings, so that even the shortest Eihlans had to enter it on hands and knees. Inside, the reason for this became apparent. The floor of the holm – which lay at the bottom of a short series of roughly made steps – had been dug deeper than those of the others, with a false ceiling of wooden planks laid across it at ground level. Through lowering the floor and reinforcing the roof in this way, the Cloudfarers – principally Tafril, Jarrid and Amik – had created a makeshift shelter.

Now everyone crowded into it, filling it up from the edges inward. This entailed much jostling and many contortions, but no-one betrayed the slightest irritation at being packed so closely together. Indeed so shocked were they by the force of the bombardment that they all behaved towards one another with scrupulous patience – as if determined that none of the discord outside should leak into their precious refuge.

Breah found herself crammed against the wall opposite the entrance with Persis and Aònghas. At her whispered request, each placed a hand under her arm and hoisted her up so she could locate her mother and sister. In their eagerness to help, they did so with such vigour that she bumped her head against the low rafters, but she didn't mind. After a few moments of scanning the curious terrain of bowed heads that filled the room, she located them, just to the left of the steps. Eithné was curled on Morveyn's lap, fear seeming to have shrunk her, while her mother murmured comfortingly in her upturned ear.

Satisfied that they were safe – or, at least, no less unsafe than anyone else – Breah squirmed back down into the space that Persis and her father had kept vacant. For a while no one spoke. Instead all the occupants of the holm focused their attention on what was happening outside. The bombardment continued, but it was hard to distinguish between the impacts of the individual shells. Muffled by the double roof, they seemed to merge into a low rumble of unvarying belligerence.

Eventually, however, isolated conversations started up again, until the holm was filled with murmurous chat.

"How long do you think it will last?" Breah asked Persis.

"Which, the bombardment or our defences?" he replied, with a grim smile.

Aware that he was pointing out, as obliquely as possible, that this was an unanswerable question, she nodded and said, "I suppose the second depends on the first, doesn't it?"

"Indeed." He shifted his posture as much as the cramped conditions would allow. "If they've established a secure supply line for ordnance all the way back to their lair – which I'm sure they have – I suspect they'll continue while there's enough light to find a target… And even after nightfall they could keep their cannons' barrels at the right elevation to pummel more or less the same area." He pursed his lips. "I'm sorry to tell you, but I think the bombardment may prove unremitting until there's nothing left of this village but one large, smouldering crater."

Breah frowned, her fears confirmed.

"In which case…"

"In which case," put in Aònghas, who had been listening to this exchange. "We need to find a way of conveying ourselves safely out of the village and into the hills."

"Exactly," replied Persis.

As if in illustration of the urgent need for an escape plan, their discussion was interrupted by the sound of a shell striking the exterior of the holm. Clamorous, emphatic, it was like a thunderclap breaking directly overhead. It rolled around the partitioned space above them, as if testing the acoustics of every corner. More importantly, it also sent a deluge of shattered clay and charred wood onto the planks of the false ceiling. They flexed in several places, but held fast. Only trickles of the finest debris issued from the narrow gaps between them, settling on the hunched shoulders of some of the Eihlans, who were too immobilised by terror to brush themselves clean – and would have struggled to manoeuvre a hand free from the crush of bodies even if they had wished to do so.

Aònghas peered up at the planks as if they had suddenly become something threatening, rather than a form of protection.

"We cannot endure if we stay here," he said, the doleful reality of the fact settling more firmly upon him.

Persis nodded.

"As soon as night falls we'll begin making our preparations." He lapsed into frowning reflection for a few moments. Then, with a grunt of effort, he raised himself on his haunches. His gaze sought out each of his fellow Cloudfarers in turn, until he succeeded in capturing the attention of one of them: Lucis. With as much fluency as his restricted position allowed, he formed a rapid series of shapes with his extended hands, the fingers interlinked in different combinations. Lucis – keen-eyed as ever – observed this display intently for a few moments and nodded. Then, twisting round, he sought the eye of another comrade and repeated the wordless message in the same way. Soon enough, he, Tafril, Jarrid, Denihr and Amik had all shared it.

Meanwhile Persis settled himself down again beside Breah and, in response to her questioning look, said, "It's a method of communicating our Cloudfaring Corps uses in special circumstances – like during an aerial battle when the recoil of the cannons makes it too loud for anyone below deck to hear themselves speak. I thought it best to use it at present, so we don't alarm any of the other villagers by telling them they're doomed if we stay here."

"Very wise," commented Aònghas, with feeling.

"But they'll find out soon enough if the roof caves in," Breah pointed out.

"True," conceded Persis. "But by the same token, a riot in so confined a space would serve little purpose. When the time *does* come to move everyone outside again, we need to avoid any sense of panic – wouldn't you agree?"

"Yes… I see what you mean."

And so they continued to wait for night to come, craning their necks now and then to see if the pale dribble of light, which lay over the topmost steps of the holm, had grown any weaker. As they did so, Breah could not help but recollect, with a keen sense of irony, the way that winter days used to seem all too brief when she was a young girl, offering so little opportunity for playing outside; yet now here she was, willing this one to finish and, in doing so, deliver them some hope of salvation.

At last the light on the stairs began to retreat, like a leak mysteriously repairing itself. The instant the last trace of it vanished, there were stirrings in different parts of the holm, as the Cloudfarers, by prior consent, began putting their plan into action. Uttering whispered apologies, mingled with broken words of reassurance, they all shuffled between the Eihlans to converge on the stairs. Then, in spite of the monitory rumble that persisted outside – growing louder now and then when a pair of shells struck simultaneously – they exited the holm one by one.

Once they had departed, Breah gradually realised that the time she'd spent anticipating the fall of night had seemed positively fleet-footed compared with the time she now spent wondering how the Cloudfarers were going to arrange an escape route for the villagers, and if any of them would be picked off by a stray shell in the attempt. Sighing, she crossed her legs, finding it difficult to derive much pleasure from the extra space that Persis' departure had afforded her.

She was just beginning to entertain the fear that *all* the Cloudfarers had perished, when a pair of feet grew dimly visible on the top step, to be replaced, a few seconds later, by Denihr's face, tilted sideways. Directing his voice over the bowed heads of the other Eihlans, he called out to Breah and Aònghas.

"I think we have found a way of conveying you all to safety – at least temporarily," he told them. "Please tell the others to quit the holm in as calm and orderly a fashion as possible."

Breah and Aònghas repeated this message to their fellow villagers, who stirred themselves fearfully. Father and daughter were then forced to loiter in a crouch at the edge of the holm until almost all of them had vacated it in single file. The indistinct sounds of wonderment that issued from the trench made her unbearably curious about the change the Cloudfarers had wrought in the world outside. What had they done to make the compound safe and – as she'd only just now noticed – mute the sounds of the bombardment?

As soon as she reached the trench herself and peered over the top of it, the answer became apparent. All around the edge of the compound, the serrated top of the stockade was sharply etched against an even higher wall of flame, which loomed, pulsating, beyond it. Gasping at this spectacle, she edged along the trench, past the other Eihlans immobilised by astonishment at it, until she found Persis. He wore an expression of grim satisfaction. The top half of his face was luridly illuminated by the flames, while the lower half remained in the shadow cast by the stockade. This lent him a furtive, half-concealed look, which did little to calm Breah's nerves.

"What did you do?" she asked him.

"We set fire to the marsh gas that collects on the surface of the water as oil," he replied. "It's just a thin layer so it'll burn off fairly soon. But it should confound the Nullmaurs just long enough for us to make our escape into the dark of the fields. There's plenty of furrows and hollows out there where we can conceal ourselves at first." He squinted up at the crest of flames, smiling. "Our enemies must be wondering what's happening. They probably think we've chosen cremation over being pounded into pieces."

Breah frowned.

"But if the marshes all round are ablaze, how can we pass through them safely?" she asked.

"Don't worry. We've thought of that."

Before she could question him any further, he heaved himself out of the trench in one decisive movement that testified to both his strength and the heaviness of his frame. Then, turning round, he proffered an outstretched hand and hoisted her with ease after him. All along the trench, his comrades were assisting the other Eihlans in a similar way. Mothers clasped babies to their hips with one arm before allowing themselves to be pulled up by the other. Young children – Eithné included – wriggled with delight at being swung through the air, momentarily forgetting their perilous circumstances.

Once everyone was in the compound again, Tafril and Amik led the way to the northern end of the village – a more unkempt area, where farming implements and other tools were stored beneath simple shelters that consisted of four corner posts and a rain warped roof. Less effort had also been made here to clear the snow, which lay around in dirt encrusted heaps.

Indifferent to everything except the prospect of escape, the villagers assembled themselves beside the stockade, as instructed. They then watched curiously as the Cloudfarers filled buckets with snow and hurried with them to the nearest holm, a dwelling large enough for three families. During their protectors' absence everyone shuffled on the spot – unable to go anywhere but lent a restless energy by the ever-present sense of danger.

The Cloudfarers, led by Lucis, returned a few minutes later with undiminished haste. They now wielded buckets full of water, having melted the snow on a wood-fired stove, which had been left untended in the holm since the siege began, but retained just enough heat for the task. The villagers' perplexity deepened when the Cloudfarers proceeded to slosh the water over one section of the stockade.

"What are you doing?" Breah whispered to Amik.

"Wait and see," he replied, before departing to fill another bucket.

Having soaked about eight wooden stakes that formed one section of the stockade, the Cloudfarers placed their shoulders against them and gave a prolonged, concerted push. Only now did Breah notice that the earth into which each stake was lodged had been partially excavated to loosen it at the base. With a decisive creak, the stakes – still soldered together – fell forward onto the burning marshes.

Flames billowing out from where they landed, the stakes flattened tussocks and carved a channel of clear air through the conflagration. Almost immediately the wood began to spit and sizzle, resin bubbling up through cracks in the bark. None the less, though the flames writhed on either side – desperate to join up again and restore their encirclement of the village – it looked as if they would be kept at bay for at least a few moments.

Seizing Breah by the arm, Persis gestured with his other hand to the makeshift bridge that the Cloudfarers had created and said, "This is it. We must go now. Tell the others to cross it as quickly as possible."

Biting her lip, she cast an uncertain glance at their method of escape, but turned, none the less, to the assembled

Eihlans and repeated Persis' instructions. Their expressions seemed to reflect, in magnified form, all the apprehension that she herself felt. Some even took a couple of steps back. Realising that the only way to embolden them was by setting an example, she turned back to face the flames. She closed her eyes and – before Aònghas or her mother could stop her – plunged forward over the slippery, uneven surface of the hissing stakes, flames harrying her on either side.

X.

Voices in the Alley

Over the following days, the fugitives continued to plan the rebellion. The problem didn't lie so much in how to *launch* it, but in how to spread the word in the first place and recruit a sufficient number of allies.

As they sat around the table after yet another meagre dinner, of which there were absolutely no leavings, not even any dirty plates, Ampliata said, "In the Laborium we're not allowed to talk much above a murmur when we're stitching the air sacs. And even then only strictly about work. There's no way we can discuss the intricacies of a full scale revolt against Titus and make it look as if we're just asking one another for more tarred wax or to get the awls sharpened."

"Doing what?" asked Theus.

She smiled.

"We use tarred wax to help the needles pass through the canvas. And awls are small pointed tools to score holes in it."

"Oh."

"Anyway, the point is," she continued. "That however I start to spread the word in the Laborium, I can't do it by talking to anyone. The guards will haul me off to be interrogated before even ten words have escaped my lips. We have to find another way."

Brebix nodded.

"It's more or less the same in the fields," he said. "We work in teams, so it's slightly easier to talk to one another up to a point. But the teams are kept separate from one another at all times. And, as you already know, we're not allowed to talk when we mingle together going on or off shift. Nor can we leave our dwellings outside working hours. So I can perhaps inform my closest workmates. But it would be practically impossible to contact anyone outside that small group."

Marcus nodded.

"Hmm…"

Thinking hard, they all lowered their gaze to the table, as if the answer were faintly inscribed in its tarnished surface and they might discern it if only they looked hard enough. Yet the problem seemed intractable: how do you spread the word without using *words*?

No solution to this question arose over the next few days. Then, one afternoon, while Brebix and Ampliata were absent on their shifts, sounds of a commotion drew Marcus, Theus and Magnis' attention to the alley outside the dwelling. Exchanging fearful glances, they rose and crept over to the top of the stairs.

Peering down them, they saw Rhea flattened against the wall on the third last step. She looked back up at them and raised a single finger to her lips, urging silence. Then she gestured to them to join her. As they crept down, the noises grew louder still. Joining Rhea, Marcus craned his neck to get a view of its source.

Just a few feet down the alley from Brebix and Ampliata's front door, a woman was kneeling and sobbing. A basket full of fruit lay overturned at her side. Marcus felt acute relief that she wasn't Ampliata. But the sense of relief was quickly followed by guilt – even if she wasn't their friend, she was still a human being in danger. A small number of Kabal guards stood around her, jeering. Several pointed hand-held crossbolts at her. Fired together, the triangular weapons, loaded with stubby bolts, would perforate her within seconds.

One of the guards stepped forward, grabbed her hair and wrenched her head back, forcing her to look up at him.

"Do you truly think you can steal from the Kabal and go unpunished? Do you?" he shouted.

The woman's face crumpled into a pitiful expression.

"I'm so sorry!" she replied, barely audible through her sobs. "My children are hungry. I meant no disrespect to the Kabal."

"The Kabal is indifferent to whether or not it has your respect," sneered the guard. "It demands absolute obedience."

"I'll never steal again, I promise!"

The guard drew his sword.

"I promise you won't too," he said. "Not without hands."

The woman blanched but could choke out no more words.

Instead she squirmed from the man's grasp, shaking her head. The other Kabal guards looked on, smirking.

As the woman began trying to crawl down the alley, the principal guard followed her. He slashed the air with his sword, practising the stroke he was about to visit upon her. His comrades followed too, crossbolts still raised. Now all of them had their backs to the doorway where the fugitives were concealed.

On the stairs, Magnis clenched his teeth, his head quivering. He looked flushed and his breath came in short, ragged gasps. All the fugitives were appalled by what was about to happen to the woman. But Magnis, being from a Farming family himself, looked positively enraged. It soon became clear that he could stand the situation no longer. Before the others were able to stop him, he dashed back up the stairs then returned with his own crossbolt. Rhea grabbed the sleeve of his tunic.

"You can't!" she hissed. "You'll give us away!"

"I've not lost my mind," Magnis hissed back. "I can do this without betraying us. Trust me."

Watching them both, Marcus could tell that Rhea was torn between fear of discovery by the Kabal and mounting distress at the woman's continued sobbing in the alley outside.

"We have only moments to save her," Magnis pointed out.

Faith in his judgement – bred by the courage he had displayed in Daldriadh and on the ascent to Heliopolis – prevailed within Rhea. With a brief nod, she surrendered her grasp on his tunic and stepped back from him.

Raising the crossbolt, Magnis rested his arm on Theus's shoulder to steady his aim. Then, leaning as far out as he dared, he pulled the trigger.

A single bolt streaked through the air and glanced off the Kabal guard's sword blade just as it descended towards the woman's neck. Knocked off course, it clanged against the cobbles of the alley floor instead. Momentarily astonished then enraged, the guard whirled round to look behind him. But Magnis had already retreated up several steps, concealing himself once again. The other guards stared back at their leader – too astonished to think of lowering their own weapons. Surveying their wide-eyed expressions, he reached a swift conclusion about what had just happened.

"Fools!" he bellowed. "Can't you even keep a steady trigger finger? You could have killed me."

Before any of them could react to this, he set about each one of them with the hand of his sword, slamming it into the sides of their heads. They put up some feeble resistance – but such was the unyielding discipline demanded by the Kabal that none of them attempted to contradict him or defend themselves in any significant way. As he continued to berate them, the woman escaped round the corner of the alley and the fugitives crept back into Brebix and Ampliata's dwelling.

In the kitchen, they listened to the guard exhaust his store of oaths. Eventually he and the others quit the alley in search of their escaped victim, his still grumbling voice slowly fading away. But Marcus, Rhea, Theus and Magnis continued to stand, motionless, around the kitchen table for some time, until they were absolutely certain the danger had passed.

"Well done," Rhea whispered to Magnis.

He smiled modestly.

"Thank you."

When Brebix and Ampliata returned much later that day, the fugitives thought it best not to alarm them by relating what had occurred. The evening passed in the now customary manner. After dinner, Ampliata sat hunched over one of the children's shawls, doing her best to patch and darn it in the paltry light of the candle on the table beside her. She kept the shawl as close to her face while she worked. After a while, however, she stopped and held it at arm's length, needle poised glinting between thumb and forefinger. Having just finished drying some bowls, Marcus caught sight over her out of the corner of his eye. She stared at the garment with unblinking intensity, brows knit.

"What is it?" he asked.

She turned towards him, taking a few moments to refocus.

"I think I know how we can pass a message to the rest of the Farmers," she said. The others gathered eagerly round the table.

"How?" asked Theus.

"Well, as we all know only too well, neither Brebix nor I can speak properly to our co-workers at any point during our shifts."

"Yes."

"But when the other women and I are in the Laborium we spend most of our time working canvasses that make up the air sacs. It's a long, tedious task. Each air sac takes a month to prepare. At the moment we're about to begin the stage where the sections of the newest one have been soldered together, but still need to be stitched more closely around the edges. We sit in a huge circle on stools, with the canvas spread out between us, draped over our laps.

"Okaaay..." said Marcus slowly, still not really seeing where this was going.

"We stitch each section then lift the canvas up and pass it around clockwise, so each person re-stitches the work done by the woman sitting on her right," continued Ampliata. "Eventually the stitching will be smeared with more heated pitch, so that the canvas becomes absolutely sealed, no matter how strong the air pressure inside it when it's inflated."

Marcus glanced at the others, who were all frowning at her. Yet she didn't seem to be put off by their perplexity.

Indeed her soft, brown-eyed gaze was lit with quiet amusement as it surveyed their faces.

"So?" said Rhea.

"So... with enough tarred wax to make the stitching easy and a sharp enough needle, I'm sure I could stitch a message into the canvas. Mind you, it'd have to be something brief and clear. But then when the canvas is passed around, the next person will get to read it and then the next person and so on. What's more, the guards tend to lurk at the fringes of the Laborium, so there's a good chance that none of them will see it, or be aware of what's happening. And when the section of the canvas with the message on it comes back round to me – which it should do, after a few hours - I'll unpick the stitching with an awl to leave no evidence."

There was silence while her words slowly sank in.

"Then, when the other women go home at the end of their shift, hopefully they'll tell their husbands the message in the privacy of their dwellings" she continued. "Before too long everyone in the layer should know what's afoot. Whether or not, having discussed it, they'll agree to help us is another matter of course. But still..."

The others said nothing, but they way they slowly shifted in their seats then assumed a more upright posture suggested a reawakened sense of hope. Marcus glanced at Rhea.

"Could it work?" he asked.

"It could," she said, inclining her head respectfully towards Ampliata. "The

most difficult thing will be to find a form of words that's brief but lets the other women know that we've returned.

Theus sighed.

"No small feat."

"Indeed"

"It doesn't just have to be one message though, does it?" offered Magnis. "I mean as long as it's done discreetly, Ampliata could split the message up into fragments, over several days – feed it to the others piece by piece. That way there'll be less chance of discovery too, because each shorter message will be easier to stitch and unpick."

"Hmm."

They all pondered a little longer. Then Brebix said, "As uncomfortable as I am about the idea of placing my wife in danger, none of us is going to come up with a better idea… It's this or nothing. But we have to make the messages as brief and clear as possible, to minimise the risk for her."

The others nodded.

"Of course," said Marcus "That goes without saying."

So Ampliata rose and retrieved some parchment and charcoal from the amongst the children's school supplies in the other room. The children's curiosity was aroused by this and they practically danced around her, insisting on being told what was going on. But she shooed them away and instructed them to return to their homework in a tone which brooked no opposition. They slunk back into the bedroom, grumbling mutinously but quietly. Then she and the others sat around the table until late into the night, drafting the message and breaking it down into the simplest phrases – ones that would present the least possible challenge to Ampliata's needlework over the coming days.

She rose for her early shift before dawn the next morning. The family's preparations for school and work had settled back into an efficient routine, now that they had grown accustomed to the fugitives strewn across their floor. Even Imlac and Nekaya, no longer so distracted by their presence, stepped nimbly over their trailing limbs.

Until now the fugitives had shared a strong but unfocused fear of discovery by the Kabal; they had laboured in its shadow, but had tried to push it out of their minds, since there was nothing they could do about it. From this point on, however, all their anxieties would be fixed on Ampliata; she now carried with her the fate of her family, the fugitives, indeed the whole of the citizenry. As she moved around the room – setting the table, preparing the breakfast with Brebix, kneeling to adjust the children's clothes and smooth down their hair – she was the object of everyone's vigilant attention and the repository of all their hopes. Sitting once again with his back against the exposed stonework of the wall, Marcus noticed Magnis gazing at his cousin's wife over the rim of his bowl of kheifra with mingled sympathy and admiration.

He did the same himself, as he sipped his own kheifra. Each time he shifted position, to reduce the discomfort of the uneven flagstones beneath him, he felt the parchment they had used the night before nestling in his back pocket. It had their future – one way or another – written on it in a series of stark, disjointed phrases. Ampliata had memorised the first two, which informed the other women that Titus had been responsible for the King's death. She would now try to circulate both of them during the day's shift, if she had time.

Eventually Ampliata rose to leave, tying her hair back and knotting her head scarf under her chin. She kissed the children, whom Brebix would take to the Juvenum before he began his own shift, slightly later than her. Then she kissed Brebix himself: a lingering kiss, which emphasised again that beneath the occasional brusqueness prompted by the exhaustion of their daily routine there still lay the embers of what had once been a true and rare love for one another. Marcus was touched to note that the children betrayed not the slightest sign of surprise or embarrassment – such displays of affection between their parents were obviously not unusual.

Then Ampliata turned to survey the others, who had risen to bid her farewell. Chin tilted up, her expression bore only faint traces of apprehension. They could already hear the tread of her co-workers, trudging along the alley outside to begin their shift.

"Well, I suppose this is it," said Ampliata.

"I suppose so," replied Marcus.

"Wish me luck."

"Good or bad luck?" asked Theus, before cursing under his breath at making so crass a joke.

Ampliata gave a mirthless chuckle none the less and the tension in the room eased a little.

"Uh, good luck," she told him. "Under the circumstances."

"All our thoughts will be with you," Rhea assured her.

"I wish there was some way we could really help," added Magnis.

"Well, you could slip into one of my dresses and come and do some stitching yourself, Magnis. Who knows, one of the guards might take a fancy to you." Her expression darkened. "That's been happening recently too."

"But your time to help will come," added Brebix. "If Ampliata succeeds, we shall be looking to you to for leadership on the next stage."

Nodding, Ampliata embraced all the fugitives in turn. The way she clasped each one to her bore none of the reserve and self-consciousness that had existed between them when she had first reluctantly agreed to give them shelter. Then she turned away and, brushing Brebix's hand with her fingertips as she passed him, she trotted down the steps to join the throng of women heading for the Laborium.

Once Brebix had left too, ushering the children out with him, the fugitives faced another tense day. It looked like being even worse than the ones that had preceded it because the fear of being discovered was now compounded by anxiety about whether or not Ampliata would succeed on the first stage of her mission. Further discussion of how the uprising might be accomplished if all did go well was enough to keep them distracted, at least some of the time. But they still found themselves often lapsing into silence and gazing through the shuttered windows, mesmerised by the comings and goings in the fields – as if, by staring at them for long enough, they could discern a pattern in the seemingly random activity there. It occurred to Marcus at one point that eventlessness and uncertainty were, in some ways, perhaps more difficult to endure than the peril and discomfort he'd experienced in Daldriadh. He had no idea, though, how soon this insight was to be put to the test.

It was just before noon when the sense of dread, which had squatted over their day to day existence, was realised, like a storm cloud finally delivering upon the threat of its appearance. While Theus kept watch, Marcus, Rhea and Magnis sat hunched around the window, trying to stay out of the cold breeze yet gleaning what warmth they could from the insipid winter sun. Their murmured conversation was interrupted by a scuffling sound on the steps that led down to the alley. Marcus went rigid and gazed in horror at the others. Magnis half rose and placed his hand on the hilt of his sword, preparing to repulse any Kabal guard who might be about to burst upon them.

Instead, Brebix practically vaulted into the room, wheezing and red faced, closely followed, at a slower pace, by a bewildered-looking Theus, whom he had barged past to gain entry. Staggering to a halt, he reached out to grip the kitchen table and stood bent over for a few moments, trying to catch his breath.

"What is it?" hissed Marcus, approaching him. "Why are you here?"

Still flushed, Brebix said, "The Kabal are on their way."

XI.

The Search Party

After leaving her dwelling earlier in the day, Ampliata had stepped into the alley and was immediately absorbed by the great traffic of jostling bodies heading towards the Laborium. It was as if she had immersed herself in a brimming, turbulent stream that somehow, miraculously flowed upwards. In spite of how closely everyone was packed together, they didn't indulge in any exchange of greetings, no matter how muted. Guards were posted along the route and would plunge the stock of a crossbolt indiscriminately into the mass of female workers if any of them uttered a word.

Head bowed, Ampliata trudged onward, glancing neither left nor right. The main alleys radiated out from the Laborium like spokes from the centre of a wheel, so her route brought her to it simply and swiftly, without any turns. After waiting for a short while amid the bottleneck of bodies that inevitably formed around her designated entrance, she stepped through one of the archways.

The Laborium was an immense closed space. Curving stone buttresses rose from floor to ceiling all around it, making its occupants feel as if they were lodged inside the ribcage of some immense beast. A broad spiral staircase in the centre – called the 'Great Staircase' – stretched upwards to where the buttresses met. From there, its steps climbed into darkness, heading towards the Artisans' layer – the only means of accessing it. Indifferent illumination was provided by tallow lamps, which sat in sconces fixed to the buttresses. The section of stonework above each candle was blackened by its rising smoke.

Sprawled across the floor lay an enormous, circular sheet of canvas, composed of overlapping sections. Bunched and puckered in some places, stretched taut in others, it practically filled the available workspace. Entering the Laborium with all the other women, Ampliata joined them in fanning out around the canvas and sitting on one of the innumerable low stools placed at its edge. Once everyone had settled into place, they all bent forward and lifted it onto their laps. Smoothing her section down, Ampliata delved into the shapeless bag she had placed beside her and drew out the necessary implements.

When she glanced around her momentarily she saw the guards positioned like statues at regular intervals around the walls of the cavernous room. The influx of hundreds of women at the beginning of each shift edged them towards the fringes, where they tended to remain for the duration. Perhaps they were immobilised by the tedium of observing so much hunched, subdued labour. Or perhaps the circle of female industry formed a kind of tightly-knit conclave, which they were reluctant to interfere with. Either way, the fact that the guards kept a certain amount of distance could only help her in what she was about to attempt.

The first phrase she was to commit to the canvas repeated itself clamorously inside her head, like a caged bird beseeching someone to set it free. Selecting the most appropriate type of twine – durable yet not too thick – she took a deep breath and set to work with nimble, practised fingers.

Well, she thought. *There's no going back now.*

In the dwelling, the fugitives absorbed Brebix's news. Such was his sense of shock that Marcus felt a sharp pressure at his temples. The walls of the room seemed to flex around the corners of his vision, moving slightly further away then even nearer than before.

"On their way? What do you mean?" he asked.

"They're searching our quadrant of the layer over the next few hours – I heard it in the fields. I made an excuse to go up to the atrium then slipped away when the sentinels weren't looking and came here as fast as I could."

"What can we do?" asked Rhea. "There's nowhere to hide."

"I don't know," Brebix replied, with a despairing look. "I have to get back or they're sure to notice I've gone. I can't help you – I can only warn you, to give you a chance… But I beg you, if you can't think of some way to conceal yourselves or distract the guards, please, *please* go down into the alley and give yourselves up before they reach our dwelling. Don't let them find you here, or they'll put me and my family to death as certainly as they will you."

Theus nodded gravely.

"Don't worry. Whatever happens, we won't give you away," he said.

"Thank you," replied Brebix with a pitiful attempt at a smile. Already backing towards the door, he continued, "I'm sorry I can't do more. But I *must* go. If I'm absent much longer they're sure to notice and I'll only have succeeded in leading them right to you."

"Of course…We understand. Go. *Go!*" Marcus told him, his tone urgent yet his voice barely louder than a whisper.

Nodding, Brebix turned and vaulted back down the stairs.

For the first few moments after he departed the others continued to stare at the doorway, as if it now framed the rapidly diminishing prospect of ever defeating Titus. Marcus sensed a reluctance on everyone's behalf to make eye contact, lest seeing the fear etched on one another's faces would force them to acknowledge how dire their situation really was. He guessed he wasn't the only one who was wondering if Magnis' intervention to save the woman in the alley had prompted this search.

Rhea looked despondently round the room.

"Well, it's not exactly a labyrinth, is it?" she said.

"Do you think there's any way we can hide from them?" asked Marcus, following her gaze.

"Oh, I'm sure we can," said Theus dryly.

"Really?" asked Magnis, surprised.

"Yes… until they hit upon the ingenious strategy of looking in the other room."

"Okay, so the only other option is to create a distraction," said Rhea.

"And how do you propose we do that?" asked Theus.

"Well, I could distract the first one who comes into the room with a crossbow bolt between the eyes," suggested Magnis. "But that might just arouse suspicion."

They all smiled. The problem lying before them was so intractable, and their fate so unavoidable, that this droll, dismissive tone seemed the only appropriate one to adopt. But it proved impossible to sustain it for long.

Rhea rubbed her forehead.

"All joking aside," she said. "However you look at it, it's an impossible situation. We've made some daring escapes together, but there's no way we can get out of this one."

"But there *has* to be," protested Marcus. "Listen, think back when we first fell through the clouds. There we were, washed up on the shore of an alien world – drenched, frozen, with our aëro:cruiser smashed beyond repair on the rocks and only a few possessions scattered around us. Didn't that seem an impossible situation? Yet we set to work and built an ice yacht out of the wreckage and set out on our journey across Daldriadh. And then when we were trapped in that tunnel of frozen trees in the heavekairts, we had the idea of firing crossbolts at the icicles on the overhanging branches to bring them down on the Nullmaurs. And later still, when we were on the last part of the ascent of the Ins'lberg, we would never have survived without being tethered to those air sacs that Magnis devised – and to each other. After all that, surely we can't allow ourselves to be cornered in this tiny room, like vermin flushed out of some crevice and exterminated."

These words were accompanied by an imploring look that fixed on each of their faces in turn. Though he had made such speeches in the past, he always felt self-conscious while doing so, fearful that the others would dismiss what he said as exuberance – more a reflection of his youthful naivety than anything else. He wondered if he would ever reach a point in his life when his bearing and tone of voice might match the sentiments he was trying to express and not make them sound so lame and deluded. Someone else his age, who had experienced a more conventional upbringing, might not have expected to be able to sway the opinion of adults by sheer force of argument. But Marcus had long since ceased to make any such allowances for himself. The loss of his father, Titus's betrayal, the realisation that so many of his past certainties had been an illusion – all these things had hardened him, creating a carapace of adulthood within which he sought a curious kind of shelter.

Rhea, Theus and Magnis did look sceptical; but beneath that scepticism lay the recollection of his past ingenuity. This in turn prompted a glimmer of guarded hope that – all evidence to the contrary – there was indeed still a route out of their current plight.

"Okay," said Rhea slowly. "Agreed. But how do we do it?" She gestured around her. "I mean what is there in this tiny room that we could possibly use to save ourselves from being discovered?"

Magnis thought about this for a while, staring at his boots, brows knit. Then, brightening just a little, he said, "What about the incendiary bombs? You know... the Nullmaur ones that we climbed with in our packs?"

Theus frowned.

"And what do we do with them? Roll them down the steps into the alley?" he said. "Don't you think that might attract a little too much attention? Or perhaps you're suggesting we avoid capture by blowing ourselves up? If so it seems a rather drastic solution."

"I'm not sure Brebix and Ampliata would thank us if they returned home from work to find their dwelling a charred shell and lots of Kabal sorting through the debris," added Rhea.

They all lapsed into silence again, heads lowered. After a few moments, Marcus's gaze wandered diagonally across the flagstone floor then crept up the discoloured copper pipe that stretched from floor to ceiling. Part of the citadel's fiendishly complicated plumbing system, it had a circumference slightly smaller than a full-grown man's waist. The longer Marcus looked at it, the more an expression of guarded optimism lit his features.

"Wait a minute..." he said. "Magnis has the right idea. But we need to create a diversion much further off, so it can't be traced back to this dwelling."

"But how?" asked Theus.

Marcus walked across to the pipe and lay the palm of one hand on it. It vibrated ever so slightly and seemed even to shiver now and then, as if another part of it, somewhere out of sight, many yards above or below, was being struck with a hammer. He pressed his ear to it as well and wrapped his knuckles against it. It emitted a hollow ring. He could also hear very faint, very remote gurgles. It was like listening to the digestive processes of a huge, slightly dyspeptic monster.

He glanced back at the others. They were contemplating him worriedly, as if this sudden urge to embrace a section of the citadel's plumbing system might be the first sign of derangement, inspired by the stress of their dire situation – and perhaps by so many hours trapped in so cramped an environment. Ignoring their evident concern, he asked, "Where does this pipe run on to?"

"It runs to the base of the fortified wall then carries on, partly covered, between the fields," said Magnis. "It emerges in a channel at the fringe of the orchards – so do several more just like it in the other quadrants. That way the citadel's, um... *waste* is conveyed over the edge of the peak, to prevent it collecting anywhere in an insanitary way."

Rhea, her gaze still on Marcus, narrowed her eyes.

"What are you thinking?" she asked.

Instead of replying, he hurried to the other room to rummage through the packs they had carried with them on their ascent of the Ins'lberg. A few moments later he returned with one of the Nullmaur bombs. It was an egg-shaped clay pot, with a pinched neck, from which a fuse protruded stiffly, coated in a yellowish waxy substance.

"I'm thinking that if we cut into the pipe, then dropped a couple of these bombs down it, with a long enough fuse attached to each one… there's a fair chance they wouldn't detonate until they rolled out into the orchard, where the pipe ends. Surely a series of explosions down there, far from us, would create enough of a diversion for the Kabal to cancel their search?"

The others stared at the pipe with renewed fascination. It was no longer just part of the plumbing system; now it represented a method of perhaps conveying them to safety – for the time being at least.

"Surely an explosion in the orchard just makes the Kabal even more paranoid," said Theus. "They'll think there's a rebellion amongst the Farmers. Wouldn't that prompt them to search all the dwellings again with redoubled effort?"

"Not necessarily," replied Marcus. "Think back to what happened just a week ago…"

Theus frowned, shaking his head. But Rhea nodded slowly.

"The Mercanteer," she said.

"*Exactly*. We all saw it breaking up as it sank into the clouds. An explosion in the orchards could easily caused by some ordnance that had fallen from its hold, but not been discovered yet."

Magnis rubbed his chin.

"It might just work," he said. Walking over to the pipe, he tapped it experimentally about half way up. "We could cut into it about here."

"But would the fuses stay lit on such a long journey down it?" asked Theus.

"They will if we coil them inside the neck of the pots. That way the bombs can't roll over them and put them out. And remember, these bombs were designed for the damp air of Daldriadh. The fuses are coated in sophorous precisely so they wont get extinguished by rain or snow. In many ways they're perfect for the job. Even with a drenching in, uh... waste, they should still work."

While the others were still pondering the idea, a blossoming of creaks over the ceiling alerted them to the presence of Kabal guards, spreading out to search the dwelling above. Glancing up, Rhea said, "I think those footsteps are telling us that whatever happens we have nothing to lose... Come on, let's get started."

This wasn't quite the hearty endorsement Marcus had hoped for, but the felt a surge of pride, none the less, that they'd decided to follow his plan. Theus and Magnis darted through to the other room and returned with the packs. Attempting to move both rapidly and quietly, they were forced to adopt a bizarre mincing gait, the spectacle of which Marcus would have found irresistibly comic were the circumstances not so dire. Dumping the packs on the floor, they handed the remaining bombs to him and Rhea then delved into them again for climbing implements, such as adzes and ice picks that might be suitable for cutting open the pipe.

Hunched over the table, Marcus and Rhea began preparing the bombs. They had to trim the fuse in each pot then coil it with immense care, so that the waxy sophorous in which it was coated didn't rub off against the inside of the neck, leaving a bare patch that might get damp and fail to ignite.

Crouching at the pipe, Theus and Magnis attacked it with the ice picks. Their initial attempts produced a clamorous ringing that, to Marcus's ears, sounded almost as loud as the pealing of bells in the Palace's towers. Wincing, he felt certain that the sound must have transmitted itself along the network of pipes all the way up to Titus's throne room, passing at least ten search parties on the way.

Theus glanced up and down the pipe despairingly.

"We need to muffle the sound somehow," he said.

"Hang on," said Magnis.

He scuttled to the other room and returned with an armful of bed linen, which he proceeded to wind as tightly as possible around the pipe above and below where Theus was labouring, so that it might smother some of the noise. With the pipe insulated in this way, they began again, while Marcus and Rhea continued with their more intricate task.

Presently, the scuffling of the search party above was complimented by a new sound. From the far end of the alley they heard the raised voices of more Kabal guards, announcing, in peremptory tones, their intention of searching each dwelling. They did this, presumably, to alert any mothers who had been allowed to stay at home to nurse babies or care for sick children.

Marcus and the others froze. Though filtered up the narrow staircase, the voices none the less filled the room to bursting point with the significance of their message. After staring at one another for a few moments, its occupants resumed work with redoubled effort.

A short time later, a hideous sound – like the wrenching of bone and muscle – drew Marcus's attention back to Theus and Magnis. Having managed to breach the pipe, they had now started to saw at the resulting hole with an adze, the blade of which was lodged deeply in it. Pausing, they wiped their hands on their tunics then grasped the protruding handle of the adze again and squared their shoulders.

They waggled the flat blade in the cleft they had created. Soon the part of the pipe above the blade was peeled back and curled upward like a sneering lip. Theus grabbed the ragged edge they had created and tugged at it with all his strength while Magnis once again sawed away at the edges of the cleft to enlarge it. Soon they had peeled away a section of the pipe large enough for the bombs to be squeezed through.

As the hole grew, it liberated a fetid smell – the residue of unmentionable substances – that slowly filled the room. It didn't prompt Rhea to look up from the table, but her nose wrinkled as she worked.

"Perhaps we should just leave the pipe open and hope that lovely aroma you've discovered will dissuade the guards from coming up the stairs," she commented.

"Sorry, can't be helped," replied Magnis gruffly.

"Let's just hope no-one above flushes anything away, or we might get better acquainted with some of our neighbours than we'd wish," added Theus.

It occurred to Marcus that if their plan succeeded they would still have to find a way of patching the pipe afterwards to avoid just the sort of cascade that Rhea had hinted at. But it seemed the least of their worries right now.

Rhea turned the pots over in her hands. About an inch of splayed fuse protruded from the neck of each, the rest nestling within. Having examined both her and Marcus's work, she said, "Okay, we're ready."

Magnis practically lunged at the table, grabbing the bombs then rolling them across the floor, one by one, to Theus, who had positioned himself at the stove. As he scooped them up, everyone heard the emphatic tread of Kabal boots on the steps of the dwelling just one door down from theirs'. Theus lit the wicks of the bombs. As soon as the white, pulsating flame, characteristic of burning sophorous, had enveloped each one, he threw it back to the others, Marcus and Rhea having joined Magnis at the pipe.

Catching the bombs, they crammed them through the hole. The bombs plunged down the pipe, which received each one with a hollow rattle. Within a few moments, however, this sound had dwindled away and the fugitives' attention was drawn back to the commotion next door. A thudding against the wall sounded like a fist pummelling it, but must in fact have been the guards opening and slamming cupboard doors.

There was nothing to do now but wait. Theus and Magnis bent the broken section of the pipe back into place as best they could and Rhea placed a chair in front of it to mask the damage. Then, keeping as quiet as possible, they all crept over to the window and peered out between the shutters. Below lay a scene of improbable order. In the fields, which were partitioned by dry stone walls, Farmers wielded scythes and mattocks with fluid movements gained through long practice. The guards who observed their work passed between them in an unhurried fashion – their loose-limbed, nonchalant progress testimony to the unchallengeable power they represented.

It was fairly windy, and streams of vapour – filtered by the trunks of the trees around the edge of the peak – lay across the fields, flexing like the tentacles of some mythic creature formed out of the cloud depths. The outfall pipe, which, they so fervently hoped, was conducting their trundling salvo of bombs towards the orchard, lay beneath the thickest of the dry stone walls.

"You know, we didn't consider what might happen to someone working in the part of the orchard where the pipe comes out," said Theus. "If they're anywhere near it, they're liable to get more than just singed."

The others exchanged an anxious look. Marcus gave a brief grimace.

"There shouldn't be anyone in the orchards – not this late in the season," Magnis pointed out. "All the last windfall fruit should have been collected by now."

"Well, if there is…" said Marcus.

Their eyes remained fixed on the part of the orchard where the pipe emerged. It was concealed from view. But they continued to stare, as if the force of their collective gaze could peel the trees back and replace it.

As fixated as they were on the orchard, however, their attention was torn from it by a sound, much closer to home, that they had so dreaded. The Kabal guards had completed their search of the adjacent dwelling and descended its stairs. From the foot of the staircase leading to Brebix and Ampliata's dwelling, the fugitives now heard the following words, many of them italicised in a belligerent tone which countenanced no opposition: "In the *name* of the *supreme* and *beatific* Imperator Titus – *grand* architect of the *New Age* of Heliopolis – all those within must *desist* and submit to inspection *forthwith*."

Without hesitating they responded to this order by dashing towards the other room and concealing themselves on either side of the doorway. Breathing as shallowly as possible, Marcus gazed around him. In spite of the anxiety of the moment, he couldn't help but be moved by the shabby dignity on display in the room – as if it were a shrine to the importance of maintaining certain standards in reduced circumstances. Covered in a meandering network of stitching, the bed linen was neatly folded at the foot of the mattress. Slumped against the wall at the top of the bed, the pillows looked emaciated but were spotlessly clean. The pile of the rug on which the bed stood – its intricate pattern clearly distinguishing it as a prized possession – was worn and shiny, but the few tassels that remained at either end of it were neatly brushed.

The Kabal guards began to ascend the staircase, the steady motion of their armour-clad limbs producing a succession of clanks and grating sounds. Marcus's heart rate grew slower yet also more intense, as if each pounding beat had the strength of three normal ones crammed into it. He visualised the clay pots travelling along the convolutions of the drainage system, spinning as they went. If they were too close together, would they block one another's progress at some sharp turn? Or would a torrent of fetid liquid overtake them and drench them too thoroughly for even the sophorous to remain lit? Once again, it seemed helplessly comic, yet awful at the same time, that something as mundane as a flushed toilet or emptied sink could extinguish all hope of overthrowing Titus's regime and placing the future of Heliopolis in the hands of its citizens.

Now the guards were in the kitchen, the curtain at the entrance wrenched aside. Marcus's mouth felt parched. He hunched slightly and began to tremble with a weird kind of excitement, as if, in spite of all the fears to which his mind was prey, his coiled body was prepared – eager even – for a confrontation.

"Tidier squalor than usual," he heard one of the guards comment.

"Still squalor," another observed. "Rustic squalor too, the most pathetic kind. Clothes with patches on patches and the smell of vegetables boiled to death."

The two men snorted with amusement. Marcus remembered what Brebix had said about only 'pure bred' Kabal from the Cloudfarers' layer being allowed to serve as guards or sentinels in the lower parts of the citadel.

That's right, he thought. *Stop and take the chance to sneer as much as you want. Just give us a few more seconds.* The tension resonated in the air like a high frequency hum so intense that all the contents of the room seemed fragile, as though, at any moment, every plate, cup or vase could shatter or explode.

He strained his ears, searching for the faintest note of discord in the fields to suggest that the bombs had detonated. Still nothing...

Instead, his faculties honed as sharp as they had ever been, he sensed a collective squaring of shoulders from just a few feet away, as the guards prepared to repeat what, to them, was a mundane task they had already performed numerous times.

Marcus closed his eyes. The imposture of the past half hour was finished. There was no avoiding the fact that time had run out for him and the others – their fate was now sealed.

XII.

The Kabal Deceived

"Okaaaay, usual routine," said one of the guards, his authoritative drawl identifying him as the leader. "You two search in here and I'll…"

He paused, interrupted by a distant rumbling sound.

"What was *that*?" asked one of the other guards.

There was a renewed scuffling as the search party hurried over to the shuttered windows. All three of the guards emitted a brief but colourful selection of oaths, provoked by whatever it was they had seen outside. This was followed by sounds of hurried departure, the table's legs scraping against the flagstones as one of them bumped against it.

Once the last footfall had died away again in the alley, Rhea lifted a small mirror off the drawing table next to her and held it out at arm's length, carefully angled. She scrutinised it to make absolutely sure that one of the guards hadn't been left posted in the other room. Satisfying herself that it was indeed empty, she nodded to the others and they all dashed over to the window. Thankfully the Kabal guards had already thrown the second pair of shutters open, offering them a clearer view of the fields than they had enjoyed previously. Though this also made them more exposed, the attention of the sentinels on the Great Wall below was focused wholly outwards. None the less, they peered around either side of the window with due caution, so they could quickly duck out of sight if the need arose.

In contrast to the order that had prevailed not long before, the scene in the fields was now one of utter disarray, with Farmers and guards alike milling around.

All the fugitives' attention, however, was focused on the orchard, where several strands of smoke emerged from amid the trees. Though fairly narrow, the strands twisted as they rose and plaited themselves into a much thicker column. This in turn was soon nudged sideways by the prevailing wind, casting a shadow over the fields. Birds wheeled around it, calling out to one another in a reedy, anxious tone.

There was no exultation from Marcus and the others: no slamming of fists into palms. Instead they were all drenched in an exquisite sense of relief. They bowed their heads, with hands either gripping the window ledge or pressed flat against the surrounding stonework.

As they continued to watch, the last of the bombs detonated, shouldering open the branches of the surrounding trees in an eruption of charred twigs and leaves. They all sighed with relief.

"I never imagined I'd be so pleased to see an explosion that close to the citadel," said Rhea. "It's strange, isn't it, how a few twists of fate can make something so appalling seem like such a relief?"

Marcus nodded.

"I know. Let's just hope we've bought ourselves a bit more breathing space."

They remained huddled where they were for a considerable amount of time, observing the aftermath of the explosions. Though the sentinels continued to pay little heed to anything other than the smoke rising from the orchard, Rhea and Magnis gently eased the shutters closed, so they could continue to stand at the windows with less chance of detection.

In the fields, the Farmers edged towards the trees. Their number was supplemented by many others, who had been working on the far side of the mountain top and were drawn round by the noise. Forming a confused, jostling semicircle, they looked like a human land slip, viewed in slow motion, as they continued to move downward towards the source of the explosions. So absorbed were they by what had happened in the orchard that they ignored the Kabal guards trying to shoulder a path between them, in spite of the vicious chastisement that normally accompanied even the slightest sign of disobedience. The object of their fascination continued to smoulder and had by now acquired a crest of flames. Distant though they were, there was something in the flames' vivid orange hue that provoked an instinctive reaction in Marcus and the others – a shrinking from heat and potential pain. They edged slightly from the window.

"It's doubly useful in a way," said Theus.

The others frowned at him.

"How?" asked Rhea.

"Well, we don't just create a diversion, we get the measure of them a bit as well; we find out how good the Kabal is at dealing with an emergency like this."

The others nodded. As they watched, a number of Kabal guards emerged from the shade of the Great Wall and assembled themselves in a chain stretching all the way down one of the rutted paths that ran alongside the dry stone walls.

"Vigiles," murmured Theus.

"Who?" asked Marcus.

"Fire fighters," Rhea explained.

"How are they going to fight the fire?" asked Marcus. Asperia, in her lessons with him about the structure of Heliopolitan society, had never deigned to mention such practical matters as firefighting.

Before anyone could reply, one of the most extraordinary looking contraptions he had ever seen emerged into view and passed along the chain of bodies, several more Kabal guards clustered round it to keep it in motion. It was a large, rectangular wooden box – partially open-topped, with a square tower at the rear. Two long bars ran parallel to the box on either side, connected by struts to a central axle that also ran the length of it. The axle was mounted on the tower at one end and on a sturdy-looking stanchion at the other. A coiled tube hung on the back of the tower and the whole assembly stood on four narrow, spoked wheels. As one of its wheels bumped into a shallow hole in the track, it tilted sideways and water sloshed out of the uncovered portion of the box. In response to Marcus's questioning look, Theus said, "It's a handtub. I trained on them in the Corps, in case we ever needed to douse fires aboard damaged aëro: cruisers that were trying to land."

"How do they work?"

"They're hand-operated. Those bars running parallel to the main body – they're called brakes or pumping arms. When you push them down on either side they operate a set of pistons that suck water out of the big tub and force it into a special chamber, which is inside that tower at the back. The air trapped in the chamber creates a consistent pressure, to make sure the water sprays out of the hose in a steady flow. The hose itself is made of canvas, waxed and smeared with hot pitch, just like the air sacs of the aëro: cruisers, but in this case to keep the water *in* instead of out. With a full crew manning the pumping arms – it's called "working the brakes" – the piston can be operated at more than sixty full strokes per minute."

"I see," said Marcus, slightly overwhelmed by so much complex information, but intrigued none the less. "And the Vigiles?"

"They hand buckets of water to one another to keep the handtub full."

As Theus finished explaining all of this, the Vigiles in charge of the handtub positioned it about twenty yards from the blaze and wrenched at levers next to the front wheels to lock them and thus prevent the vehicle from rolling any further. Then two of them hurriedly uncoiled the hose while the other six took up position on either side, their hands resting lightly on the parallel bars. Already their comrades further up the fields had started to hand buckets of water to one another, in expectation of the water in the tub rapidly diminishing. Meanwhile the flames continued to spread, vaulting between tree tops with each powerful gust of wind. Some of the earliest branches to catch fire broke from the trunks and fell, sending up dense showers of sparks.

A few seconds later, the six Vigiles at the handtub began to work the pump, heaving their shoulders and bending at the waist, gripping it tightly. The hose, sagging between the arms of the other two, twitched just a little at first. None the less, both men stiffened visibly, preparing themselves to wrestle with it. Sure enough, a few seconds later, it convulsed as a large volume of water surged into it. At first the jet of water sprayed at random over the surrounding fields. Then they seized the thrashing tube and directed the neck of it towards the blaze.

While the assembled Farmers and guards stood around watching the Vigiles gradually brought the fire under control. Those in the chain that stretched all the way back to the Great Wall, continued to pass buckets, struggling to do so as swiftly as possible without slopping too much of their contents over the sides. With every looping gush of water, a patch of flame was quashed and co-mingled smoke and steam rose in its place, drifting out to merge with the banked edge of the cloudscape.

Eventually the fire was extinguished completely and a succession of shouted orders, relayed along the chain of Vigiles, halted the supply of water. The six manning the pumps on the handtub stood back from it and rubbed their chafed, aching palms on their thighs. The two holding the tube let it fall to their feet, where it writhed with diminishing energy as the water pressure diminished.

"Very disciplined, very efficient," observed Theus glumly, in answer to the question he himself has earlier posed.

Rhea nodded.

"Hmm."

After warning the fugitives, Brebix had hastened back along the maze of alleys, in the hope of returning unnoticed to the fields. Clipped, stentorian voices, just up ahead, had obliged him to duck down narrow side passages a couple of times and take a more complicated route to avoid Kabal search parties already embarked on their mission. Arriving at the atrium beneath the Great Wall, he peered round the half-opened, mildew mottled entrance doors. He heard more Kabal voices, not far along the alley behind him. They seemed to acquire a physical force, impelling him forward, so keen was he to escape their owners. Fortunately the atrium was filled with enough activity to distract the few guards posted there. Slipping inside, he grabbed an unattended basket and hoisted it onto his shoulder. Then, lowering his head and assuming his usual posture of cowed obedience, he headed towards the carved archway and back out into the fields.

In the fields he rejoined his work party. Though puzzled by his prolonged absence, they greeted his return with studied uninterest, lest any frowns or questions draw the attention of the roaming guards. For the next quarter of an hour or so, he laboured in a state of tranced unreality, as if the frantic activity in which he'd recently been engaged had been a dream. To calm himself, he focused wholly on the crunch of the mattock he wielded plunging into the ground and the slap of the turned earth. He tried as best he could not to wonder how the fugitives were faring – no amount of anxiety on his behalf could help them.

Lulled by the rhythm of this task, he was wholly unprepared for the first explosion. The sound wrenched his gaze towards the orchard. He was in the wrong portion of the fields to see any flames. But the way the shockwave flattened a wide radius of treetops, like the palm of an invisible hand sweeping across them, left little doubt about what had occurred.

He felt a hot flush of excitement at Marcus and the others' ingenuity, followed by a stab of chill fear at what the consequences of their audacity might be for him and his family. For a few moments, these contending emotions were almost too much for him. He remained rooted to the spot, while the surrounding Farmers and guards edged towards the source of the uproar for a better look. Sweat beaded his brow. Yet he maintained as calm an expression as possible. No one would have guessed that he was gripping the handle of the mattock so tightly because it was the only thing keeping him upright.

For the fugitives themselves, the rest of the afternoon passed with a surreal and unaccustomed air of serenity, as if all their anxieties had been temporarily suspended by the eruptions of flame and smoke in the orchard. They mainly busied themselves with repairing the damage to the pipe – in case a reeking inundation came spilling across the floor; a development which, they all agreed, could only add to the indignity of their situation, while doing little to endear them to either Brebix and Ampliata.

They worked at the edges of the bent-back section of pipe until it more or less fitted again with the contours of the rest. Distant but unignorable gurgling encouraged them to work as swiftly as they could. As soon as they had finished, they wrapped the broken section of pipe in a spare pillowslip, which they knotted, as if applying a bandage to a wound.

Standing back to examine their work, Theus said, "Well, it doesn't add much to the elegance of the dwelling. But hopefully it'll hold for the time being.

"I don't know," said Rhea, with a thin smile. "It looks quite festive to me – almost like a bow."

Having completed this task, they returned to the window. Or rather, Theus, Marcus and Rhea did. Though it seemed unlikely that there would be any other attempts at searching the dwellings that afternoon, they thought it prudent to post a guard on the stairs again anyway and Magnis elected to go first.

The crowd in the field had thinned. Corralled by the Vigiles, (who managed to convey an air of menace, in spite of the fact that they were still wielding half-full buckets of water), the Farmers returned to work. Many of them trekked round either side of the Great Wall, with only a few lingering glances back at the scene of the explosions. Though now extinguished, the flames had gouged a charred cavity out of the tree tops, which still smoked thinly. Some of the other Vigiles began the laborious task of pushing the handtub back up the rutted track – though only after releasing a sluice valve, which voided the rest of the tank in a gush of surplus water. A few of the guards ventured into the orchard to check the damage. They moved cautiously, in case any more 'ordnance' detonated without warning. But Marcus had counted the explosions and knew there were no more to come.

As they continued to watch, Rhea said, "In all the excitement I'd almost forgotten about Ampliata in the Laborium. I wonder how she is getting on."

"Perhaps work was suspended there on account of the chaos in the fields?" suggested Marcus.

"I doubt it," countered Theus. "Remember, the Laborium lies at the core of the layer. And it's well soundproofed. I wouldn't think that anyone in there is even conscious of something amiss – guards included. I hope not at any rate. What we've done might postpone a search of the dwellings for a few days, but no longer than that. It's more important than ever that she spreads the word as quickly as possible... We don't have much more time..."

He paused and surveyed the others.

"All these events are gathering towards something decisive," he told them. "If we're not prepared to take full advantage of them, we'll be lost – they'll overwhelm us.

"Well put," acknowledged Rhea, though she seemed, understandably, to derive little pleasure from his eloquence.

XIII.

Ring of Fire

Breah reached the end of the makeshift bridge that cleaved an uncertain path through the flames and fell into darkness. It was darkness so absolute that she felt she was being immersed in an element far thicker than air. She landed on the rough, uneven terrain that fringed the far side of the marshes. The ground here was smothered in a variety of long grass – matte in texture – that seemed to devour every trace of light thrown out by the burning surface of the oily water.

It took her a few seconds to regain any comprehension of what was happening around her. But when she rolled over and looked back where she had come from, she saw signs of movement within the ring of fire. From this distance, the gap in it created by the wooden stakes was barely visible. As a consequence, the figures of the first few Eihlans following her lead seemed to emerge from the heart of the conflagration itself. Arms pinned protectively at their sides, they stumbled forward. The glare of flames slenderised their already meagre outlines, making them seem even more dauntless in their frailty. One after another, they landed on the ground beside her, flattening the grass in random patches. Many of them carried threadbare packs, hastily stuffed with provisions. With an acute sense of relief, Breah saw Morveyn among them, clutching Eithné to her chest, and Aònghas close behind. As soon as she had satisfied herself that they were safe, she shuffled backwards, further into the darkness, to avoid being pinned beneath a tumbling body.

Gradually more and more of the Eihlans gathered beside her. Breah noticed, when their faces drew close to hers, that the simple act of confronting and surviving this ordeal had lent them a new air of fortitude, which many of them had never displayed before. It was almost as if, in passing through the scorching barrier, they had been momentarily reborn: cleansed of their innate timidity by the flames.

As she continued to watch, the last, most reluctant stragglers amongst the Eihlans reached safety. The conflagration showed no signs of diminishing. Indeed, it had begun to insinuate itself between the different sections of the bridge. With mounting horror, Breah watched the stakes begin to roll apart – flames springing up in between – just as the Cloudfarers ventured onto them.

Arms thrown wide for extra balance, Jarrid and Denihr came flailing forward in the lead, leaping between the ever more separate stakes. Reaching the other end with seconds to spare before the marshes became impassable, they hurled themselves towards safety. The others followed suit. Tendrils of flame played around their bodies, like the outstretched arms of a spurned lover, but failed to get a grip on any of them.

Persis was the last to cross the burning marsh. He landed with a resounding thud close to Breah. Unlike the others, he had not quite managed to escape unscathed; a pelt of flame covered the back of his tunic. He rolled back and forth several times to extinguish it, colliding with hapless Eihlans as he did so, before lying still.

Finally, with the oil almost consumed, the conflagration began to ebb too. The flames writhed less and less then adopted a sickly green pallor before rapidly shrinking. Soon all that was left of them was a thin glaze that rippled across the surface of the water, with charred tussock protruding from it here and there.

The shrinking of the flames brought no resumption of cannon fire from the Nullmaurs. Instead all that could be heard was the intermittent rustling sound of the scattered Eihlans assembling themselves into family groups once again. They did this mainly by touch, moulding the darkness with outstretched fingers until they came into contact with a familiar outline. Once everyone had been reunited, Aònghas edged his way towards the Cloudfarers and asked, in tones as muted as possible, "What happens now?"

Breah, who had remained close to Persis and the others, awaited their answer with as much curiosity as anyone else. Doing so, she noticed how acute the remaining senses became when the eyes could see so little. She felt as if she could almost hear the Cloudfarers' collective thought processes as they pondered this new situation.

Eventually Tafril said, "We need to get everyone as far away as possible from the Nullmaurs' cannons while it's still dark. Our only option is to head north into the hills."

"Wont they follow us?" asked Breah.

"Probably," said Amik. "But when daylight comes we'll at least be able to keep track of them from higher ground."

Though no one could see her, Breah nodded in agreement with this. Then, drifting through the night, she heard an increasingly familiar sound: her father's weary groan of assent.

"Very well," he replied.

A few moments of irresolute silence followed, while everyone peered out at the dark landscape, trying to discern even the faintest contour in it. They needed the cover of night to escape, but night itself would make the escape immensely difficult to accomplish. Thankfully, however, the marshes' thin covering of flame was bisected by the fallen stakes – all still fitfully illuminated and all pointing north like splayed fingers. Glancing back at them would at least allow the fugitives to set off in the right direction until they reached higher ground and gained the cover of trees. In accordance with Jarrid and Denihr's whispered instructions, therefore, they all set about assembling themselves into single file – hands joined – so that no one who foundered in a trough or hollow would run the risk of being left behind. Having formed this chain of mutual support, they shuffled into the impenetrable darkness.

The initial stages of the journey – across the hummocky scrubland that separated the marshes from the foothills – were, as anticipated, agonisingly slow, with much stumbling along different sections of the chain. When the ground began to curve upwards, the going became even more difficult. Compacted snow, which lay deep between the fir trees, made it all too easy for several Eihlans in succession to lose their footing and slide down the incline, dragging others with them until a luckily positioned rock interrupted their descent. In spite of this, the simple fact of being amongst the trees, with their feathery, interlaced branches, proved a consolation for all the fugitives, making them feel far less exposed than before to the Nullmaurs' malevolence. Thus emboldened, they continued to toil upwards.

Dawn found them miles from the village. They had left the tree-clad slopes behind and entered a new, more precipitous terrain. Here, narrow but deep water-eroded channels wound upwards between monstrously twisted, overhanging rocks, to which vegetation clung in sparse patches. All day they traversed these channels, offered only the briefest glimpse of the surrounding landscape by an occasional fissure in the rock. They could make out no signs of Nullmaur pursuit, but at the Cloudfarers' insistence they pushed on none the less.

Breah trudged along beside Persis. She found it comforting to be near his height and solidity, though she kept her family, who were slightly farther ahead, in her sight at all times. By midday it had started to snow. Too cold already to feel self-conscious, she moved even closer to him and he raised his arm to accommodate her and afford her a little shelter beneath his cape.

Peering up at the flakes, she said, "I suppose I should be used to this, considering it's the only world I know, but I hate it."

"Just because you're familiar with something, doesn't mean you have to like it," Persis pointed out with a smile.

"But it never used to occur to me before whether I liked it or disliked it," Breah replied. "It's only since I met Marcus and you and the others that I've realised there's anything else."

Persis smiled again. Though she sometimes referred to Marcus in an oblique sort of way when they talked, she rarely mentioned him by name.

"You make it sound as if we've done you a disservice," he said.

"No, I don't mean that, I just…"

"It's all right, I understand. There isn't any shame, you know, in imagining how things might be different. Do you think there isn't a day goes by when I don't imagine how my life might have been different if the Kabal hadn't forced me to become involved in its treachery by threatening my loved ones?"

Breah nodded sympathetically.

"The only danger," he continued, a slightly reproving note slipping into his voice. "Is to spend so much time imagining such things that you rob yourself of the will to make them a reality."

"But how can they be a reality?" she protested. "It's impossible for me to be part of any world but this one."

Persis frowned.

"Why should you think that?" he asked.

"Surely you've heard my father talk about our ancestors who tried to climb the Ins'lberg; how they were forced back down and bled from…" She raised her hand to her mouth and nose, in a hesitant, fearful gesture.

Persis inclined his head. Breah sensed that he was not wholly convinced by such evidence, but didn't wish to dismiss it out if hand.

"That may be true," he said eventually. "But I think such symptoms might have more to do with climbers inhaling ice crystals that have sublimed from the glacier," he said.

"Sublimed?" asked Breah.

Persis smiled.

"It's when rising temperatures cause a solid object to turn into a kind a granular vapour that can damage the lungs. It's dangerous, for sure. But I'm not convinced it means that the world above the clouds is inherently lethal to you or your people."

He paused and stared at the walls of the channel. They had both been so absorbed in the conversation that neither had noticed the tiny showers of pebbles, which trickled down either side of it, keeping pace with their progress. Eyes focused on the ground, due to the continued snowfall, no-one else had noticed them either. Now, however, the showers grew more dense and frequent. Persis looked around, straining to see over the sides of the channel.

"What is it?" asked Breah.

"I'm not…"

Before he could go on, however, there was an eruption of shrieking from up ahead. The channel was so tightly packed with bodies that Breah couldn't make out the source of the discord. But Persis, being taller, spotted it instantly. Cursing, he reached for the wall closest to him and hauled himself up. Then, sword drawn, arms outstretched to balance himself, he moved forward as quickly as he could over the crumbling serrations of rock that stretched along the top of it.

Finding a foothold in the opposite sidewall herself, Breah scrambled up it just far enough to see what was going on. To her horror, she saw an Eildritch – identifiable by its hairless grey body and the webs of skin which extended from its elbows to its torso. It had leaped into the channel and sunk the teeth which crammed its obscenely wide mouth into Jarrid's shoulder. Though close to the predator, Tafril and Denihr were struggling to engage it in the narrow space; as they tried to do so, their elbows jostled against one another and their sword blades clanged against the walls. Persis, however, having drawn alongside, was able to hurl himself on top of it unobserved. Driving his sword through it vertically, he used the weight of his body to hold it down, its face pressed into the packed snow, until it stopped struggling.

The aftermath of the attack was necessarily brief. Though Jarrid's injuries were far from minor, he insisted that a simple bandage would be enough to staunch his bleeding in the meantime. The most important thing, he and the other Cloudfarers agreed, was to keep moving. And so they did.

XIV.

Ampliata's Mission

In Heliopolis, the day – riven with so much anxiety and uncertainty – drew to a close. The end of the shift in the fields was signalled, as always, by horns blown on the Great Wall. And, once again, in the fading light, Marcus watched as Farmers all around the peak were drawn back into the citadel, like a ragged tide, leaving behind them the flotsam of their abandoned implements.

Though a familiar, subdued rumble, caused by the collective shuffling of innumerable weary feet, soon filled the alleys outside, Ampliata, rather than Brebix, was the first to return. As usual, she was preceded by the children, who vaulted the last couple of steps, threw the curtain aside and headed straight for the bedroom. While covering the short distance in between, they somehow managed to drop their bags, kick off their shoes and shrug off their capes without slowing down for even an instant. Nor did they offer a single glance towards the fugitives, to whose presence they were now so accustomed.

Ampliata appeared a few moments later, considerably less blithe, and somewhat florid-faced from the effort of keeping up with her offspring. Marcus and Rhea stepped forward to greet her, while Theus and Magnis edged sideways, hands clasped behind their backs, to conceal the pipe for as long as possible.

In their eagerness to distract her from the fact they had used part of the plumbing system in her precious dwelling as a conduit for high explosives, they had all adopted smiles of such fatuous affability that they appeared slightly gormless. Scrutinising each one of them in turn, she frowned and said, "What's going on?"

"Oh, nothing, nothing," said Marcus airily. "We had a slightly close call, but everything is fine now. What happened in the Lab…"

"How close a call exactly?" she asked, in her usual sceptical tone. "Close, as in footsteps along the alley right outside, or close, as in there's a Kabal guard gagged and hidden under the bed?"

"Somewhere between the two," conceded Rhea.

"You see, there was a search of the dwellings and..." began Marcus.

But before he could go any further, Ampliata, unfoolable as ever, craned her neck to look past Magnis's right elbow and spotted the pillowslip tied round the pipe, as well as the remnants of debris scattered over the flagstones.

"I know you've felt pretty bored stuck indoors this past week, but you didn't have to start redecorating," she commented. "I must admit, though, the bow is a nice touch, even if a bit unconventional."

Magnis and Theus exchanged a despairing look and stood apart to reveal their handiwork. Sighing, Rhea began to relate all that had happened during the afternoon. Ampliata listened intently, but offered little clue to her true sentiments upon hearing how close the Kabal had come to discovering her and Brebix's defiance of its authority. Only when Rhea mentioned the bombs exploding in the orchard did she cross to the window to check on the damage – and drew in a sharp breath upon seeing the leafless tree-tops, their charred, arthritic branches groping upwards towards the evening sky. She remained standing there, with her back to them, for some time. Since the familiar view could have done little to beguile her, she was clearly contemplating her response.

Eventually she turned back from the window, arms folded.

"Very ingenious," she remarked, with a less than ecstatic smile.

The others needed little insight to guess what she was brooding on. Such a gambit could only be accomplished once: more explosions in the same area of the orchard would draw the Vigiles' attention to the mouth of the outfall pipe.

And aside from that, if they tried the same thing again, bombs might get stuck in some earlier part of the sewage system and explode there – there was no guarantee they would be lucky a second time.

"So how about you?" asked Rhea, clearly keen to change the subject. "What happened in the Laborium?"

Ampliata sighed.

"I made some progress. The stitching was more time-consuming than I'd expected. But I managed to at least convey that you were back; that you were planning an uprising; that we needed assistance. I had to rush a bit towards the end and nearly stitched 'cup' instead of 'coup'. You can imagine how much confusion *that* would have caused."

They all laughed appreciatively at this, grateful for some relief from the prevailing air of tension.

"Anyway," she continued. "The canvas got turned clockwise as I expected. I couldn't afford to look up from my work too often. But I stole the occasional sidelong glance when the guards weren't too near me and saw a few of the woman peering at it pretty closely. They were frowning and a few of them looked over at me. I tried to nod as discreetly as I could, but I'm afraid very few of them nodded back. I think they were too shocked – or perhaps even puzzled, given my stitching skills – by what they'd just read."

Marcus nodded.

"So now there's nothing to do but wait," he said.

"*Please* prompt them tomorrow, if they don't seem inclined to make any response" put in Theus. "We don't have much time left." He glanced towards the window. "Today's events have left little doubt of that."

"I will, I will," replied Ampliata. "Though they may ask for longer to think about it – and discuss it with their husbands."

"Well, we'll just have to wait and see," said Rhea.

The others gave a collective sigh. They had done this so often recently that they now exhaled in perfect unison – a fact which seemed to amuse Ampliata.

"So, have you added any other decorative touches that I should know about?" she asked.

"Not yet," said Magnis.

"I'm relieved to hear that at least."

Nodding briskly, she busied herself with collecting up the children's discarded possessions. Her back ached from being hunched over her work all day, so each time she bent down she emitted a martyred groan, until Rhea darted forward to help her.

Meanwhile the others softly closed the shutters and lit candles on the table and sideboard. Then they began preparations for dinner, allowing Ampliata to go to the other room for her nightly remonstration with the children about doing their homework before it got too late.

Brebix returned after another hour. In spite of his weariness, he still braced himself to receive the greeting of his children, who hurtled from the bedroom and clasped him round the waist – a twin salvo of unquenchable adoration. Patting their heads reluctantly only because his hands were so dirty, he looked up and offered the others a half-smile.

"So… I was working in the fields, wondering how long it would take the Kabal to reach our dwelling, secretly hoping you'd be at least fifty yards away in the alley and greet them with the utmost civility," he said. "And suddenly there was this uproar in the orchard."

The fugitives arranged their features into an expression of perfect innocence and Marcus replied, "Yes?"

"From what I could overhear the Vigiles all seem to be agreed that it must have been caused by unexploded ordnance from the Mercanteer."

Still betraying no flicker of comprehension, Theus said, "Yes?"

"Yes, though I couldn't help but wonder if it had a slightly different origin."

"Hmm."

"So...how exactly did you engineer it?" he asked.

Unable to keep up the pretence of naivety for any longer, they broke into broad grins.

"Well..." began Magnis.

Brebix drew out a chair and, sitting at the table, listened while Magnis described the events that had transpired after he'd warned them about the Kabal's search. He listened with evident fascination, tinged with a mutinous delight, casting only the briefest glance towards the damaged pipe. As Magnis concluded his description of the explosions, Brebix slammed his fist into his palm and said, "Yes!"

His enthusiasm quickly subsided, however, when he caught Ampliata's eye. Now busying herself at the stove, she gave him a look, which, though not exactly reproving, reminded him that the events of the afternoon had done little to lessen the danger that harbouring the fugitives had placed their family in.

"Anyway..." Trailing off, he rose to help her at the stove and enquire, in chastened tones, how she had managed in the Laborium. She offered clipped replies at first, but gradually elaborated on them, the tension in her shoulders ebbing in response to his playful nudges and one-armed hugs as they worked side by side. The others huddled around the table, to afford them a little privacy.

At dinner they all talked in an undertone about the decisive events which would surely soon occur. They had no way of knowing when the crucial moment would arrive; or, for that matter, whether it would be caused by Ampliata's message seeping through the layer's dwellings, or by the Kabal's renewed attempt at searching them. All they could hope for was to be ready when the time came.

Early the following morning, Ampliata once again joined the procession of workers en route to the Laborium. It occurred to her that most of the women with whom she jostled elbows in the confined space of the alley had probably heard, from their husbands, about the explosions in the orchard on the previous day. Yet no attempt was made – even in the most fleeting undertone – to raise the subject. The constant presence of the guards was enough to ensure absolute silence. Surely though, she speculated, the women who had seen her message the previous day must be wondering if the explosion had a cause slightly different from the one the Kabal was already (according to Brebix) assuming.

When she entered the Laborium the usual dispersal took place, with everyone spreading out around the canvas. Settling into place, she reached down to grasp the outer rim and, having done so, surveyed the great semi-circle of women around her, to ensure that they too were ready to hoist it onto their laps. To her surprise, she saw that many of them were staring at her rather than at it. In slow and deliberate succession, from left to right, they nodded meaningfully at her. Some also allowed an encouraging smile to play around their lips – though their expressions still bore faint traces of uncertainty.

This display continued just long enough for her to understand the significance of it, but not so long as to provoke the guards' suspicion. A few moments later everyone raised the canvas, conjuring the usual inrush of air and dust that stirred the hems of their long skirts. Then they settled to work. Doing likewise, Ampliata fumbled with an awl, her dexterity held temporary hostage by agitation at what had just occurred. To regain it, she reminded herself that what she had just witnessed was an acknowledgement, at best, from only some of her co-workers. The question of whether or not they would actually help remained unresolved – so far, anyway.

The next couple of days offered no resolution to this problem; but they were not entirely eventless. Returning from the Laborium each evening, Ampliata reported that she had circulated the messages again twice and that an increasing number of the other women had nodded furtively to her. There was, however, no gainsaying the fact that this amounted to something less than an actual promise of help. Brebix had described a similar reaction in the fields - unaccompanied, due to the constant proximity of the guards, by any words.

On the third day, however, Ampliata returned with a brighter expression and movements quickened by the news that she had to impart. Tossing her canvas bag of stitching implements and swatches of material onto the table, she said, "Well, there was a message in return at last."

"*Really*?" responded Rhea, eagerly.

She nodded.

"It was slipped to me on a piece of parchment during a short break half way through the shift. It bore the signature of Urmila – she and her husband live in the third tier, second quadrant. I'm guessing she'd been deputised by some of the other women to give a response. I got rid of it as soon as I'd read it."

Marcus felt a vice-like tightness of anxiety in his throat; suddenly it was difficult to inhale enough air to make his response audible.

"What did it say?" he asked, hoarsely.

"In essence it said that she and the others were intrigued by what I had told them but they want some kind of sign; some token of good faith, before they'll commit themselves any further."

Theus rubbed his chin.

"A token of good faith? Like what?"

"I don't know exactly. Maybe something that could only come from you." She gestured towards Marcus. "To prove your presence here."

Marcus looked around the room, frowning. What could he possibly provide, amongst the few possessions he had managed to haul up leagues of rock face from Daldriadh, that would offer proof of his identity?

"Wait a minute," said Rhea, vanishing into the bedroom, to the others' puzzlement.

She returned a few seconds later with Marcus's frayed, dirt encrusted cloak and proffered the section that bore his personal crest – unique to his former status as Prince. No garments other than his bore it. As he scrutinised it, the intricacy of its design made it seem like an alien artefact; he could scarcely remember the kind of life – pompous, formal – that it represented. And in the plain but dignified surroundings of Brebix and Ampliata's dwelling its supposed finery seemed unblushingly vulgar.

"What about this?" Rhea asked him. "I know it's a bit more visible than a discreetly stitched message. But sewn onto a section of the air sac then passed around the Laborium…well, who else could it have come from?"

Marcus glanced at Ampliata.

"You'd be the one taking the risk again," he said. "What do you think?"

She took the crest and fingered the stitchwork around its border.

"I think your tailors had far too much time and gold thread at their disposal in the old days," she replied.

Marcus laughed.

"Agreed. But do you think it'll help?"

"Well, I don't relish the prospect. But I don't see that we have any alternative, having come this far already."

And with that she crossed to the drawer beside the sink, took out a knife and set about cutting off the crest.

The following morning she departed again for the Laborium, this time with the crest hidden in the voluminous pocket of her skirt. The fugitives, meanwhile, occupied the day – yet again – by pacing around the dwelling as quietly as possibly and occasionally staring out of the window. They also remained vigilant at all times for noises in the alley that might signify a renewed Kabal search and the dissolution of all their hopes.

Returning at the end of the day, Ampliata's mood was hard to interpret. It didn't convey the lively optimism of the previous day. But nor was she obviously despondent.

In spite of the danger which attended her every move at the moment, Marcus sensed that she was deriving no small amusement from the desperate eagerness which greeted her every time she arrived home.

"It's all right," she said, in response to the question no-one could quite bring themselves to put to her. "I managed to pass the crest around without being observed. I made sure it was only half visible by putting it beneath of the pleats in the canvas – enough for the other women to notice but not enough for the guards to spot. Anyway, it went round as far as Urmila, but by then the shift was drawing to a close. I saw her unpick it with an awl and slip it in her pocket. She's probably taking it home to show to her husband." She sat down at the table and yawned, arching her sore back. "I think we'll have our answer soon."

An answer *did* come, albeit not quite as quickly as they had hoped. The next day limped by, as if crippled by the sheer weight of anticipation it bore. But the one after brought a response.

"They're willing to help," announced Ampliata breathlessly, as soon as she reached the top of the stairs. "There was a message stitched under one of the outermost pleats. It was very discreet and bore Urmila's initials again. It simply said, '*We with you.*' Not very grammatical, but clear enough. I don't think we'll know if the 'we' means everyone in the layer until we make our move. The most important thing is that they're aware of what we're going to attempt."

"Good, good," said Marcus, acutely relived.

Rhea touched Ampliata's arm.

"Thank you for taking such a risk," she said.

"It's okay," Ampliata replied with a smile. "Once you settle down and have children there tends to be a certain lack of suicidal danger in your life. It can be quite invigorating now and then."

They all laughed. Then there was a protracted lull while everyone absorbed the fact that the first stage of their plan, which had seemed so impossible when they dreamed it up, actually appeared to have worked.

"Of course, the next stage is even more difficult," commented Theus, his expression darkening. "The support of the Farmers alone won't be enough to let us prevail. We need the Artisans on our side as well, to create a force big enough to overwhelm the Kabal in the lowest layers. And, even more importantly, to hold these layers against more Kabal from the Admins' and Cloudfarers' layers, who'll surely try to force their way down."

"Well, contacting them shouldn't be impossible in principal," said Ampliata.

"How would you suggest doing it?" asked Rhea.

Taking the crest out of her pocket, Ampliata turned it over in her hands.

"The canvas we're working on right now in the Laborium will get sent up very soon to the Artisans' layer, where it'll be waterproofed. I could sew the crest onto it again, just visible beneath one of the pleats, but with a note concealed behind it."

"You mean a stitched message?" asked Magnis.

"No, not this time. I mean just a note, on a piece of parchment, folded up – like the one Urmila passed to me. That way we can convey a message to them in one go, instead of having to break it down into small stitchwork phrases."

"Okay good," said Rhea, nodding slowly.

"But getting some kind of response back will be much more difficult, won't it?" said Theus.

Brebix nodded.

"You have to keep in mind the way the citadel is organised," he said. "Everything – produce, resources – all flows upwards. The only things that travel in the other direction are pointless directives. They all come from the Admins' layer and we mostly ignore them."

"So there's no way at all for the Artisans to send us a response?" asked Marcus.

"No easy way that I can think of."

"Don't they send you tools and implements quite regularly?" asked Theus.

"Yes. But every consignment is checked by Kabal guards before it leaves the Factorium in the Artisans' layer."

"What if they hollowed out the handle of a chisel or a sickle and placed a rolled up message inside?" suggested Theus.

Ampliata shook her head.

"The guards handle every item when they check them. They would notice the difference in weight immediately."

"Hmm."

In the protracted silence that followed they all stared at the floor with unseeing eyes, each one of them seeking an answer to this new problem.

Eventually Marcus said, "You know, there *is* one other thing that doesn't flow upward through the citadel."

The others looked at him.

"Yes…what?"

He hesitated, somewhat abashed.

"It's sort of obvious, really," he said, hedging.

"It'll be more obvious if you tell us what it is," Rhea pointed out, though not unkindly.

Marcus blushed.

"Well…you know…" He reached over and tapped the pipe. "*Waste.*"

"Waste," echoed Rhea.

"Yes, waste. Sewage, effluvia – whatever you want to call it. All of it running down through the plumbing system and…"

"And expelled through the outfall pipes in the orchard," said Brebix.

"Exactly. I mean if we can send bombs down that way, surely we can ask the Artisans to do the same with some kind of message in reply to ours," Marcus pointed out. "And surely you or one of the other Farmers might be able to edge away into the orchard and retrieve it when the Kabal guards aren't looking."

"The Kabal guards are *always* looking. It's their defining characteristic," commented Theus dryly.

"They are," agreed Brebix. "But it's still an interesting idea."

He considered it a little longer, lips pursed.

"No-one, not even the guards, wants to go near the outfall pipes normally because they smell so rank," he said. "So any message the Artisans send should be able to lie there undiscovered until I can get to it. The only problem I can see is that there are three other big outfall pipes as well as the one you sent the bombs down. But luckily they all emerge in our quadrant, fairly close together, so checking them isn't impossible – just a bit tricky."

"Why do they all come out in the same place?" asked Marcus.

"Prevailing wind," replied Brebix. "On our side of the peak it usually blows any unpleasant smells out over the cloudscape instead of across the citadel." He smiled. "I'm not surprised you've never noticed. Such aromas don't usually percolate up to the Palace... Anyway, the point is that there's no way of knowing which pipe a message – whatever form it's going to take – will come out of. If I *did* manage to slip away from my work party into the orchard I'd have to check all four. *That* could be a problem. It would mean I might be out of sight of the Kabal long enough to arouse suspicion."

He pondered this point a little longer.

"Then again, I'm not sure if the guards really pay that much attention to the details of our work rota. I could sort of *migrate* discreetly around the edge of the fields, and labour in various places, so I can check a different pipe each day."

"Always assuming the message, if it's on a piece of canvas, doesn't blow away with the autumn leaves before you find it," said Magnis.

"Or worse than that, float up between the bare branches, up to the Palace and right into Titus's hand as he's standing on a balcony," added Theus.

"I think that's unnecessarily alarmist," Rhea told them both, with a reproving smile.

She looked back at Brebix.

"Are you willing to do it: to take such a risk, when the time comes?"

Brebix smiled and reached out to clasp Ampliata's hand.

"Well since my wife has taken just as great a risk right under the gaze of the Kabal several times already," he replied. "I think it would be a poor tribute to her courage if I didn't do the same. So… yes, I'll help in any way I can."

"Good."

Rhea drew a deep breath and looked at the others.

"So. We have the Farmers with us. We have a means of contacting the Artisans. And we have a means for them to respond, when they wish to… It looks as if this really might happen."

They all nodded pensively. The impending crisis was unignorable now. Marcus sensed that the others felt the same as he: part of him dreaded the risk it represented and the pain it might entail, but part of him was eager for some, *any* resolution of the tension that governed their every waking moment.

XV.

On the Edge of Disaster

Ampliata departed again early the next morning for the Laborium, carrying the message for the Artisans. More adept now at this strange new method of communication, which required both speed and dexterity, she returned that evening to report that she had indeed managed to stitch Marcus's crest to the canvas – partially covered, with the message hidden beneath it. The canvas, she went on, had been folded numerous times towards the end of the shift then secured with rope and hauled up the Great Staircase to the Artisans' layer.

The others received this news with satisfaction tempered by uncertainty. There was no way of knowing how long it might be before the message circulated amongst the Artisans, or how long it would take them to formulate a response – or, for that matter, whether the guards might discover the message before the Artisans themselves did.

None the less, out in the fields Brebix embarked on his new, perilous routine of slipping away from his work party at some point during the day to check the outfall pipes in the orchards. Each evening he drew the curtains at the top of the stairs aside with a despondent expression and shook his head before anyone could ask him if he had found anything.

Three days passed in this fashion. On the evening of the fourth, however, Brebix's demeanour was somewhat different.

"What is it?" asked Marcus, fearing the worst.

"It's all right," replied Brebix. "The Artisans haven't refused us – not yet anyway. It's the men I work with. I had to explain to them as secretively as possible why I kept on creeping off between the trees every day. They've been working closer and closer to the misty edge of the fields to make it easier for me to slip away. But now they've, uh…

indicated that they'd like to see you in the fields before they risk the attentions of the Kabal guards by concealing my absences any more."

Rhea, Theus and Magnis looked appalled at this idea.

"But they've seen him before, in the orchards, when we first arrived back," Theus pointed out.

"Only some of them," replied Brebix. "The others say they need proof. To be honest, I think they just want him to show good faith by coming out in the open."

"But that would be suicide for him!" exclaimed Rhea.

"Not necessarily," Brebix told her. "We have labourers as young as Marcus in the fields. His shorter stature would not alone be enough to draw attention to him. And on these early winter mornings – with the first chill weather upon us – we all wear cowls over our heads to keep them warm. As long as we're careful I can lead him out safely out to join my work party."

Rhea didn't seem much reassured by this. And the others still exchanged concerned looks.

"We have no choice but to do this," Marcus told them. "We *need* the support of the Farmers – without it there's no way we can progress any further with our plan. If they want some kind of reassurance through seeing my face, so be it."

Secretly, though he was abundantly aware of the danger it would place him in, the idea of exchanging the confinement of the dwelling for the open spaces of the fields – even if under a literal cloak of secrecy – exhilarated as much as alarmed him.

Rhea sighed.

"Very well," she said.

Theus smiled at Brebix.

"Let's hope the portraits in your co-workers' dwellings weren't as, uh… vague as the one in yours, otherwise they might not recognise him at all," he observed.

"If that's our biggest problem," replied Brebix. "I'll be perfectly happy."

So, early the next morning, Marcus and Brebix departed for the fields, covered heads scrupulously lowered as they descended the stairs from the dwelling. The alleys they trudged along smelt musty as the living stone breathed out its trapped moisture with the slight rise in temperature brought by the new dawn. In the canopied atrium, the listlessly patrolling guards, who had also just begun their shift, looked too tired and beset by too many jaw-breaking yawns to pay them much heed. None the less, they tried to remain as unobtrusive as possible while selecting – at Brebix's whispered instruction – long-handled hoes and rakes from amongst the mass of implements stacked against the walls. Having done so, with the required equipment balanced on their shoulders, they manoeuvred themselves through the carved archway flanked by sentinels. Marcus was careful to move in a straight line so neither end of his hoe inadvertently scraped against it – or, even worse, clipped one of the sentinels on the side of the head, thus drawing their attention to his inexperience.

Stepping into the fields, he took the first deep draught of fresh air that he had enjoyed in nearly two weeks. Chill and bracing, it seemed to clarify his vision, making everything look twice as sharp. Stretching down before him, the wide crescent of the fields lay as yet undisturbed, seeming to slumber beneath a fragile few inches of mist. He and Brebix joined the other Farmers in descending one of the rutted tracks. Still studiously looking down, Marcus concentrated on the way the mist swirled and eddied around him with each foot fall. Presently, they reached the portion of the fields that abutted against the orchards. Here, three members of Brebix's work party were already assembled. Marcus recognised none of them. Moving irresolutely about – bending and stretching – they gave the impression, for the benefit of the Sentinels, of beginning their labours, but were actually awaiting Marcus's arrival. As he and Brebix approached, they forgot their half-hearted pretence and stood motionless, eyes fixed on the shorter of the two figures.

Marcus glanced around, to check if there were any members of the Kabal loitering in the immediate vicinity. But, being less vulnerable to the threat of chastisement than the Farmers were if they tarried in the Atrium, the guards had not yet fully dispersed over the fields. So, turning his back to the Great Wall, Marcus peeled back his cowl just enough for Brebix's three co-workers to see him.

As he watched the men watching him, it seemed to Marcus that he was being presented with a triptych of the human face in various states of astonishment. In the case of the Farmer on the left, the astonishment was tinged with fear at the realisation that the uprising could not now be avoided. The centre Farmer wore, instead, an expression of guarded satisfaction at the prospect that the Kabal's oppression of them might soon be cast off. The one on the right seemed overcome by a sense of deep sympathy for all the travails, which, he knew, Marcus must have endured to return to Heliopolis after being lost in the cloud depths. For his own part, Marcus nodded to each one of them in turn, trying to convey as much confidence as he could summon.

He held their wordless gaze for a little longer, before replacing the cowl. Then, as the first of the guards arrived in the fields, straying into their orbit, all the members of the work party bent to their labours, turning and aerating the soil. Marcus remained close to Brebix and copied his movements as best he could, hoping that his lack of skill wouldn't draw undue attention to him.

Morning passed. The sun burned off the mist and continued to climb the sky. To Marcus – confined for so long in Brebix and Ampliata's cramped dwelling – the great span of blue above him seemed more invigoratingly limitless than it ever had before. Throughout the morning, he continued to snatch glimpses of it whenever he could.

The work itself turned out to be awkward and demanding. Towards midday, Marcus grew conscious of all sorts of aches and pains radiating through various parts of his body. He therefore felt both relief and apprehension when, in the early afternoon, Brebix nudged him and indicated, through discreet gestures, that now was the best time to slip away. Marcus glanced around him. Sure enough, a change of shift had temporarily thinned the number of guards in the fields.

Nodding, Marcus followed Brebix in edging towards the orchard. Then, at the moment when the fewest pairs of beady eyes seemed to be directed at their portion of the fields, they darted together between the trees. As soon as they were out of sight, they hastened through the resinous shade, which was skewered at many different angles by narrow shafts of light. Brebix moved swiftly and assuredly, heedless of the rotten fruit that he squeezed to a pulp beneath the heel of his shoe. As Marcus struggled to keep up, Brebix said, in a whisper, "I check the outfall pipes in rotation. Today it's the centre one, over here."

With that, he peeled off to the left. And, sure enough, when they reached the outer edge of the orchard, the designated pipe lay just a few yards away. It emerged from amid the trees and terminated where the grass gave way to a barer terrain of shale and pebbles. Beyond lay the banked cloud. They hurried towards the pipe and crouched at its mouth, which was warped and encircled by cracks. Stretching away from the end of it, the downward sloping ground was streaked with a miniature riverbed of discoloured soil. Marcus knew only too well what had caused it to become discoloured, but didn't want to think about it too much. Donning gloves, Brebix began sifting unenthusiastically through the soil.

"Not my favourite task," he muttered.

"I don't blame you," replied Marcus.

They scanned the residue of sewage and the area surrounding it in vain. Their search was somewhat hampered by the fact that they didn't really know what they were looking for – other than something that looked alien or incongruous. But there was nothing.

Brebix sighed resignedly. They were just about to give up and hurry back to the fields when Marcus spotted an object poised at the lip of the pipe. Leaning forward, he plucked it from its resting place and turned it over in his hands. It was a wooden tube, slightly curved at either end, with a deep incision running around its circumference about half way along. Though very simple, its sleek contours testified to the Artisans' craftsmanship. Gripping it at either side of the incision, Marcus twisted. The two halves unscrewed to reveal a rolled up piece of parchment protruding from one of them. He lifted it out and unrolled it.

His crest, folded inside the parchment, fell out. Brebix caught it before it landed in the brown mulch at their feet. The parchment itself bore one simple phrase. Soldered on in a cursive script – elegant yet perfectly clear – it said:

We Are With You

Somewhat puzzlingly, however, it was surrounded by an intricate stitch work border, composed of numerous different symbols. At first, Marcus thought that the Artisans' much celebrated flair for design had got the better of them, but Brebix soon corrected him.

"They're blaizes," he said, taking the parchment. "Even within their own layer, the Artisans have a strict hierarchy. They wear these symbols on their clothes to show which level of accomplishment they have reached." He fingered the parchment, stroking the blaizes almost reverently with his thumb. "This is their way of showing that Artisans from all strata are prepared to…"

"You there!"

They leaped to their feet, heads snapping round in the direction the voice had come from. Brebix slipped the parchment in his pocket. The tall figure of a guard emerged from between the trees. Drawing his sword, he broke into a run, moving towards them with unmistakable intent. Marcus was instantly reminded of his first encounter with members of the Kabal, just after the Mercanteer's foundering. This time, however, he had no comrades to fight alongside and no sword with which to defend himself.

Motioning Marcus to stay well back – in the hope that he might still fail to be recognised from a distance – Brebix snatched up his rake just in time to block the first vicious swipe of the guard's sword. The force of the blow none the less sent him staggering back against the pipe. He was obliged to roll sideways to avoid the next one, which connected clamorously with the pipe itself.

Watching this unfolding spectacle, in which Brebix struggled to parry yet more lunges with the frail handle of his rake, Marcus boiled with frustration. There had to be *some* way he could help. Yet as he looked around him, the bare terrain offered no inspiration at all. Then, in a flash, he remembered the climbing equipment he and the others had been forced to leave buried when they first emerged from the cloudscape. Since they'd met Brebix and his co-workers in the orchard almost immediately, surely that meant that the pile of stones beneath which the equipment was concealed couldn't be too far away.

Skirting round the thrashing, jostling bodies of Brebix and the guard, his face still averted from the latter, he ran as fast as he could along the curved alley formed by the undecided area between the pines on one side and the banked cloud on the other. In some places the cloud had encroached further up the mountainside, making it difficult to see where he was going. This fact became all too readily apparent a few seconds later when he tripped and grazed his shin. Wincing, he clasped both his hands across it as tightly as possible to staunch the rapidly blossoming pain.

Acute discomfort was soon replaced by exquisite relief, however, when he realised that what he'd tripped over was the object of his search. The outline of a plan already sketching itself in his mind, he clawed at the partially crumbled heap of stones. Beneath lay the canvas balloon. Swollen and randomly bulging, due to all the items – adzes, ice picks, empty proleyne stoves, stale oaten bread – crammed inside, it looked like the larval stage of some huge insect. He ripped the cinched neck of the canvas open and began to pull out the long rope that he, Rhea, Theus and Magnis had used to tie themselves to one another during the ascent of the Ins'lberg.

Hastily untangling the rope, he threw it around his neck, picked up one of the larger stones and rushed back to where the sounds of close quarters combat between Brebix and the Kabal guard were growing both more desperate and more laboured by the second. Skirting round them again, he looped one end of the rope round the trunk of the nearest tree, knotted it as tightly as possible, and tied the other end around his left wrist.

Returning to the antagonists, weighing the stone in his hand, he discovered that he'd done so just in time. With a final, vicious stroke, the guard had splintered the shaft of Brebix's rake, rendering it useless. Brebix had lost his footing and fallen to the ground as a consequence. Now gripping his sword in both hands, the guard hoisted it above his head, preparing to administer the final thrust, plunging the blade into the soft flesh just above Brebix's sternum.

Marcus hurled the stone at the back of the guard's head. It didn't connect with enough force to cause any real damage, but that had not been his purpose. It did, however, attract the guard's full attention. He whirled round, with a growl. As soon as his gaze settled properly on Marcus's face for the first time, his eyes widened with recognition.

Satisfying himself that proper contact had been established, Marcus set off down the incline at full tilt, the guard close on his heels. Within a few moments, they had both been swallowed by the opaque yet penetrable wall of damp mist. The ground became glossier and more treacherous beneath Marcus's feet, yet he knew he couldn't afford to slow his progress. He was counting on the fact that the guard, who was running diagonally towards him, had been too astonished by the recognition of his identity to notice the rope curiously trailing from his wrist. Once they were both deeper into the mist it would become even less visible. Marcus only hoped he'd judged its length correctly.

The ground grew steeper, his footing less sure. All his instincts told him to slow down. But he ignored them and hurtled on into nothingness. His pursuer's pounding tread kept pace, close behind him. He could feel a gentle, whispered breath on the back of his neck, which he knew was caused by wild sword strokes just missing it. The guard had clearly decided that the ideal outcome would be to take his scalp back to Titus.

But just a few yards further on, as Marcus knew it would, the ground vanished beneath him. He sailed over the precipice and began to fall.

XVI.

The Eve of Battle

He threw his free arm up and grabbed the rope, so he was holding it securely with both hands, then braced himself. Within seconds it drew taut. Horribly jarred, he swung back like a pendulum and slammed against the nearly vertical wall of damp rock.

Wholly focused on capturing Marcus, the guard had no time avert his fate. He too sailed over the precipice. But he continued to plunge in an indistinct flurry of arms and legs. The scream he emitted faded with merciful speed, muffled by the thickening cloud.

Marcus hung motionless for a few moments. His desperately improvised gambit had worked. Though his right wrist was encircled with chafed skin, he scarcely noticed it. He stared into the saturated void that surrounded him. Yet it was not the cloud that had doused the light in his eyes; it was the realisation of what had just occurred. He was responsible for a man's death. He had not strangled him or stabbed him in the heart, but he had led another human being ineluctably to his doom. No matter that the man in question was about to kill Brebix; no matter that the series of events that had led to this calamity had been set in motion by Titus, not him. The fact remained that he had passed through a door in his life. Already he felt a new, slightly different sense of his own identity settling upon him. It did so like the moisture that steadily beaded his face, flattened his hair, and even gathered on his eyelashes, pre-empting the tears he might otherwise have shed.

The pain swarming down his arms as the blood drained from them reminded him that there was little time to reflect on these things at present. Kicking against the rock, he twisted his body round to face it. Then, gripping the rope, surrendering it only briefly to pass hand over hand, he began to 'walk' up the precipice as best he could. Progress was difficult. Twice his feet slipped and the rope again took the full weight of his body. It wasn't as wrenching a drop as the initial one, but the muscles and tendons in his arm sockets – already tender – pleaded as if it were. He had just started to wonder if he would make it when he felt a sharp tug on the other end of the rope.

"Are you all right?" shouted Brebix.

For a brief moment Marcus reflected that this was a rather obtuse question to ask someone who had just hurled himself off a mountain peak several miles high attached only to a frayed length of rope. But the anxious sincerity with which it was delivered affected him like a benediction. In the acute discomfort of the moment, he felt indescribably consoled by Brebix's concern.

"More or less," he shouted back. "Though I think my arms are a few inches longer than they were before."

In spite of the trauma of what they had just been through, Brebix chuckled at this. Digging his heels into the shale-littered ground, he pulled hard on the rope and helped Marcus scramble up the last part of the precipice. Hauling himself over the edge of it, Marcus lay face down for a few seconds, catching his breath. Brebix crouched solicitously beside him and, as gently as possible, untied the rope from around his wrist. Marcus rolled over and crossed his arms over his aching chest, eyes still closed.

"That was very ingenious," said Brebix.

Marcus grimaced. He thought of the guard tumbling through endless grey fathoms of cloud.

"Small consolation to our friend," he replied glumly.

"He would have cleaved my skull in two if you hadn't acted as you did," Brebix told him. "You know that as well as I. And having done so, he'd have captured you and revealed your presence to the rest of the Kabal. My family would have been condemned to death…"

He trailed off. Marcus nodded wanly. He understood that Brebix was reproving him not for his concern at the guard's demise but for assuming too great a burden of guilt.

"If he hadn't died, many other lives would have been forfeit," he said cautiously, as if exploring the notion to see if he could make himself believe it.

"Exactly."

Marcus wanted to accept Brebix's rationale – to clad himself in it like armour and thus maintain his resolve for the challenges yet to come. But doing so too quickly felt somehow callous. Sensing his confusion, Brebix drew both their minds back to more urgent matters.

"Well… one thing is certain: we can't delay acting any longer." He drew the parchment from his pocket and twitched it between his fingers. "Whether the Artisans' message is genuine or not, there's now a guard who'll fail to sign off at the end of his shift tonight. The Kabal will launch a search for him first thing tomorrow… Events have overtaken us."

Marcus nodded again, more resolutely this time.

"We'll begin at first light. There's no gong back now."

He rose to his feet. Concerned that they had been absent from the fields longer than intended, they quickly set about erasing as much evidence as they could of what had just occurred. Marcus loosened the other end of the rope from around the tree trunk, allowing it to slither away down the incline. Brebix hurled the Artisans' wooden vessel into the mist. Then they made a brief detour to completely dismantle the small pile of stones and throw away the rest of its contents. They did so in case the other guards came looking for their missing comrade later in the day. Having accomplished these tasks, they threaded their way back up through the orchard.

At the far side of it, lingering in the embrace of the shadows, they assessed the situation in the fields. The day's work continued. The Farmers still congregated in work parties that dotted the sloping peak, bristling with upswung scythes and other implements. Most of the groups remained in the same place, but two sometimes merged where there was especially demanding work to be accomplished.

Marcus and Brebix's own work party had lingered as close as possible to the trees, awaiting their return and hoping that the guards wouldn't become suspicious of the attention they seemed to be lavishing on one relatively small patch of soil. Giving silent thanks for their loyalty, Marcus followed Brebix in darting amongst them once again.

Having retrieved his hoe from between the trees, Marcus was able to resume work immediately. But for a few surreal moments Brebix had to endure the indignity of miming work with an invisible rake until one of the other Farmers noticed his plight and handed him a spare one.

They all worked on through the rest of the day. As the hours passed, Marcus found that his sense of exertion lessened as he grew better at emulating the Farmers' measured rhythms. He began to feel as if the work party was a single entity and he one of its many limbs, moving in perfect time with the others. Given how fresh memories of his isolated upbringing still were, the sensation was oddly comforting; in spite of the constant observation they were all under, he was able to immerse himself in it until the end of the shift. It also helped to allay his lingering sense of guilt at the guard's fate – at least temporarily.

Finally the crimson winter sun began to set. The shadows of the trees in the orchard lengthened, seeming to nudge them back up towards the citadel. Collecting their discarded implements, Marcus and Brebix's work party followed the others up the rutted tracks and through their archway. Marcus again kept his head lowered and face covered beneath the cowl. But given the throng of activity in the atrium, it was relatively easy to pass through it and along the alleys to the dwelling.

Once inside, they were greeted eagerly by Rhea, Theus and Magnis. In response to their questions, Brebix unfolded the fragment of parchment and smoothed it out over the tabletop. The others scrutinised it then listened as Marcus related what had happened at the outfall pipe. They sensed, from the clipped tones in which he described it, that he was seeking no balm of sympathy for what he had just done; rather he simply wanted to push it out of his mind for the time being, in order to focus on what they had to accomplish. So, after a few brief but sincere words praising his daring, they settled to discuss preparations for the uprising. Though their plans were already well established, they went over every detail again, conscious that this was their last chance to do so.

When Ampliata returned a couple of hours later with the children, they quietly told her what had happened during the day. Then everyone settled again to the more practical task of preparing what little ordnance they still had for Brebix to use it at dawn the next day.

"It's strange isn't it," commented Marcus at one point. "Last time we desperately hoped that the Kabal wouldn't be suspicious about an explosion, yet *this* time we're hoping the exact opposite."

The others smiled in acknowledgement of this. They all feared how the events of the following day might develop: at what human cost an uprising against the Kabal might be accomplished, if it succeeded at all. And not one of them was unaware of the fact that the hoped-for intervention of the Selenopolitans had failed to materialise. But their fear was leavened by a sense of relief that the waiting was almost over. The little conversation that they exchanged as the evening wore on remained muted and reflective. Every now and then one of them paused and looked up from his or her work, catching the eye of another. The two would exchange a brief nod and then return to the task at hand.

In this way, sustained by mutual infusions of support, they completed their preparations. Then Brebix and Ampliata bade everyone a grave goodnight, while the others prepared wordlessly for sleep, conscious that they would need as much rest as possible to sustain them on the following day – or, rather, later on the same day, since it was now the small hours of the morning.

Lying on the floor, Marcus found it impossible to get to sleep – indeed rather than 'drifting off,' he found himself fighting against an advancing tide of wakefulness. The more he shifted position, the more the ridges of the flagstones imposed themselves uncomfortably in his torso. So eventually he allowed his restless thoughts to range as far and wide as they wished. Somehow this made it easier for him to lie still.

He thought of the citadel, slumbering beneath cloudless skies and stars that barely glimmered, due to the high, thin air. So keyed up were his senses that he felt he could mentally inhabit every part of it, even the ones he had never visited. It was as if the citadel were enclosed within him, instead of he within it.

He imagined the Farming and Artisanal families around and above where he lay. He knew only too well how apprehensive they must be. Like him, they doubtless felt as if they were being stretched on a rack of contending impulses: borne up by the prospect of freedom, but at the same time oppressed by the fear of death. He also imagined, albeit more indistinctly, the Kabal in *their* quarters – each guard sleeping with an unmerited ease, complacency hugging the contours of his body like an insulating blanket.

His thoughts then roved higher, in questing spirals, to the Palace. Gliding along corridors, through successive gateways of light cast by proleyne lamps, they sought out Asperia. Had she been left to starve in a cell, lying on her side – the shrinking of her stomach drawing her knees up towards her chest? Or had she been set to obscure tasks in the archives, perhaps to prove that Titus's new status was justified by his lineage? Was she being given just enough food and water to sustain her as she laboured amid stacks of books and scrolls? Then again, perhaps neither of these images was accurate. Perhaps she had been eliminated as soon as Titus seized power. And what of Synvadis? Did he languish in fetters or had he too been swiftly disposed of? Marcus realised that he had pondered his fate far less than he had Asperia's. The Prime Minister's stiffly formal air – which preceded him everywhere, like an ornate shield upraised – had meant that any sense of closeness to him was impossible to achieve. Allied to his self-love, it had made him an unendearing character, whom Marcus felt had stalked through his childhood world with a perennial air of disapproval. Yet he felt guilty for ever having doubted the man's honour, and thought of him now, in spite of all his foibles, with unmixed fondness.

As for himself… Well, what did he think of himself? Though he hadn't mentioned it to the others, he had turned fifteen only a few days earlier. He was quite happy for the event to pass unmarked – principally because, after everything that had befallen him, he felt twice as old as his actual age. This was a mixed blessing, he reflected. On the one hand he was glad to bid farewell to the callow mixture of exuberance and naivety that had once prompted him to blurt out foolish things. So many times, when he was younger, he'd voiced opinions that had been greeted by the adults around him, like Asperia, with, at best, wry indulgence, at worst, stern correction. On the other hand, he did mourn slightly the cheerfulness that had once animated his every waking moment. But the loss of his father had put an end to this. The sense of bereavement had not left him, but it had adopted a new guise. He no longer felt the uncomprehending pain that had tormented him in Daldriadh. It had been replaced by a low-level, dolorous ache, which, though far from welcome, was containable.

Everything at the moment seemed uncertain to him. He didn't feel fully alive, but rather as if he were suspended between two lives. There was the old one: secure, but filled with so many strictures and prohibitions. And there was the possibility of a new one with Breah: aglow with closeness, perhaps even love, but uncertain in every other respect. The prospect of the sacrifices he would have to make to attain this new future didn't disturb him – he knew that the odds against vanquishing Titus were so great that there was little point in fretting about what might come after.

Yet the idea of Breah had given his life a purpose beyond simple revenge. He wanted to survive and he wanted to be happy – in spite of knowing all too well that she, the author of his renewed sense of hope, might already be dead. Though not often given to self-pity, he did fear he might be doomed to repeat a dismal series of events: he had been unsure whether or not his father had survived in the cloud depths; he had gone in search of him and discovered that he had not; he had found Breah instead then fought his way home; yet now here he was, back in the citadel, unsure if she too had perished, many leagues below where he now lay.

Sighing, he turned on his side. Resigned to being unable to sleep, he stopped trying and did, therefore, eventually succumb.

The morning dawned stormy. Winter, so far mainly just the retreat of warmth and light, had acquired teeth at last, barging round the citadel's walls and harrying the shutters of the dwellings in the lowermost layers. In Brebix and Ampliata's dwelling, everyone rose and made themselves ready with the same subdued purposefulness they had shared the night before. They all tended to keep their heads lowered and shoulders squared while moving around, as if the events of the coming day were an actual physical barrier that they were preparing themselves to run at full tilt. Even the children, who normally engaged in murmurous bickering over breakfast that erupted into occasional mutual hand slaps, kept perfectly quiet. It was as if some familial telepathy told them that their parents had far greater concerns to preoccupy them today. Ampliata shot them the occasional anxious glance, evidently praying that they would remain safe in the Juvenum with the other children while violence raged around them.

Presently she and Brebix prepared to leave. All of the fugitives hugged both of them in turn and bade them "Good luck" in grave, tender tones. Then Brebix hoisted the bag of clay pots onto his shoulder, Ampliata herded the children towards the door, and both departed in their respective directions. Marcus, Theus, Rhea and Magnis were left to pace the room – so accustomed to the confined space that they weaved round one another and the table as if engaged in a stately dance. They were kept in restless motion not just by anxiety about whether or not the first stage of the uprising would succeed, but also by the prospect that a search for the missing guard might lead the Kabal to them before Brebix could even attempt his opening gambit. Whatever transpired over the next hour, however, the decisive moment was almost at hand…

XVII.

Into the North

The channel that the Cloudfarers and Eihlans had been trudging along finally opened onto an uneven plateau, just wide enough for them to congregate on it and consume some meagre provisions. Jarrid's wounds were also attended to. How they would all survive when the provisions ran out was a question almost everyone was acutely conscious of but no one dared to express. Only the youngest children seemed unconcerned. In spite of the attack by the Eildritch, they still seemed to labour under the blissful misapprehension that they were participating in some kind of communal adventure. Consequently, they tore back and forth across the plateau – exulting in their freedom – until drawn close by their parents and ordered to sit still as the empty space filled up with more and more weary families.

Perched on the edge of the plateau, Breah looked back the way they had come. This was the furthest she had ever been from home and her first experience of the northern reaches – uncompromising in their fissured, contorted geology. Realising this, she was struck anew by how remote from anything familiar her world must have seemed to Marcus when he first found himself in it. She felt her heart swell with sympathy for the bewilderment and anxiety he must have experienced – not only gazing out on an alien terrain, but also knowing full well that home had become so dangerous to him. Now that she had been forced to abandon her own home, it seemed as if he were slipping further and further away from her. If he ever did manage to return to Daldriadh, she wondered, how would he know where to find her? Beset by such fears, she found herself cherishing memories of him even more intensely, as if they were glowing embers that she was trying to protect against an encroaching coldness. Yet in spite of how urgent these emotions were to her, she felt no desire to share them with anyone else. Somehow, cradling them to her allowed them to retain their intensity.

Musing on these things, she kept her back to the rest of the Eihlans and cast a despondent gaze over the landscape. It swelled – sometimes slowly and regularly, often in convulsive surges – until it reached the elevation where they now sat. Shadows were starting to brim amid the folds and creases, in preparation for the advent of night.

Breah remained absorbed in her thoughts a little longer, until a stirring amongst the hunched bodies behind her drew her attention back to them. Looking round, she saw that some of the Elders had risen on their haunches and congregated in a tight circle. Heads bowed in concentration, they were rummaging in their packs and distributing between themselves objects that she could not see. But the words they began to intone – gravely, reverently – left her in little doubt as to what they were doing. Squirming her way between the other watching Eihlans, she drew close to the circle then smiled with mournful recognition when her guess was confirmed.

The Elders were tapping themselves lightly on their limbs with polished, intricately carved pieces of bark – ritually cleansing themselves in preparation for offering prayers. But Eihlan prayers were no mere verbal messages, transmitted to a hopefully sympathetic deity. They were, instead, actual written messages, written with charcoals on thin fragments of parchment. These fragments were folded into neat pyramid shapes. Then, having had a lit candle suspended beneath them with twine, they were released to float up into the clouds.

Breah watched as the Elders continued their preparations. At first the Cloudfarers seemed uncomfortable at the notion of releasing illuminated objects into the air – doubtless concerned that doing so might give away their location to any Nullmaurs tracking them. But Aònghas assured them that the interiors of the parchment pyramids glowed too weakly to be seen from any distance. Breah noticed, with a renewed sense of pained sympathy, that in spite of lending the Cloudfarers these assurances, he displayed no inclination to take part in the ceremony himself. None the less, he observed it with a smile that bore little trace of bitterness. And, when the prayers finally drifted upwards, nudged this way and that by contending breezes, before being lost amid the all-devouring blankness of the low sky, Breah herself could not help but feel consoled by the long-cherished delicacy of the ritual.

Hours later, in the middle of the night, she woke from a bad dream. Pinned so tightly between her mother and father, she knew she would find it hard to get back to sleep. Within a few seconds of realising this, she felt an idea form. It was far from logical, but her brain was too sleepy to analyse it in any objective way. Instead, rising gingerly, she picked her way between slumbering bodies to where the prayers had been offered. Then, having collected up a fragment of parchment, a candle and a few other discarded items, she turned and tiptoed back towards the edge of the plateau. Reaching it, she stepped back into the channel that they had all toiled along to reach open ground. She followed the channel's twisting descent for fifty yards or so, until ensured of privacy, then sat down and assembled the materials on her lap.

Using two pieces of flint to light the candle, she leaned into the uncertain glow it cast and smoothed out the parchment. Then, haltingly at first, but with increasing confidence, she wrote the following:

Marcus,

I scarcely know why I am writing these words, since you will never read them. I can only think that I need to do this not to reach you, but to lighten my own heart of the feelings that press so much upon it.

*We are lost. The Nullmaurs have at last driven us
from the soil we cleaved to for generations. If it were not
for your comrades we would be dead already. They have
exceeded in every way the belief you placed in them. Yet
now we wander the Marches – between Daldriadh and
the northern lands – seeking shelter and sustenance, but
finding little of either. As we do so, I think more and more
of how it must have been for you when you first found
yourself in our world. I see now that you were braver than
I ever understood and I use the example of your faith as a
light to guide me.*

*From the first moment I saw you, I felt our lives
would somehow be entwined, and that feeling grew as we
talked – though the lives we described to each other could
not have been more different. But how can we ever be
together? If you survived the journey home, you will have
returned to a place as hostile to you as it could be. And
even if you do prevail there, I know that the chances of
you finding your way back to me are remote. There is no
point in hoping that it might be otherwise. These are facts
which we cannot alter.*

*I realise that I alone would not be enough to make you
return here to stay. Even if you do come back, it is more
than likely that every one of us will already have died.
Knowing this, I wish to say only one thing… I love you,
and will think of you for as long as I am spared.*

Breah

As she scratched out this message, bent over it like a
supplicant, tears gathered on her lower lids, threatening to
erase the words as soon as they were written. She therefore
held the parchment at arm's length to keep it unblemished
while she folded it. Having done so – obliged, all the while,
to blink her vision clear – she attached the candle to it then
took a deep breath and let it go.

The parchment ascended in a flawless vertical between the walls of the channel before being snatched at by the breeze and quickly straying into darkness. Breah sat staring up at the point where it had vanished for some time. Then, at least somewhat consoled, she crawled back towards the plateau, to rejoin her slumbering kin.

The following morning they moved on through the labyrinth of water channels. They had only been travelling for an hour, however, when a storm swept down upon them from the north. Icy winds raced along the channels, stinging pellets of ice borne upon them.

Just when their situation seemed irretrievably desperate, they came upon a gap in the rock that opened into a large cave. Though damp and cold, it offered the best chance of shelter that they had yet seen. And so, one by one, they crawled into it.

"It won't serve as a new home," said Tafril. "But it'll at least keep us safe until the storm abates."

Aònghas nodded grimly.

"However long that may be."

XVIII.

The War for Heliopolis

When Brebix entered the fields by one of the archways, the winter sun, still low in the eastern sky, shone almost vertically across Heliopolis. The citadel's immense shadow therefore fell over the fields and orchards on the western side of the mountain top and stretched out onto the fringes of the storm-wracked cloudscape. In order to conceal better what he was about to do, he strayed from his work party and stole round the curve of the tree-line until he was in part of the fields where the sunlight drew a thick shroud of vapour from the damp ground. Knee-high, it streamed over the mountaintop, driven by the wind.

Glancing around once, he wedged his hoe under a stone, which he then stepped on. He gave the handle a sharp downward tug and the blade snapped. Then, setting his features into an expression of innocent imbecility, he wandered over to the nearest guards and asked if he could borrow another hoe from one of the other Farmers. Bored, already perspiring in their armour in spite of the morning chill, they said nothing, merely offered an irritable wave of assent. Smiling to himself, clay pots clanking together in the bag slung over his shoulder, he hurried off across the fields.

Agitated not only by the tense wait but also by the amount of kheifra they had drunk, Marcus, Rhea, Theus and Magnis continued to pace back and forth in the dwelling. Every few moments Marcus went over to the window and peered out of it, trying to check on Brebix's progress. But he had long since worked his way round the fields and out of sight. Marcus leaned out of the window a little further and squinted back up at the battlemented wall of the Artisans' layer. He caught only occasional glimpses of the Kabal sentinels when they passed the gaps in the battlements. All he could see the rest of the time were the glinting crowns of their helmets and the tips of their spears.

Slightly less than an hour later, Brebix returned to where he had first been working. He waved his new hoe cheerily at the guards, but they were looking the other way, having long since forgotten about him. He worked on for a while. Then, when the second hour was almost up, he slung the bag off his shoulder, crouched down and drew from it the one clay pot he had left. (He had distributed the rest to the other Farmers on the pretext of asking them for a replacement hoe.) Cradling the last one in his hand, he lit the wick.

Pausing to take a deep breath, he let go of the pot. It rolled down towards the orchard. Nothing happened for a few moments. Then it came: an eruption of leaves and splintered wood from amid the trees, accompanied by a booming sound that rolled over the fields and up the walls of the citadel, causing the Farmers and sentinels to reel backwards. Severed, burning branches spun through the air and landed in the fields, starting small fires. A few seconds later this was followed by more explosions all round the curve of the mountaintop as Brebix's comrades followed suit. Throughout the fields, the guards looked stunned. They struggled first to comprehend that this circular fusillade could not possibly have been caused by ordnance from the Mercanteer. Then they began to work out its true origin. Taking advantage of the shock that had immobilised them, the Farmers leaped upon them, brandishing implements. The sentinels on the Great Wall, shouting in alarm to one another, turned from watching the rapidly developing fray in the fields and rushed down towards the archways that led there.

Up at the window Marcus slammed his fist into his palm and exclaimed, "Yes!"

He looked up again at the edge of the Artisans' layer. The few sentinels he had been able to see before had vanished. Hopefully they were hastening through the interior of their layer, heading for the Great Staircase, intent on helping their fellow Kabal below.

"It really is working," said Marcus, scarcely able to believe it himself.

"But this is only the start," replied Rhea, peering out of the window beside him.

Retrieving his sword from the possessions stored in the other room, Marcus dashed across the kitchen and down the stairs. Similarly armed, the others followed. At the foot of the stairs he paused and peered into the alley. Several guards rushed past, heading for the fields. Once the alley was empty, he, Rhea, Theus and Magnis all set off in the opposite direction.

They ducked inside one of the unguarded archways to the Laborium just in time to be greeted by an impressive – and inescapably bizarre – sight. Kabal sentinels and guards tore down the broad spiral steps from the layer above, cloaks fluttering as they descended. The women, Ampliata amongst them, sat around the edge of the latest canvas they were working on, heads meekly lowered.

In the interests of speed, the Kabal troops began to cut across the expanse of canvas, heading for the archways, with no regard for the women's work. When the majority of them were trampling over it, the women sprang to their feet, hoisting the edges up. Though the women were not as strong as the troops, they significantly outnumbered them and were able to exert considerable force. With a startled yell, the troops all lost their balance and fell against one another in a cacophony of clanging armour. The women hurriedly drew the edges of the canvas together and, having done so, began to stitch them closed.

No one was under any illusion that this gambit was going to contain the Kabal troops for long. But if it kept them entangled and disorientated for just a few minutes it would have served its purpose. So while Magnis and Theus, with powerful sword strokes, disarmed the few who had eluded capture, Marcus and Rhea rushed out to the fields in search of reinforcements. There, inspiringly, the Farmers were beginning to gain the upper hand. The Kabal guards already present when the bombs went off had been subdued and herded into groups of five or six. Some Farmers kept an eye on them. Others, having taken their weapons, engaged the Sentinels – newly arrived from the Great Wall – with increasing confidence. The sentinels fought more adeptly: their sword blades made the smoke that drifted across the fields from the explosions swirl around them in elegant patterns. But they were, once again, outnumbered. And the Farmers fought with all the force of their pent-up anger at the oppressiveness of Titus's regime.

Moving amongst the fray – dodging the wild back swing of swords and stray spear thrusts – Marcus and Rhea rounded up as many Farmers as could be spared then ran back towards the Laborium. While the Farmers engaged the troops who were now cutting their way free from all over the bulging canvas like angry bees from a hive, Marcus rejoined his comrades and they tore up the Great Staircase. Passing through the thick stratum of stone, they encountered a number of bewildered Artisans, milling around on the last few broad steps that led to their layer.

From the moment he had stumbled out of the clouds and been overwhelmed by the spectacle of the citadel shining on the mountaintop, Marcus wondered if he would finally get the chance to see all the parts of it that he had longed to visit as a child. So far he had scarcely had time to notice, let alone absorb anything. But, entering the Artisans' layer, he stopped and gazed around him at its main workplace.

The Factorium was even larger than the Laborium, but seemed, if anything, smaller, due to being so crammed with the paraphernalia of manufacture. Everywhere he looked he saw partially completed objects – furnishings and farming equipment identified themselves most readily to his eyes – sitting on work benches or caged within scaffolding. Chains were festooned everywhere too, like the vines and creepers he had seen in paintings of walled gardens in tropical citadels. A network of cables with pulleys attached ran, criss-crossing, from one side of the great space to the other. And, squatting all round its fringes, were sturdy kilns, which shed half circles of red light over the floor. Together they basked the Factorium in an infernal glow quite appropriate to the scene unfolding within it.

Those Kabal sentinels and guards newly arrived from the Admins' layer above had been waylaid by the Artisans, who set about belabouring them with whatever tools lay to hand. Initially astonished by this development, the Kabal had swiftly regained enough composure to engage their attackers. Now, throughout the Factorium, Kabal and Artisans were viciously embroiled with one another. Pairs of bodies slammed into scaffolding and rolled under benches, neither displaying even the slenderest regard for the craftsmanship that had threatened to be destroyed in the process.

Marcus was profoundly affected by the spectacle of the Artisans' courage. He noticed also that Rhea and Theus were scanning the turmoil around them with an even keener intent – trying to locate, amongst the thrashing bodies, the recognisable outlines of a family member. But there was no time for reunions at present; too much remained to be accomplished.

So the three of them climbed half way up the next section of the Great Staircase then stood facing in different directions and rallied, in as loud a voice as possible, any Artisans not already fighting. A few weaved towards them, ducking to avoid stray backswings of weapons or tumbling antagonists. Having collected as many reinforcements as they could muster, Marcus, Rhea and Theus continued up the staircase, a rising tide of inflamed humanity at their heels. Their destination was the Admins' layer – home to the citadel's bureaucracy.

So great was the fervour that now boiled within Marcus, his arrival in the Admins' layer proved to be somewhat of an anticlimax. Climbing the last steps, he found himself in a circular hall, from which long narrow corridors fanned out all around. Apart from the discreetly recessed tallow lamps that lit them, neither the hall nor the corridors bore any trace of decoration. And although they were, on the face of it, much cleaner than any part of the two layers below, there was something disquietingly sterile about them.

Frowning, Marcus and the others began to move along one of the corridors. There were windowless doors set into it at regular intervals on either side. Picking one at random, Marcus opened it gingerly. Before him lay the smallest room he had ever seen. It was really just a cupboard with pretensions to grandeur. A desk, almost as wide as the room itself, sat in the middle. All round it towered stacks of paper that nearly touched the ceiling. Each stack leaned at a crazy angle, prevented from toppling over only by the others leaning at equally crazy angles against it. Hunched behind the desk, seemingly unaware that he might be smothered by an inundation of paper at any moment, a man scratched with a quill at a roll of parchment that spilled off the desk and unspooled onto the floor. He looked painfully thin and careworn.

"Um, excuse me," Marcus said.

The man failed to look up. Instead, he shook his head – as if troubled by an insect buzzing around it – then, rocking slightly back and forth, began to mutter under his breath as he worked. Terms such as 'memo,' 'itemise' and 'triplicate' were pronounced over and over again in an urgent tone, as if to ward off some unidentifiable threat.

Marcus was at a loss to understand the reason for the man's behaviour, until Rhea, who was also peering into the room, shook her head and said, "Poor fool. The Admins never did have much of a grip on reality. They were always so obsessed with their work – even though no-one else was ever quite sure what they did. It looks as if the harsh treatment from Titus has been too much for this one. He's just sought refuge in meaningless details. I doubt if even *he* knows what he's doing anymore… and I'll bet the others are the same."

Together they looked into a couple more offices and the spectacle presented to them each time confirmed Rhea's diagnosis.

Closing the last door gently, Marcus stared at the floor for a few moments then, looking up at the others, said, "I think we may not be able to count on the wholehearted support of our Administrators."

"It doesn't matter. We can manage without them," Theus replied in clipped tones. "Titus has already committed most of his Kabal troops to the layers below us. There can't be many more left in the layer above now. It should be populated mainly by Cloudfarers who only obeyed him to stop their families from being hurt. But their families have made the decision to rebel. So they no longer have to protect them."

Marcus nodded.

"What we need now, though, is a way to get up further," he said. "Any ideas?"

"There are several lifting stations that go up through the Cloudfarers' layer to the Palace," said Magnis. "We could try them."

"Okay, where's the nearest one?"

Magnis looked around him, frowning.

"Um…I think it's down one of these side corridors."

"Lead the way."

With Marcus, Rhea, Theus and the assembled Artisans following, Magnis searched for the lifting station. For some time, they marched along a series of almost indistinguishable corridors. Occasionally, when they passed an open window, the sounds of continued fighting drifted up from far below. Most of the Kabal troops had now been subdued in the fields and more and more Farmers, no longer occupied with fighting, were hastening up, through the Artisans' layer, to join them.

Eventually they found the lifting station. Or, at least, they found an empty shaft. To its right, lay a deep alcove, crammed with a complex array of gears and levers.

"You operate the mechanism by hand and it brings the lifting station down," Rhea explained.

She took a step towards the mechanism, but then paused and looked back at the others, puzzled. A rumbling sound was issuing from the shaft. It grew rapidly louder and the floor began to tremble.

A look of comprehension dawned on Rhea's face. She grabbed Marcus and Theus, pulling at them, and yelled to the others, "Get back!"

The lifting station – a rectangular box, with a timber frame and mesh walls – plunged into view, ablaze. Having been dropped all the way down from the top floor of the Palace, its cables severed, it struck the floor of the shaft at great speed and shattered, sending a maelstrom of flame, smoke, twisted mesh and fragments of wood hurtling into the corridor. Marcus and the others threw themselves on the floor. The fireball caressed their legs and shoulders then retreated down the corridor. Sitting up, Marcus patted himself. The back of his tunic was smouldering a little but otherwise he was okay.

There were a few moments' silence. Then Theus commented, "Like I said, Titus must have realised he didn't have enough loyal troops left to hold the Cloudfarers' layer, having sent so many of the Kabal down to combat the Farmers. So he's withdrawn to the Palace and tried to cut off all access to it."

The others nodded grimly. They were still sitting on the floor, hunched against the wall, absorbing the significance of this development. But they were soon distracted by a renewed rumbling from above, though this was different in tone.

"What's that?" asked Rhea, looking up.

"I'm not sure," replied Marcus. "But I don't like the sound of it."

Fighting their way through the smoke, they ran down a side corridor, looking for the nearest window. Finding one, they peered out of it. Rhea scanned the fields below. Only a few, localised skirmishes were still raging. But then Marcus nudged her and pointed upwards.

The prow of an aëro:cruiser was nudging over the edge of the landing stage, directly above them. Soon it was floating away from the citadel, trailing mooring lines. Another aëro:cruiser quickly joined it. Then, however, both vessels, instead of picking up speed, slowed. Turning ninety degrees, until their starboard sides lay parallel to the landing stage, they hung, motionless, in the air. Their cannons tilted downward.

"Oh no," said Marcus, suddenly realising what was about to happen.

A volley of shells ripped from the cannons. They streaked through the air, slamming into the fields and into the walls of the Farmers' and Artisans' layers. Bricks, earth and bodies were hurled into the air. The whole citadel shook. In the Admins' layer, plaster dust drifted down from the ceiling and settled over Marcus and the others' shoulders.

"Air power," he said despairingly. "I didn't think about that."

"Do you think Titus is on board one of them?" asked Rhea.

"I doubt it. I'd guess he's directing them both from one of the Palace balconies. He's probably using flags to communicate with them, like the lookouts do."

"But the fields are full of Kabal. By ordering an attack like this, he'll kill his own people," pointed out one of the Artisans.

"He doesn't care," replied Marcus. "No one's life means anything to him besides hanging on to power."

"But if the aëro:cruisers fire more shells on the layers below they could bring down the whole of the citadel," said one of the newly arrived Farmers. "The layers above depend on those below."

"If Titus can't control Heliopolis," said Rhea. "He'd probably prefer to see it destroyed."

"Still," said Marcus. "I don't think he'll order them to fire on *this* layer just yet. He'll want to see if he can quash the uprising before he risks throwing everything away. So that buys us some time."

"We need to get up to the Palace," said Theus.

"But how?" asked Rhea.

"We've no option. Titus will have destroyed all the lifting stations by now," said Marcus. "We have to go up the outside."

XIX.

Marcus Ascendant

Half an hour later, Marcus was standing on the sill of the same window, gripping the end of a rope, looking up the sheer side of the Admins' layer. The wall above was dotted with small wrought iron balconies and unpainted, shuttered windows. The rope stretched between them then vanished up over the sloping side of the Cloudfarers' layer. To either side of him many more ropes also stretched upwards, with Artisans and Farmers already attached to them. Some of these 'rebels' – which, he supposed, was now the proper term for them – were making good progress.

After they grudgingly conceded that climbing was the only way to proceed, Rhea and Theus had dispatched a group of Artisans back down to their layer to search for equipment. Having found as many ropes as they could, the Artisans had improvised by tying sickles, the blades of scythes and even clawed hammers to the ends of them. Then, running back up to the Admins' layer, they leaned perilously far out of the windows, spun the weighted ends of the ropes round as fast as possible and hurled them up the wall towards the Cloudfarers' layer. Though most quickly snagged on something, the Artisans tugged at them a number of times to ensure that the improvised hooks were secure.

Now, Marcus started to climb. He swung himself out sideways from the window and planted his feet flat against the wall. The ever-strengthening wind pummelled him. Looking up from his new vantage point, he could now see that every elegantly carved window ledge in the Palace had lethally sharp spikes protruding from it. This seemed an eloquent symbol of the fact that although Titus had power over Heliopolis, he had gained it by violence and therefore had to protect himself against the threat of violence from others.

More shells slammed into the fields far below, sending rippling shock waves up through the whole structure of the citadel. Marcus struggled on regardless. But just a few seconds later, something struck him hard in the shoulder. Losing his footing, he spun wildly, hands chafing against the rope. As the world flashed past him – cloudscape, wall, cloudscape again – he also heard a desperate shriek. It grew rapidly fainter. Regaining his footing, he looked down. One of the Farmers lay crumpled on the wall of the Admins' layer, severed rope still clutched in his hands.

The Kabal in the Cloudfarers' layer had obviously seen what Marcus and the others were trying to do and were starting to repulse them. He climbed faster. Many of the Farmers and Artisans, he noted with relief, had already vanished over the top of the wall. He reached the guttering that ran round the base of the Cloudfarers' layer. The slope ahead of him led up to one of the innumerable windows that protruded from it. And there, framed in the window, was a Kabal guard sawing at his rope.

"No!" shouted Marcus.

The rope snapped. Plummeting, he threw his arms up and grabbed the guttering. It sagged and creaked but stayed in place. He hauled himself up just far enough to see that the guard, with a malevolent grin on his face, was crawling out of the window, spear clutched in one hand. The guard leaned out onto the sloping wall and began jabbing his spear at the guttering. Though loath to let go of the guttering, even for an instant, Marcus kept on shifting his grip on it in an attempt to avoid the spear's tip severing his fingers. His arms soon ached unbearably with the effort.

Just when he was convinced that he must lose his grip at any moment, the guard, with a holler of astonishment and distress, tipped, head first, out of the window. He rolled over twice then found himself hanging from the guttering beside Marcus. He was no longer grinning. Yet he managed to recover within a few moments and began aiming a series of vicious, sideways kicks at Marcus, indifferent to the fact that doing so imperilled them both by making the guttering sag even more.

Rhea appeared at the window and threw a rope down to him. It dangled just next to him, on the side opposite to the guard. Grabbing it, Marcus hauled himself upwards. As he did so, he heard the guttering sag slightly more and the guard whimpered, newly conscious of his fate.

Rhea was perched on the ledge of the window. She pulled him inside and he flopped down on a couch.

"Thank you," said Marcus breathlessly.

"Don't mention it."

Marcus sat upright on the sofa and looked around. He was inside a typical Cloudfarer's quarters. It was larger than a Farmer's and less sparse than an Admin's. In addition to the sofa, several shapeless but comfortable looking chairs were dotted around it. A low table sat between the chairs, smothered in charts and diagrams. The fireplace was unfussily carved and had a neat, smoke-blackened grate. The mantelpiece above it was crowded with bric-a-brac: old fashioned compasses and sextants and other, even more intricate looking navigational instruments that Marcus didn't recognise. A telescope stood on a tripod in one corner. Sepia tinted nephograms of foreign citadels – taken from approaching or departing aëro:cruisers – hung on the walls. The volumes that crammed the small bookshelf had titles written on their spines in languages that Marcus couldn't read. So intent was he in observing all this that for a few moments he forgot everything else.

Returning to his senses, he jumped off the sofa and both he and Rhea headed for the door. Just then another explosion shook the room. Once again, a light sprinkling of plaster dust settled over Marcus's shoulders. Several of the navigational instruments fell off the mantelpiece, smashing over the grate, while some of the charts slithered from the table to the floor. The explosion sounded different to those that had preceded it: deeper, more concentrated. Marcus darted back to the window.

"Oh no," he said.

"What is it?" asked Rhea.

"The aëro:cruisers are firing together at only one part of the fields, just below the Great Wall... He's really going to do it. He's going to create a landslide and destroy the whole citadel."

"He must have seen our forces getting into this layer."

"We have to get up to the Palace. Like I said before, I'm sure he's on the Throne Room balcony. We have to get him to call the aëro:cruisers off."

"But how? You must have seen all those spikes sticking out from the Palace windows. Every balcony is probably booby trapped too. There's no way we can climb up there. We need to secure this layer first."

"There isn't time, Rhea! If we don't stop those aëro:cruisers there won't be a citadel to save." Her expression told him that she saw the truth in what he said, but she could offer no solutions to their plight. He paced round the room for a minute or so, staring at the floor. Then he said, "We need to get to the landing platform."

"Why?" asked Rhea warily.

"I'll explain on the way. Come on!"

They ducked out of the Cloudfarer's quarters into a large, octagonal atrium. Doors lined its eight walls, leading to more quarters, and a fountain splashed at its centre. In different parts of it, rebel Farmers and Artisans who had scaled the wall alongside Marcus were already engaging the Kabal troops. As Theus had predicted, there didn't seem to be that many troops left in the layer. But so few rebels had thus far managed to reach it that the antagonists were more or less evenly matched in numbers – with the Kabal, as always, better equipped and drilled. Already the rebels were struggling. Seeing this, Marcus and Rhea leaped into the fray.

After several minutes' exhausting combat, Marcus began to fear that unless reinforcements arrived swiftly, the Kabal might successfully repulse the rebels. But just then events took an inspiring turn: one which he had hoped for but had not dared to anticipate. A group of armed men appeared at the end of the wide corridor that led into the Atrium. The absence of black bands encircling their arms showed that they were ordinary Cloudfarers – unwilling recruits to the Kabal, loyal only for the sake of protecting their families. Taking only a few seconds to assess the situation, they drew their swords and began to fight alongside the rebels. Some even displayed fleeting delight at recognising a relation amongst the Farmers and Artisans, though, once again, the urgency of the moment offered no chance for proper reunions.

Liberated from the immediate struggle by the arrival of these allies, Marcus and Rhea sped off down one of the corridors that led from the atrium. Along the way, they encountered further groups of rebels – Theus and Magnis amongst them – fighting the Kabal with the assistance of ordinary Cloudfarers. So fierce were the battles that they were forced to duck, flatten themselves against the walls and even slid across the floor to dodge them. While doing so they also kept their swords raised, deflecting the odd glancing blow that came their way. Approaching the end of the corridor, Marcus breathlessly explained his plan to Rhea. When they eventually emerged, panting, onto the sunlit expanse of the landing stage, she commented, "I wish I could say there was a better way to do this but unfortunately I can't think of one."

The landing stage was deserted – all the Kabal troops had been sent into the heart of the layer to deal with the rebels. Marcus and Rhea dashed across to the hanger and plunged into its dark interior. Moments later they re-emerged, dragging an ornithopter by the wings. They dragged it all the way over to the launching track and hoisted it on. Then they began pushing it into position, straining against the coiled strength of the launching mechanism, which would accelerate it out over the cloudscape. Once Marcus's feet slipped on the smooth floor and the ornithopter sprang back slightly. Spotting a couple of Artisans – the first to fight their way past the Kabal – emerging onto the landing stage, Rhea called them over. With their help she and Marcus were able to get the ornithopter all the way back up the track and locked into position. Then, dashing over to the apron of the landing stage, they retrieved one of the grappling cables that were used to pull returning aëro:cruisers back into dock. They tied the end without the hook attached to the tail of the ornithopter. As prepared for launch as circumstances allowed, Marcus and Rhea squeezed, side by side, into the ornithopter's cockpit. Marcus had the cable coiled in front of him and clutched the hook in one hand.

"I can't believe we're doing this," muttered Rhea.

"Don't worry," replied Marcus. "I have complete faith in your piloting skills."

In spite of his reassuring words to her, he briefly reflected that an escapade like this would, just a few weeks ago, have terrified him. Now, though still scared, he did it without a moment's hesitation, such was the intensity of his resolve.

"Go!" he shouted to the Artisans.

They wrenched the release levers on either side of the mechanism. The ornithopter hurtled down the track. The wooden cage that enclosed Marcus and Rhea creaked alarmingly. To his embarrassment Marcus found himself involuntarily screwing his eyes shut. When he opened them again the ornithopter was airborne, already banking hard to avoid the two aëro:cruisers. The few Kabal crewmembers on their decks who were not fully occupied with firing cannons pointed as he and Rhea soared past, gaining height all the time.

It grew rapidly colder and thermals buffeted the ornithopter. With Rhea expertly twisting the controls, they completed a tight circle then plunged back towards the citadel. As they passed over the landing stage Marcus saw the tiny figures of more rebels spilling onto it. The two who had helped launch them were still standing next to the catapult, gesturing to one another and pointing out over the cloudscape. They seemed to be discussing something important, but what?

He had little time to speculate about this. They were now sweeping over the Palace battlements, which, as Rhea had pointed out before, were smothered in lethal-looking spikes. By a mixture of her piloting skill and a favourable air current they dodged the many turrets, towers and spires. There were no Kabal guards on the walls – they had all been sent below to help deal with the rebellion.

"Now!" shouted Rhea.

Marcus hurled the hook out of the cockpit. It fell rapidly, the cable uncoiling behind it. Soon it was dangling thirty feet below, thrashing around in the rush of air. Marcus watched hopefully as it trailed over the battlements. The idea was that the hook would snag on something solid and the cable would stretch taut, slowing the ornithopter down enough for them to jump safely from it.

The fringes of the Hortoreum swept by beneath the ornithopter in a blur of colour, the foliage shivering in its slipstream. The birds in nearby trees squawked as their cages swayed back and forth. But still the grappling hook had not snagged on anything.

"No good!" Marcus shouted.

"Hang on!" Rhea shouted back. "We'll have to try the pool."

Given what they were about to do, it occurred to Marcus that "Hang on" wasn't really the most appropriate piece of advice. None the less, the instant he saw the first glint of water below he slipped the catches that held the side of the cockpit shut. Rhea tilted the ornithopter to port. The hatch fell open and first Marcus then Rhea rolled out into the hurtling air.

XX.

The Hortoreum

Tumbling towards the pool, they both stretched their arms in front of them to try and dive more smoothly into it. However the instant Marcus's chest slapped the surface he felt all the breath being knocked out of him. He speared downwards through the icy water, lungs throbbing, desperate to inhale but knowing he didn't dare. Kicking his legs, he clawed his way back up. The instant he broke the surface he took in several gulping breaths. Rhea appeared a few seconds later, doing the same. Though one of its wings had brushed the pool when it tipped sideways, the ornithopter gained height again and soared over the hills on the far side of the pool, the grappling hook that still hung from it skipping across the surface of the water.

"Nice flying," gasped Marcus.

"Thanks," replied Rhea, hair plastered in strands over her forehead. "Do you think Titus saw our antics?"

"There's only one way to find out," replied Marcus. "Come on."

They swam for the side of the pool, helped one another up onto the path that fringed it and stood looking around them, dripping on the gravel.

"There are several staircases going down into the Palace," said Marcus.

"You still think he'll be on the Throne Room balcony?"

"Oh I have no doubt about it."

"Okay, then I think we should split up. That way if there are any Kabal guards lurking around one of us has a better chance of getting to him."

Marcus nodded. Having had Rhea at his side almost every second since they fell into the cloud depths, he felt reluctant to be separated from her now, as if she were a talisman. Without her, would the luck that had carried him through so many perils forsake him?

"The stairwells are at each corner of the Hortoreum. We should go in opposite directions. And stay off the paths," he said.

"Right. Good luck."

"You too."

Turning from her, he skirted the fringes of the pool then stepped onto another gravel path that branched off from it. However, instead of following the path itself, he scrambled up one of the hills and vanished into the bushes that clung to it.

As he crept along he couldn't help remembering the last time he had done this. It seemed an eternity ago. Then he had been eagerly taking part in a charade: a mock set-piece of adventure, devoid of true fear, that had none the less turned out to be a prelude to unimaginably terrible events. Now his world had, quite literally, been turned upside down and he could remember little *but* fear. And, in some part of his brain where illogical thoughts are free to flourish, he hoped that this time the opposite would happen: that a full awareness of just how treacherous the world could be would enable him to elude whatever dangers might lie in wait for him once he had left the fragrant Hortoreum behind.

At first it seemed that this might indeed be the case. Reaching the top of the hill, he straightened up a little and peered across the gracefully undulating artificial landscape. Lying diagonally to the right, some way distant, was one of the ornate, wrought iron structures – like a three quarters dome – from which staircases descended. It was unguarded. Marcus had just allowed his hopes to rise a little at this sight when a large pair of gauntlet-clad hands emerged from the heart of a frangipani bush right in front of him and parted it roughly. A scowling face thrust itself through the gap. Crying out in shock, Marcus realised that there was no time to jump up and draw his sword. Instead he threw himself backwards and rolled down the hill. A rose bush scratched his arms as he raised them to cover his face. He landed in a narrow gully, water rushing over him. Dazed, he shook his head. Something slid rapidly up his back and scratched the nape of his neck. He squirmed desperately at first, not knowing what it was. But then, looking upstream, he saw the hooked end of the grappling cable trawling through the water as the ornithopter soared, pilotless, overhead. If he could just reach it...

He staggered up the gully, arms outstretched, in pursuit of the cable. The fast running water frothed round his ankles. But he had only gone a few steps when the Kabal guard cannoned sideways into him, having launched himself down the hillside. Marcus was slammed against the other side of the gully. His sword arm crunched painfully into rock and soil, going numb instantly. The guard lost his own balance and fell into the water. While he struggled to his feet Marcus scrambled up the opposite hill. But the guard recovered quickly. Grabbing one of Marcus's ankles, he hoisted him into the air until he was upside down. Meanwhile the dangling cable swung back round from a different angle, whipping across both of them as the ornithopter passed by overhead again. The guard swatted it away as if it were a minor irritant.

Perhaps it was the extra blood rushing to his head that lent Marcus his inspiration. He grabbed the guard's leg and sank his teeth into it. The guard howled, dropping him. Marcus tried to roll out of his reach but he wasn't fast enough. One hand pinned him down at the shoulder while the other struck him across the face. The blow stung excruciatingly, the shock of it speckling his vision. None the less he spotted the ornithopter swooping around again. This time it flew much lower, with most of the cable dragging across the hills, between the bushes.

The guard shifted his grip on Marcus's shoulder, preparing to strike again. The cable came into reach. Squirming free, Marcus grabbed the hook at the end of it and rolled forward between the guard's legs, which the man had planted wide apart to steady himself while he pummelled his victim. The guard wheeled round, staggering slightly on the slope. Though he was large and muscular, Marcus sensed that he wasn't especially agile.

He rolled back between the guard's legs. The guard twisted this way and that trying to regain his grip on Marcus. So intent on this was he that he didn't seem to question Marcus's purpose in weaving around him rather than trying to escape. Nor did he seem to feel anything when Marcus, dodging behind him once again, managed to attach the hook to the belt of his tunic.

The ornithopter sped on across the Hortoreum, heading towards its fringes. Oblivious to it, the guard stamped a foot on Marcus's chest, pinning him down at last. He unsheathed his sword. But he swung it too hastily and only managed to slash open the front of Marcus's tunic. Cursing, he adopted a firmer, two-handed grip on the sword and prepared to bring it down vertically, drilling his victim into the ground.

At that precise moment, however, the cable pulled taught and the guard reared back helplessly from Marcus. First he was wrenched sideways through ninety degrees then he doubled over, as if punched in the abdomen by an invisible fist. He reached frantically behind him to detach the hook from his belt, but to no avail. Instead, bellowing with outrage, he found himself dragged, at considerable speed, over the tops of hills and down gullies. At some stages in this journey his flailing limbs thrashed shallow water into foam, at others they conjured maelstroms of petals.

The bellowing stopped abruptly when he slammed into the battlemented wall at the far side of the Hortoreum. Going slack, still dangling from the cable, he slid smoothly up the battlements and vanished over the other side, as the ornithopter, riding another powerful air current, soared out over the cloudscape. Watching this, Marcus kneaded his numb arm until the feeling returned to it. Then, drawing his sword, he jumped down onto one of the pathways, ran as fast as he could to the nearest staircase and rattled down the steps. He wondered if Rhea had encountered any other Kabal guards and, if so, whether or not she had managed to dispose of them. But there was no time to stop and find out.

When he reached the bottom of the staircase he found himself standing in one of the Palace's many interior courtyards. Once again, a fountain splashed at its centre. Sunshine poured in through the domed skylight and threw the water's sparkling reflection back over the walls.

Creeping round the fountain, he entered one of the cool, well-lit corridors that led off the courtyard. Here he was on surer ground. He knew every inch of the Palace – mainly from a childhood spent sneaking from his apartments to explore it when he was supposed to be studying. He moved swiftly and confidently along the maze of corridors.

The Palace seemed eerily similar to the way it had before. A deceptive air of calm reigned within its marble walls. Only the occasional, distant rumble of an explosion suggested that anything was amiss – though Marcus did notice that all the portraits of his father, which used to be dotted along the corridors, had vanished. Passing his apartments, he peered in very briefly. Nothing had been disturbed. Indeed the drawing room looked a good deal tidier than it had before – like a mausoleum that had been preserved in honour of his memory. Shuddering, he hastened on.

He had just reached the far end of the corridor that led to the Throne Room when a series of strange noises – a hurtling roar followed by a resonant *whump* – drew him over to the nearest window. The two Kabal-crewed aëro:cruisers still hung in the air a couple of hundred yards off. Pointed towards each other, presenting port and starboard sides respectively to the citadel, they continued to pummel it, seeming to shiver with pleasure each time they loosed another broadside. So focused were the crews on their common target, however, that they had failed to notice a new development.

Cresting a cloudbank less than a mile further out, the sleek outline of a Selenopolitan aëro:cruiser had appeared. It was a warship-class vessel, its prow tapering into an iron-clad ramming post. Marcus was seized by an exquisite sense of relief. For more than a week now, the hope that emissaries from the great eastern citadel, seeking to discover the fate of the Mercanteer, might come to their aid had slowly shrivelled within him. Yet now it blossomed once again – all the more intense for having been so despondently cast aside. The sound he had heard was the Selenopolitan vessel's latest salvo, fired at long distance to shock the Kabal aëro:cruisers into desisting, if only for a few moments. Sure enough, their cannons fell silent.

Taking advantage of the Kabal crews' disarray, the rebels on the landing stage prepared their own response. They hoisted an ornithopter onto the launching track. Having locked it into position, they doused it with liquid proleyne, set it alight and released it at a slight angle. It streaked across the landing stage and shot unerringly through the air towards the Kabal aëro:cruisers. A few seconds later it slammed into the clustered air sacs of the one on the left. Instantly, a mass of orange flame blossomed over the bulbous contours of the canvas. The rebels cheered wildly. Mindful of where he was, Marcus resisted the temptation to cheer with them. Instead he hastened along the corridor, fists clenched, determined to match their courage and ingenuity with his own.

When he reached the Throne Room, he found the huge double doors ajar and unguarded. Stepping inside, he looked around him. The ceiling was an immensely complex network of interlocking domes. The domes were decorated with frescoes that depicted citadels elsewhere in the hemisphere. The concave shape of each dome forced its fresco to be drawn in a weird perspective that only seemed normal if you looked up at it from directly below. Otherwise, simply glancing around the ceiling, as Marcus was doing now, you caught glimpses of a series of weirdly elongated or compressed images. The central dome was made of normal glass, studded with jewels at the corner of each pane. These jewels speckled the dais on which the throne sat with lozenges of coloured light. The throne itself

– carved from oak and upholstered in rich fabric – was squat and seemed to sprawl over the dais, as if attempting to impose itself as much as possible on the room, even when unoccupied.

Already moving forward somewhat irresolutely, Marcus stopped altogether when he caught sight of the throne. Though he had seen it before many times, its bulk, added to all the redundant curlicues of its design, struck him with renewed meaning. It reminded him forcibly of Gorloch's throne in Daldriadh, which, though lacking same ornament, shared similar dimensions. During the recent past, he had found no trouble in equating Gorloch with Titus: two implacable dictators, seeking to enlarge their power, albeit in two utterly different worlds. But now, for a fleeting moment, he sensed a similarity too between the absolute authority wielded by the Nullmaur chief and the elite status of his own ancestors over so many generations. But, though this insight gave him momentary pause, it also lent the next step he took a renewed determination.

Every corner and recess of the room was populated by statues. Some of the tall figures were frozen in attitudes of profound reflection, with a deeply chiselled frown bisecting their marble brows. Others stood sentry, shoulders thrown back, heads raised, and conveyed an impression of absolute superiority. Once these figures would have intimidated him as much as any flesh and blood Minister or Seneschal. Now their self-conscious postures seemed vaguely ridiculous.

He moved further into the room. Over to the right, a carved archway led to an acreage of balcony, wider than any other in the Palace. Above shoulder height, the archway's curving outline became a series of crescents, which grew wider as they rose, supposedly showing the phases of the moon. They possessed no purpose beyond demonstrating the amount of craftsmanship that could be lavished on what was essentially a hole in the wall.

Marcus paused again. The archway was hung with silk curtains. He heard something beyond them: a raised voice.

Though he could make out nothing of what it said, it altered so frequently in tone between aggressive, despairing and exultant that it sounded like someone having a furious argument with himself. There was no mistaking its resonant timbre however – Marcus's ear was attuned to it through years of experience. Even so, when the curtains stirred and he was afforded his first glimpse of the figure beyond, he caught his breath. The broad, muscular back with its jutting shoulder blades; the thick neck; the square cranium, topped by close-cropped grey hair – all these features combined to create an impression of indomitable power that was all the more intense for being so compact.

As the curtains continued to part now and then, Marcus saw the figure framed in different positions: one moment he was standing with hands clenching the balustrade, shoulders hunched in fierce concentration; the next he was lunging first to the left then to the right, fists smiting the air; the next he was bolt upright, arms pinned to his sides, as if briefly immobilised by frustration. And all these changes in posture were accompanied by an unbroken soliloquy that ranged in tone between triumph and despair, paying visit to every shade of emotion in between. He was clearly engaged in a running commentary on the battle, aware that none of his troops could hear the instructions he bellowed, but unable to contain himself none the less.

Slipping between the curtains, Marcus approached Titus. So obsessed was the Imperator with the spectacle unfolding before him, that he heard nothing. The aëro: cruisers continued to engage one another as best they could. Unable to manoeuvre freely due to the closeness of the citadel and the danger of ramming into it, they sought to elude enemy ordnance by gaining or losing height and tilting their cannons up or down accordingly. Coils of dark smoke – the residue of cannon fire – writhed between them, slow to disperse, besmirching the otherwise flawless winter sky. The continued violence in the fields and on the walls below lay out of sight but could be heard in the form of a muted roaring sound that seemed to be constantly rising in pitch, without ever quite reaching its conclusion.

Marcus focused on Titus's back and broad shoulders: an inverted triangle of tightly packed muscle. Moving closer still, he allowed hatred to devour him at last. Since first being plunged into Daldriadh, he had kept it more or less at bay within him, drawing upon it only when he needed an extra burst of resolve to accomplish some near-impossible uncomfortable task. Now though, he felt his whole body become merely a vessel for the rage he felt: an implement of vengeance, clad in flesh braced with bone. He drew his sword. It would be so easy to slip the blade between Titus's shoulders while he remained distracted by the colossal discord in the air and on the mountainside. But he felt compelled to see his nemesis's face.

"*Titus,*" he said emphatically.

XXI.

Face to Face

The figure before him froze and fell silent. While the rest of the body remained motionless, the head twisted round. In his agitated state, which lent an unreal sharpness to all his senses, it seemed to Marcus than it turned just a fraction further than was natural, like the head of a predatory bird. The face, in three-quarters profile, was as sharply defined as Marcus remembered it. The expression it wore was less than joyous already, but the effort required to survey Marcus over a hunched shoulder drew the corners of the mouth down even further.

Eventually Titus swung his whole body round, feet planted well apart, as if he were still standing on the unpredictably tilting deck of an aëro:cruiser, as he had been when Marcus last saw him.

What amazed Marcus was how normal Titus looked. He had brooded on the elder man's perfidy and dreamed of revenge through sunless days and starless nights in Daldriadh, as well as on the long climb back through the grey fathoms of cloud. As he did so, Titus had, in his imagination, become monstrous. His features had acquired a brutish cast: the brow lower, the bridge of the nose thicker, the teeth fang-like, the chin more prominent. Yet here he was – now almost lounging against the balustrade, having composed himself after the shock of Marcus's appearance – barely altered. Indeed, his deep-set eyes, which looked like frozen slivers of the winter sky behind him, were lit with exactly the same droll indulgence that he had displayed on so many of their previous sparring sessions. Marcus felt much more disturbed by this apparent equanimity than he would have been if Titus had dropped into a crouch and snarled at him. It made the Impetrator's reaction to his reappearance impossible to interpret – and his next move, by extension, impossible to predict. Marcus did notice, however, that his left hand had inched discreetly from the balustrade to rest its fingertips on the hilt of his sword.

Silence prevailed between them for a few more moments. Marcus's natural instinct was to say "I'm back" or "I've returned," but this seemed self-evident. Oddly enough, he didn't much care about dying at Titus's hand, but he did care intensely about appearing foolish before him. Yet what words could open an encounter freighted with so much intense emotion? What greeting could adequately convey what he felt: a mixture of hatred, fear, perplexity, humiliation and sense of trust betrayed?

Eventually Titus extracted him from his quandary by addressing him in a nonchalant tone, as if resuming a conversation they'd been having only a few moments before.

"When I saw your vessel plunge towards the water in that other world," he said, gesturing over his shoulder towards the cloudscape. "After the cables snapped and we were lifted back up, I did wonder... I wondered if it was possible that you might survive. But I suppose I assumed that any attempt to return here would dispose of you satisfactorily enough... even if you hadn't already been devoured by some nameless beast."

"Perhaps I'm more resourceful than you thought," replied Marcus.

"Oh I had few doubts about your resourcefulness... I taught you, remember?"

Marcus flinched at this; he didn't want to recollect any part of their former relationship that might temper his resolve now.

"And now I'm back," he said.

"Indeed... Doubtless athirst for revenge and tormented by the acute injustice of it all."

"Something like that."

"Well, I can hardly blame you... You know, if I really were as void of all decency as you obviously seem to think, I would slit your throat with one stroke right now and let you watch your life's blood ebb away without ever knowing why any of this happened."

"I think that would satisfy you even less than it would me," Marcus pointed out.

Titus smiled.

"Perhaps you're right."

He narrowed his eyes, scrutinising Marcus in greater detail.

"You *have* changed, haven't you? I mean the moment I set eyes on you I noticed you'd acquired a bit more length of limb, a bit more breadth in the torso... But it's more than that, isn't it? I can see it in your eyes."

Concerned that this oblique flattery might just be a gambit to distract him, Marcus kept one eye on Titus's sword arm while asking, "What do you mean?"

"Oh you were an amiable enough youth, don't get me wrong. But you were so impenetrably *naïve*. It's an insufferable characteristic, you know; an affront to those of us who're forced to shed their innocence so much sooner. In your case, it clamoured with every callow phrase you uttered to be destroyed."

"Are you actually suggesting that I should be *grateful* to you for what you did to me?"

Titus leaned forward slightly.

"Don't pretend that you're not aware of it; don't pretend that you can't feel the change that's come over you... I know *exactly* how you must have reacted to being marooned in that other world when you began to realise how privileged your former life had been. I can just imagine you sentimentalising your fellow survivors as 'comrades'; insisting, in earnest tones, that you shouldn't be treated as special in any way. As if your former status was a sin that you could absolve yourself of by denying it." He snorted. "I must say I'm glad to have been spared so gruesome a spectacle."

Marcus flushed. There was a mortifying amount of accuracy in all this. Yet he sensed that it was being said precisely in order to unsettle him and therefore distract his gaze from those long, bony fingers, still resting lightly on the sword hilt. Having deduced this, he found it easier to swallow his anger. His whole body felt like a clenched fist, impelling him towards violence. But he held back. There was more he wanted to understand.

"And my father, did you reserve just as much contempt for him?" he asked.

"Your father, your father..." said Titus, in a ruminative tone, as if the King was, to him, a marginal figure, already fading from his recollection. Marcus found this pretence of vagueness far more insulting than any of the previous comments he had endured about his own flaws.

"Antior was a cipher," Titus resumed. "The last in a long and inglorious line of figureheads with nothing to offer but emollient manners and a refined appearance. He represented everything that had held us back for so long. He dwelt in a cocoon of privilege, yet tradition had granted him the right to meddle in any affairs of state that took his interest, no matter how remote from his own experience. The territorial gains we made in the Hemispheric Wars he handed away like a child who has received too many gifts on his birthday. That was when I realised we would never endure with him presiding over us. All the 'breeding' he was supposed to possess had bred out any trace of courage and ambition."

Once again Marcus was forced to restrain himself. Since the first shell had been fired upon the *Noble Quest* by the *Valorous Mission* he had been engaged in a long, miserable process of coming to terms with the fact that his father had been something less than perfect. Having wrestled with this notion during the long struggle to return home, he had learned, if not come to terms with it, then at least live with it.

The inheritor of centuries of rigid protocol, Antior had been protected by status from appreciating what life was like in the over-populous stew of the citadel's lowest layers – or even realising what mutinous sentiments were brewing among the members of the Kabal. But this failing had not been deliberate. He'd simply not had the chance Marcus had been granted to see the world from a wholly different perspective and profit from that change. It was not his fault. None the less, Titus's assessment of the King, honed through years of increasingly sour observation, felt like a succession of blades plunged into Marcus's heart.

His voice shook, but the power of the emotion he felt was galvanic, lending him renewed energy.

"I've lived amongst the humblest of all the citizens for the past month," he said. "It's true my father never went there, never sought to learn about their lives. But nor have you Titus. And I can assure you, their lot isn't improved through being part of your 'strong' new citadel – far from it. Not matter what you tell me about my father, all I hear is you trying to justify your own vainglory and the love you seem to have for inflicting pain on people. But you'll thwart yourself: your ambition will be its own undoing…. Look behind you, it's happening already."

Titus didn't look round, even though the sound of continued battle in the sky grew stronger with every passing moment. Nor did his body language betray – in even the slightest respect – any hint of diminished self-belief. But Marcus did notice the last drop of affected benevolence drain from his gaze.

"Bold words indeed from a young man poised on the brink of perdition," he said. "Whatever happens out there, you don't imagine you can prevail against me, do you? Surely you can't have failed to notice how unequal we are in size and strength?"

"I'll take my chances."

"Well then, at least we both know where we stand."

Marcus took a few paces back from Titus and drew his sword.

"Yes," he replied.

Titus nodded and drew his own sword.

"So be it," he said. His tone was sorrowful, but only in the sense of conveying regret at the amount of effort that killing Marcus would involve. Otherwise, he seemed eager for the chance to shed blood.

They began to circle one another. The positions they assumed bore eloquent testimony to their different levels of confidence. Marcus gripped his sword with both hands, his arms rigidly extended, the blade vertical. He crouched slightly too, bidding every muscle in his body to be as responsive as possible. Titus held his sword in one hand, the blade raised at an angle of only partial preparedness. In contrast to Marcus's prowling gait, he edged sideways in an appraising manner, as if wandering around a small statue whose unimpressive workmanship would benefit from a few choice strokes to cut away a chunk here or there.

This process continued for a few more moments. Then a stray shell from the Kabal aëro:cruisers' fight with the Selenopolitan warship slammed into the Palace wall, just a few yards below the balcony. The resultant explosion seemed to shock both Titus and Marcus into action, precipitating them towards one another. Their first clash of sword blades sent reverberations through the whole of Marcus's body. He was barely able to master them. He felt his legs buckle but willed them not to give way. Leaping back, just out of the circumference of Titus' sweeping sword arm, he was better prepared for their second collision, but it still jarred him painfully.

It swiftly became apparent to Marcus that there was no way he could prevail against Titus through direct confrontation. His only hope was to exploit the agility his size had lent him, dodging each feint or thrust until his larger opponent tired. Only then might he be able to offer a thrust of his own that Titus would not be fast enough to repel. So defensive a strategy did nothing to slake his thirst for revenge; indeed all his instincts revolted against it. But he realised that the only other option was a swift and painful death.

And so the duel continued, weaving its way across the balcony, back into the Throne Room, then out onto the balcony again. At no point did Titus seem to entertain the idea that he might be slain by his smaller, younger foe. But as Marcus continued to elude his blade, in a manner which forced him into the most awkward manoeuvres possible, his air of complacency ebbed slightly. His strokes, almost negligent before, grew firmer. His breathing became more laboured and his features assumed an expression of perturbed inconvenience, perspiration gathering in the furrows of his brow.

Though Titus's increased focus on his sword craft made him even more dangerous, part of Marcus welcomed no longer feeling condescended to. In spite of this, however, there were moments when his stomach curdled with fear, so close did he come to sustaining a mortal wound. Once Titus managed to pin him against one of the fluted columns that stood on either side of the balcony where it joined the Palace wall. He then swung his blade sideways with scarcely credible force, as if planning not only to behead his victim but to fell the column itself like a tree trunk. Marcus slid down and out of the way just in time – and so the pursuit continued.

At another point, Marcus found himself bent back over the balustrade. Titus loomed over him, sword now gripped in both hands and raised high. Only by twisting rapidly from side to side was Marcus able to avoid the blade, which clanged fruitlessly against the marble each time, barely an inch to the left or right of him. Eventually he managed to squirm free and roll across the balcony, springing to his feet again in preparation for the next onslaught.

Chastened at how recklessly he had just flirted with death through being cornered by his opponent not once but twice, Marcus now attempted to remain in the centre of the balcony, with plenty of room for manoeuvre on all sides. He drew guarded satisfaction – the only kind available to him right now – from the fact that Titus seemed to be growing more florid, though no less murderous in intent.

"It is ironic," commented the Imperator, during a brief pause in the duel. Though he wasn't quite gasping for air his breathing was a good deal more laboured than before.

"What is?" asked Marcus.

"Here I am, seeking to kill you, at the precise moment when you've finally grown into someone I could respect. You've acquired a stature – a *substance* – that you never possessed before. It almost seems a shame to extinguish such rare qualities in someone so young."

"Almost?" asked Marcus.

"*Almost.*"

Their blades clashed again, with a force that was more equal, now that Titus had tired somewhat. This was followed by a flurry of strokes, during which both of them sustained glancing flesh wounds. The elegance of the swordplay diminished from moment to moment and assumed instead a ragged, feral quality. Both combatants perspired freely, struggling to maintain a firm grip on their weapons. At one point they backed away from one another, gasping, and Titus said, "It needn't be like this."

"Like what?" responded Marcus.

"It's clear that you have a gift for leadership. You could join me. Our Kabal could extend its rule across the entire hemisphere. People in every citadel would pay homage to our names – mine and yours. What a glorious apotheosis for one so young! And it could become a reality, if only you would let go of the past."

"The past in which you murdered my father and tried to kill me? *That* past?"

"I set you free… I liberated you from stultifying tradition – from becoming a mere vessel for all Antior's outmoded principles, created in his own insipid image."

Again Marcus shook with more than mere indignation. When he heard his father so belittled it stoked the murderous rage that smouldered within him.

"Don't ever speak his name again," he said, barely able to get the words out.

Ignoring this warning, Titus with evident difficulty, assembled his features into a sympathetic expression far more chilling than the mocking scowl he had worn before.

"I taught you, Marcus," he said. "I equipped you with the skill you've used to survive. Every feat of intrepidity you owe partly to me... Think of all those hours of tutelage while Antior was absent. I've been more of a father to you in many ways than he ever was. You practically conceded it yourself once. And I can continue to be so..."

He extended his free hand, fingers outspread. He was so unused to making any kind of solicitous gesture that his movements seemed painfully awkward, almost arthritic. But Marcus could bear no more false words or gestures. With a howl of anguish, he aimed a wild, diagonal stroke at Titus. His blade opened a deep gash in the palm of his foe's outstretched hand. Wincing, but emitting no sound louder than a grunt, Titus snatched back his hand. He sucked on the wound – a gesture that left his mouth smeared with blood – and then hurled himself at Marcus.

In an instant they were savagely embroiled with one another again. Perhaps because he had initiated it in so reckless a manner, Marcus felt himself at an immediate disadvantage in the latest bout. Much more frequently than before, he had to fend off thrusts he couldn't avoid.

As they fought on, events in the citadel's airspace reached a decisive point. The Kabal aëro:cruisers outgunned their Selenopolitan opponent and had positioned themselves parallel to it on port and starboard sides to alternate their fire upon its deck. Yet they themselves were subjected to constant bombardment by the rebels on the landing stage, who launched one burning ornithopter after another at them. Enough of these found their target to clad the right hand Kabal vessel in a pelt of flame. In spite of this, its cannons continued to blaze at anything within range. It was like a blinded predator – besieged on all sides by threatening sounds, conscious that it was more vulnerable than ever, and therefore all the more eager to assert its dominance. A fair proportion of the shells it released pummelled the Palace walls at random.

Eventually, however, the flames that had enveloped its air sacs began to gnaw at its rigging too. They leaped between different sections with restless appetite. First one then another lanyard snapped. The cannons recoiled one more time but failed to re-emerge from their casings. Revolving slowly, the vessel drifted. Then, as if drawn towards its tormentor by a helpless attraction, it collided with the Selenopolitan warship.

The force of this event jarred both vessels. But in the Kabal aëro:cruiser's case it finally severed the last charred sections of rigging. Deprived of any support, the hull plummeted, stern first, dragged down by the weight of its aft castle. It clipped the edge of the orchards – taking a ragged, semi-circular bite out of the trees. Then, instead of pausing, as the Mercanteer had done, it heeled over into the banked cloud, vanishing within seconds. Its untethered air sacs, meanwhile, soared at liberty into the stratosphere, still ablaze and shedding lustre as they went.

The other Kabal vessel, having received fewer strikes from the burning ornithopters, had moved slightly further off, nudging towards the citadel itself, though its cannons continued to fire at its Selenopolitan foe with scarcely diminished fervour.

On the balcony, Marcus was sent reeling backwards by a rapid series of blows. Behind every one of them, now that he had been rejected, lay the force of Titus's redoubled enmity. The Imperator swung his sword as if he was determined not merely to dispose of his opponent but to hack him into very small pieces. Marcus felt just as much enmity himself. But there was no denying the fact that Titus still had the advantage. Though his face was crimson and wisps of steam issued from the collar of his tunic as he fought on, his sheer bulk gave him a momentum that fatigue could do little to diminish. Again and again his blade descended with scarcely believable force. Finally, unable to resist the onslaught any longer, Marcus was driven to the floor. His skull cracked against the marble and his sword spun away under the curtains to lodge in some recess of the Throne Room.

Sprawled at Titus's feet, head throbbing, Marcus blinked rapidly. He had barely collected himself before he saw Titus's sword yet again descending towards him like an executioner's axe, gaining solidity and definition as it approached through his blurred vision. He rolled to the left just in time to avoid a partial beheading – but the blade left a neat incision in his ear lobe on the last stage of its descent.

Copious amounts of blood soaking his shoulder, Marcus spent the next few minutes rolling desperately back and forth as the blade continued to plunge, spitting chips of marble every time it hit the floor. Soon, however, he realised that no matter how energetic his writhing, he couldn't hope to postpone the inevitable for much longer.

Despair was just about to enfold him, when, face down, he noticed two deep cracks in the floor advancing towards him from either side of the balustrade, where it met the Palace wall. The relentless shelling had clearly done its work with the masonry supporting the balcony – in particular the two thick columns on which it sat. As erratic as the path of each crack was, the speed of their progress left little doubt that they would meet very soon.

Wholly focused on his victim, Titus remained unaware of this new development. But as Marcus rolled over twice more, he saw that the cracks had grown closer still, like arms groping towards each other. The only question now was whether their joining would create an event decisive enough to save him. With this thought uppermost in his mind, he began trying to shuffle back towards the Throne Room. Very soon, however, he realised that he hadn't enough strength left to do this while still avoiding the slashing blade. He had to think of some other way to distract Titus.

So, in spite of scarcely being able to draw breath, he managed to choke out a few hoarse words.

"It seems like I'm no match for you after all," he said.

Titus paused, his sword upraised. Though re-energised by the awareness that he was about to prevail at last, he was clearly unable to resist a moment's gloating. He licked lips as he savoured the prospect.

"I'm glad to have afforded you that insight at least," he replied. "I hope now you'll die with a decent sense of your own limitations – as is only proper."

Nodding, Marcus rose unsteadily to his feet. He now stood on the other side of the advancing cracks from Titus. Glancing down, he saw that they were just inches from creating a single fissure. His legs trembled at the thought of the impending gambit. He returned his gaze to Titus's smirking face. His own features conveyed a doleful acceptance of the inevitable. Many men far less arrogant than Titus would not have found it difficult to misunderstand what the 'inevitable' actually was.

Marcus tilted his head back, exposing his throat.

"Please... give me a clean death," he said.

With the unhurried movements of someone whose dominance easily allowed him to be obliging, Titus adjusted his grip on the hilt of his sword for the final stroke. At his feet the newly created fissure began to widen.

"You were correct about one thing if no other," Titus told him. "Now we both truly know where we stand."

Marcus allowed himself the faintest of smiles.

"*I* do, Titus," he replied. "But do *you*?"

Barely registering this question, Titus swung at Marcus' throat. Yet even with his sword arm fully extended, the tip of the blade did not make contact as he had expected. He frowned, more puzzled than alarmed at first. Then he glanced down. A full-throated chasm was now forming between the outward tilting balcony and the Palace wall. His eyes widened with horror. But his unslaked thirst for Marcus's blood seemed to eclipse any sense of self-protection. Struggling to keep his footing, he aimed another, much wilder stoke at his young foe.

Marcus, however, hurled himself out of range, enveloped by the curtained entrance to the Throne Room. Still swinging his sword wildly, with a look of fulminant outrage contorting his features, Titus toppled backwards against the balustrade. In doing so, he imparted a decisive load to the rest of the balcony, which tilted at an even sharper angle. Its supporting columns pivoting, it sheared away completely from the Palace wall and plummeted.

The last thing Marcus saw was Titus glancing briefly below, then, in a final act of desperation, casting his sword aside and vaulting over the balustrade. Marcus guessed that he did this not out of an instinct for self-preservation but rather as a final gesture of conceit: he didn't want his broken body further mangled amid shattered masonry – a humiliating resting place for the self-styled "Imperator."

But Marcus was far too exhausted to speculate any further. Unable to believe that he had not only survived but prevailed, he lay back on the floor, eyes closed. After only a few seconds' stillness, he began to grow aware for the first time of just how many bruises, torn muscles, strained ligaments, cuts and grazes he had sustained. Each pinpoint of pain seemed to radiate outward, joining up with all the others to swathe his whole body. And the more aware he became of them, the more they hurt, as if petitioning, with increasing stridency, for his attention.

He was just absorbing the fact that the sounds of discord on the walls and fields below seemed to be diminishing in volume, when, through his closed lids, he sensed an abrupt darkening above him. It was as if a hand had been passed over his face. He opened his eyes. What he saw made him sit up and gasp, instantly indifferent to all his aches and pains.

Just a few yards away, a mass of clustered air sacs – their canvas taut and creaking – was rising to fill the entire view of the sky framed by the archway. They looked impossibly close; he could see every wrinkle and blemish that veined their contours, as if he were viewing human skin through a magnifying lens.

The air sacs belonged to the other Kabal aëro:cruiser: the one that had somehow avoided being destroyed by the rebels' hurtling fireballs. The collapse of the balcony had allowed it to manoeuvre itself parallel to the Palace wall. But as Marcus continued to gaze at its rising contours, astonishment was replaced by anguish.

There, hanging from one of the looped ropes that were woven all round the air sacs – binding them together and allowing them to keep their shape – was Titus. His leap from the balcony had been no valedictory act after all. He must have spotted the aëro:cruiser approaching, or at least heard the whine of its labouring impellers, and seen his chance for salvation. Now he clung to it, struggling to swing himself like a pendulum towards the next loop of rope and from there to one of the lanyards. Having reached it, he would be able to shin down to the gunnels and leap onto the deck. His face was turned away, but Marcus could well imagine the look it wore: one of relief, tinged with triumph, which would soon harden into his usual mask of arrogance.

Sitting in the archway, legs dangling over the precipice where the balcony had been, Marcus continued to watch this dismally unfolding spectacle. The crew of the Kabal aëro:cruiser were assembled along the gunnels, leaning back to peer up at Titus and shouting encouragement to him. Their voices somehow contrived to sound raucous yet at the same time convey cringing respect. Having almost accomplished the rescue of their leader, they seemed in no hurry to quit the scene of conflict, in spite of the fact that the Selenopolitan warship was now rapidly approaching, its ramming post pointed towards them. Marcus guessed that they assumed their opponent wouldn't fire on them while they remained so close to the Palace, lest the shells inadvertently kill any rebel occupants who were struggling to regain control of it.

Though Titus landed heavily and gracelessly on the foredeck of the Kabal vessel, his subordinates greeted him with cheers and hastened forward to help him up. As they did so, the aëro:cruiser continued to rise, further disclosing the sleek contours of its hull towards prow and stern. Also rising into view was the threat of its many squat, short-barrelled cannons.

Marcus's every instinct told him to put as much distance as possible between himself and it, but he was mesmerised by the sheer scale of the destructive power it conveyed. He also felt a strange debility come over him. In spite of how fiercely he'd fought in the past quarter hour – and how roused his blood still was – the dismal realisation that his nemesis was slipping from his grasp left him suddenly void of purpose and energy. And into this void a sluggish, low-level death wish imposed itself. He greeted its advent without surprise or alarm. If he couldn't achieve the revenge he'd so long dreamed of, did he really want to live any more? And if he didn't, was there really any point in avoiding what was about to happen?

Whatever the reason for his immobility, he continued to stare as Titus strode across the deck, barking orders, then turned back to face the archway. Their eyes locked. The air between them crackled with the discharge of their unresolved enmity. Though triumphant, Titus seemed to derive less sneering amusement from the fact than Marcus had expected. His expression was even tinged with a grudging respect. But there wasn't the faintest trace of mercy in it.

Titus quit the gunnels with a wordless salute and directly below him the snub nose of one of the cannons began to retreat into its square-cut housing. Appalled at the prospect of being left unavenged, Marcus didn't notice the cannon's movement until almost the last moment. But he knew only too well what it portended.

He hurled himself sideways into a near corner of the Throne Room and sought shelter behind an ornate table just as the cannon discharged. A shell streaked past at shoulder height where he had just been standing. Trailing cinders, it slammed into the far wall. Within seconds, the room was filled with a choking maelstrom of debris and plaster dust. The section of the wall where the shell had impacted was replaced by a ragged hole. The glass dome shivered and went opaque, then multi-coloured glass rained down on the centre of the room. Several of the statues were sent sprawling over the floor. The largest shower of debris strafed the throne itself, shredding the upholstery and toppling it from the dais.

Curled up as tightly as possible, hands clasped over the back of his head, Marcus huddled in the corner of the room, absolutely motionless, for a few more seconds. Then, very gingerly, he unfolded himself. The plaster dust was already beginning to disperse – escaping through the shattered dome. He had felt debris glance off his back and patted himself down with some wariness, but he seemed to have escaped serious injury. His hair, however, was caked with dust that cascaded down his neck in tiny rivulets whenever he moved his head. But the most apparent effect of the explosions on him was that he had gone deaf – or rather, he could hear nothing other than a high-pitched whine.

Disorientated, he staggered back to the archway and peered round it, tensed to leap aside in case the cannons were about to fire again. But instead he was presented with a clear view of the sky. Titus's aëro:cruiser had peeled away from the citadel and was now heading southward, rapidly gaining speed, the blades of its impellers a blur. Marcus could just make out Titus himself standing at the prow beside the pilot, the staunch certitude of his posture unmistakable. But the Selenopolitan warship was swiftly drawing level. Summoning what Marcus guessed was every last scrap of ordnance aboard, its crew loosed a devastating broadside. The shells pummelled every section of the Titus's aëro:cruiser, including its air sacs.

It heeled over sharply. Crew members fell from its starboard side; the decks all along the port side were exposed. Punctured in innumerable places, the air sacs began to collapse. Just before they did so fully, Marcus caught his last glimpse of Titus – still at the prow, gripping the railing; unflinching in the acceptance of his fate. Then the yards of deflated canvas wound themselves around the hull like a burial shroud and the aëro:cruiser vanished into the cloudscape.

In spite of feeling smothered by exhaustion, Marcus had remained standing in the archway and even leaned out, with slender regard for safety, to have a better view of Titus's demise in all its inexorable grandeur. The desire to see it as clearly as possible had seemed to place invisible hands beneath his armpits. Their grip as warm and strong as his father's had always been, they kept him upright for the duration of the vessel's foundering. As soon as it vanished, however, his body seemed – for the first time in more than a month – to comprehend the fact that he no longer required anything from it. With the last particle of strength he possessed, he hauled himself back from the precipice. Then his legs crumpled beneath him like dry straw and he collapsed.

He had done it; he had prevailed. The realisation came stealthily upon him, bringing no joy in its wake. Everything that had happened to him – the loss of his father, the perfidy of Titus, the discovery of a new world beneath the clouds – had left him too spent of emotion to summon anything other than a weary sense of relief. All he knew for sure was that his old life – an illusory haven of peace and security – was over. As for the possibility of a new life, one lacking the certainties of the past, but lacking also its abiding solitude… well, it remained as uncertain as ever.

With this thought barely formed in his brain he passed out, his skull saved from cracking open on the marble floor by the newly arrived Rhea, who, having finally fought her way to the Throne Room, dashed across it just in time to grab his shoulders and ease him down into unconsciousness.

XXII.

Lost and Gained

One month later – on the day of the hibernal equinox – Marcus stood on the edge of the main landing stage, looking out over the cloudscape. Its ever-shifting terrain, raked by the wind, was covered in the familiar architecture of its winter state: twisting towers, swollen buttresses and crazily leaning arches. Whole cloud bergs detached themselves and cruised along with the prevailing winds. Occasionally, their paths would intersect with Heliopolis, sealing it for several hours in a grey opacity, which left every exterior surface beaded with moisture. And all of this occurred beneath a dome of higher, thinner cloud that covered the sky.

The architecture of the citadel itself was slowly being repaired. On the landing stage close to where Marcus stood, craters were still being filled in. And as he lowered his eyes to the walls shelving away below him, he could see teams of workers collecting up shattered chunks of masonry. The ravaged battlements were having to be patched up as far as possible from debris, stuck together with loam. Further down, in the fields, charred trees were being uprooted and seeds planted in the cavities their roots left behind. As a consequence of all this activity, Heliopolis was just beginning to look restored – albeit to a somewhat dilapidated version of its former self.

In the immediate aftermath of the uprising, all had been confusion. Yet Marcus remembered none of it. With the help of the rebels who had finally managed to scale the Palace walls, Rhea had carried him to his bed. There, under the influence of a potent sleeping draught, he had remained unconscious for two whole days. Upon waking, he remained swaddled at first in the illusion that the events of the past month had not taken place. But reality soon intervened, in the form of countless aches that swarmed

over his body when he rose and shuffled out into the Palace
corridors. He hadn't ventured far before he encountered
one of the Administrators, who was hastening towards the
Cabinet chamber on some obscure errand. Taking one look
at Marcus's hunched posture and the wound on his shoulder
that had already started to bleed again, the Administrator
ushered him back to bed before summoning Rhea, Theus
and Magnis.

They arrived looking pensive. Yet at the same time there
was something in the quickness of their movements that
showed they were still energised by the recent victory over
the Kabal. In measured tones, respectful of his ability to
absorb such news, they confirmed his fears. Asperia and
Synvadis had indeed perished – sacrificed, along with all
the latter's fellow Ministers, to Titus's paranoia, which
had apparently grown like a canker during his brief and
inglorious reign.

Marcus sensed pain at hearing this, but he didn't really
feel it – not at first anyway. It was as if someone had slid a
blade into part of his body where the nerves were already
dead. He knew that in time he would grieve for Asperia in
particular. But at the moment he was too worn out, both
physically and emotionally. Instead, he simply added her to
the lengthening roll call of people who had departed early
from his life – and did so with the sobering realisation that
a fourth or fifth bereavement, though terribly sad, could
never have the impact of a first. A series of images flashed
through his mind, depicting her imperious but always
loving authority, and he paid silent tribute to them. At the
same time, however, he sensed that he would, eventually,
be able to accept her death without being crippled by grief
because his thoughts and feelings were no longer focused
on his old life in Heliopolis. He had set off on his journey
from the shoreline in Daldriadh to regain that life, but his
intentions had changed along the way.

So there were to be no tearful reunions. In some
treacherous corner of his heart he felt almost relieved. If
as Asperia had once told him, physicians speculated that

person had only so many heartbeats inside them, did they also have only so many tears? Were that so, he felt as if he had shed a lifetime's supply already.

Instead of weeping, therefore, he sat up in bed and listened to Rhea and the others report what had happened over the past couple of days. Mindful that no such joy was available to him, they mentioned being reunited with their own families as briefly as possible, though they were unable to conceal their exquisite relief at the fact. They went into much more detail when it came to describing the changes occurring throughout the citadel. Already, they reported, there was increased traffic between the different layers. The upward surge of humanity during the battle seemed to have erased the barriers that had kept everyone in their place over so many centuries. Now, Artisans moved freely wherever they were needed, using their skills to help with repairs. The Farmers, so accustomed to cleaving to the foundations of Heliopolis, were somewhat more reluctant to trespass upon its upper reaches. But even they were gradually being coaxed out of their layer by the assurance that their physical strength and adeptness with tools were crucial to the task of restoration.

"Brebix and Ampliata have set an excellent example in this respect," said Magnis. "They seem fascinated by exploring the rest of the citadel – and not at all daunted."

Marcus nodded.

"I'm glad. Please tell them to come and visit me with the children. I'd love to see them again."

"Of course."

Rhea went on to report that no one had really begun to think about the details of how Heliopolis's democracy would actually work: elections, a new style of government and so forth.

"Though with regard to a Head of State, the whole populace seems to consider you their natural figurehead," Rhea told Marcus. Seeing his unconvinced expression, she added hurriedly, "But of course you must decide for yourself what path you want to choose. It's entirely up to you."

In the meantime – she went on to explain – she, Theus and Magnis had been asked to form a kind of interim authority, supported by the most senior Administrators, to oversee the early stages of rebuilding Heliopolis.

"Now that they've recovered from the discord and upheaval of battle, our Admins seem positively enthused by having some real work to do at last," Theus told Marcus with a smile.

As for the surviving members of the Kabal, they had been corralled into a recess of the Factorium, where they currently languished – neither penned nor mistreated, but kept under constant guard none the less. There had been talk throughout Heliopolis of putting them to death. But the current plan was to send them into exile on one of the uninhabited mountain ranges in the north of the hemisphere. There, furnished with enough basic supplies to get them started, they might just stand a chance of surviving – their struggle to do so being a form of purgatory, from which they would hopefully emerge having repented their past misdeeds. In the meantime they were to be put to work each day, helping to erase the damage they had wrought.

Marcus listened to all of this with keen attention. It was impossible not to derive pleasure from such news of reform and repair. But, once again, he felt inescapably detached from it all.

This fact became apparent to Rhea the following day when she called by his apartments once again, to check on his wounds.

"I can't help but worry about what will happen in Daldriadh," he said by way of greeting, as she pulled up a chair beside his bed.

"What do you mean?" asked Rhea.

"Well, we found our way into that world by accident – it was a sheer quirk of fate that allowed us to survive the descent. But now that we've defeated Titus, sure enough trade will start again. Our aëro:cruisers will visit other citadels. And no matter how hard we try to keep it a secret, some crew members on a layover will talk about it. If they go anywhere south, a single flask of Brescian mead will loosen their tongues. So word will spread; it'll spread faster than we can imagine."

He looked at her. Though she had listened carefully, she seemed not yet to have gathered the implication behind what he was saying.

"Think about it," he continued. "What a temptation for some ambitious Head of State! All over the hemisphere there are citadels like ours with just a few hundred acres of solid, fertile land around them and limited seams of minerals in the rock they're founded on. It's only through trade that any of us survives."

"That is true," conceded Rhea. "We won't be able to restore the Palace, for instance, unless we import a lot more Tholian marble."

"Exactly," continued Marcus, nodding. "Now though there's the prospect of a new world, of unlimited territory, almost inexhaustible resources to be plundered – and I don't just mean in Daldriadh. Surely it won't be long before Cloudfarers from another citadel make an attempt to descend there. At first they might just want to harvest and cultivate a relatively small patch of land. But no ruler with any ambition will leave it at that for long. They'll seek to conquer a larger and larger area and prevent any other citadel from encroaching on it... And what about those who live there? Remember how the Nullmaurs seemed to you when you first encountered them? Stunted, pallid, unevolved, sub-human? The rulers of the Northern Citadels sacrificed thousands of Cloudfarers – their own and others – to try and gain control of the trading currents. What would the native races beneath the clouds be to them? Slave labour, pure and simple. Little more than animals to be worked without respite: kept in cages and fed a few scraps."

"Would any of us worry about seeing the Nullmaurs brought to heel like that?" asked Rhea "At least they would be some sort of use, instead of a scourge on the people our comrades have ended up forced to protect."

"But that isn't the point, is it?" countered Marcus. "However brutish and loathsome they might be, land-dwellers like the Nullmaurs still have rights, like every living creature. We might wish to see them banished from Daldriadh, but we can't allow them to be enslaved or wiped out. If we accepted that, what's the point of striving to create a better life for everyone here in the Polis?

"I suppose we would be fighting for human rights in one place and ignoring them in another," she said.

"But it goes beyond even that," added Marcus. "Just imagine for a moment. One citadel gains control over a piece of territory – encloses it, mines it, and transports the produce back up to support its people. Over time it becomes more self-sufficient, trades less. Other citadels witness this. They're jealous of its independence. They feel compelled to do the same. They seek their own territories below the cloudscape – which expand, of course. Soon the territory of one citadel encroaches on that of another. Border disputes begin. There's competition for the most fertile land, the areas most densely populated with slave labour. All across the hemisphere they're fighting over territorial rights. Every citadel is at odds with one another…"

Rhea nodded solemnly.

"It'll be a bloodbath – a conflict both above and below the cloudscape. It'll make the Hemispheric Wars look like a squabble in the Juvenum."

"Yes. And who will suffer most?" asked Marcus, with a rising note of emotion in his voice. "The smallest, the most vulnerable – the Eihlans and other races like them."

Since then, however, events had rapidly moved on. A mere week after the defeat of Titus and the Kabal, two aëro: cruisers were dispatched – well-supplied and heavily armed – to seek out the Cloudfarers still marooned in Daldriadh and rescue both them and the Eihlans. Winter had deepened further since the end of the battle for Heliopolis. But it quickly became apparent that the citadel's nephologists had already, under orders from Titus, formulated a new method for descending into the cloud depths. The method exploited precisely the weather conditions that had once seemed to make a descent impossible. It involved flying high, almost into the mesosphere, above an already burgeoning tumult then descending into the eye of it – where, it was postulated, the air would remain calm. Earning Marcus's profound gratitude and admiration, two full crews of Cloudfarers volunteered immediately for this mission and embarked as soon as their vessels were ready. Only his still healing injuries prevented him from accompanying them.

The two aëro:cruisers had been absent for nearly a month now and Marcus was starting to worry. What if they had been unable to find a suitable tumult as a portal to Daldriadh and had instead been blown off course? What if the method of descent had proved misconceived? What if they had been unable to locate their comrades, or had done so only to discover that they and the Eihlans had perished?

All these possible disasters had swarmed constantly through his mind over the past few days, as he spent every hour of light limping back and forth across the landing stage and straining his eyes towards the western horizon.

How often in his life had he done this? Yet he could scarcely remember the person he had been when standing on the same spot a few months earlier. As a child he had watched the horizon so many times for the return of his father's aëro:cruiser, fervently hoping that it would not have strayed into the cloud depths. Today – as impossible as it would have seemed to his younger self – he longed to stray back into the cloud depths himself, in search of Breah and her family, before the chance of finding them slipped away.

Though his thoughts were focused almost wholly on the future, it was impossible not to reflect from time to time on the past as well, especially now that his perspective on almost everything had changed so much. His upbringing had sought to persuade him that the world was all pattern and purpose. He saw now that this was a delusion. Never again, he told himself, would he try to predict how life would turn out, or impose upon it any fixed expectations. The folly of doing so had become clear to him. You just had to cope as best you could with whatever fate dealt you, improvising (sometimes desperately) as you went along.

In the gloom of another late-afternoon, he was just beginning to resign himself to the idea that this day too would end in disappointment when he caught sight of an indistinct shape in the far distance. Presently it split into two and he was able to discern the unmistakable outlines of a pair of aëro:cruisers.

The instant he shouted to the labouring Cloudfarers scattered across the landing stage, they abandoned their repairs and made ready for the approaching vessels. Both floated in with a surreal lack of drama and settled gently into their designated berths. From his position at the hanger doors, looking up at their great hulls, Marcus couldn't see over the gunnels to discover who was on board. But as soon as the mooring lines had been secured, boarding planks were rolled into place amidships and a succession of figures – silhouetted against the great red globe of the setting sun – stepped onto them.

First came the vessels' crewmembers, looking more or less as upright in their bearing and vigorous in their movements as they had done when they departed. Then came their rescued comrades, much more hesitant and stooped. As they descended the boarding planks, Marcus recognised the faces he feared he would never see again: Tafril, Lucis, Persis, Amik, Jarrid and Denihr. He breathed a sigh of relief. Though unmistakably pale and haggard, they had all survived.

And then, last of all, came the Eihlans. Many could barely walk and had to be supported down the gangplanks by crewmembers. Set against the imperial scale of the surrounding architecture, they looked even more vulnerable than they had in Daldraidh.

As soon as the first of them emerged into view, Marcus began moving towards the moored aëro:cruisers. When he spotted Aònghas, cradling Eithné in his arms, he quickened his pace. And when he saw Breah unsteadily following Aònghas, holding her mother's hand, he broke into a run.

She had barely placed a foot on the landing stage when he gathered her up and hugged her tightly. Too exhausted to display even the slightest surprise, she allowed herself to nestle against him, wheezing softly. Overwhelmed by the reality of her presence – which exerted a power over him out of all proportion to her slender frame – he heard the Cloudfarers proudly narrating their rescue mission, but could barely register what they were saying. Only disjointed phrases reached him:

"…more than a week to get down safely…shed enough ballast to scout round just beneath the cloud base…nothing for ages…a few well-aimed bombs to seal up Nullmaurs' lair…*still* couldn't locate…streaks of light in distance… cross-shot bolts coated in sophorous, fired up like flares… found them in a cave…almost starving…all kinds of beasts prowling round…"

He looked up and smiled at them. He tried to speak but nothing came. All he knew was that they had delivered him the chance of a future – and for that no words of thanks could suffice.

Marcus thought the events of the past few months had rid him, once and for all, of every trace of naivety. It soon became apparent, though, that life would never exhaust its ability to yield up the unexpected. Breah and most of the other Eihlans had survived the ascent to Heliopolis. But to survive was not the same as to thrive. Put simply, the air was too thin for them. Their lives were not imperilled but they were robbed of all their strength. This effect was most evident among the young, who were normally the most vigorous. And who amongst them was the most vigorous of all?

A week after the Eihlans had arrived in the citadel, Marcus entered the Palace apartments where Breah was staying with her family. He found her installed in what had become her customary spot: seated beside the bedroom window, insulated against the winter's chill, but trying to get as much fresh air as possible into her lungs. He drew up a chair and sat beside her, taking her hand. She turned to look at him. Though her delicate, youthful features remained unchanged, her eyes were as dull and her movements as laboured as an old woman's. Given her chronic shortness of breath, they had not talked much over the preceding days. Yet the absence of words had forced them to communicate in a different way – through steady looks and gentle touches – that had already led them to a far deeper understanding of one another.

He gestured towards the cloudscape and asked, "Shall we go back?"

For a few moments an almost forgotten clarity came to her eyes and she gripped his hand as tightly as she was able in acknowledgement of the sacrifice he proposed making for her. She couldn't prosper in Heliopolis. But he possessed greater strength in the dense, invigorating air of Daldriadh. So they would return there and make the best of their lives together.

"Yes," she whispered.

A few days later he stood on the balcony of his apartments. It was only mid-afternoon, but the light had already started to fade. At his back, the archway leading to his drawing room was filled with the glow of tallow lamps, which softened its ornate design. Inside, comrades had gathered at his request for a belated celebration of their victory over the Kabal. The gathering was not triumphal; rather the atmosphere was one of quiet but profound relief that the uprising had been achieved with so little bloodshed. He had also used the event to announce his intentions to Rhea, Theus and Magnis. They had looked alarmed at first, then saddened. But they understood his reasons for his choice. And once he had assured them that he, Breah and the other Eihlans would not attempt their journey until the passing of winter, they had accepted it.

He gazed out at the cloudscape, as if trying to see the map of his future inscribed upon its churning surface. So much had been lost, yet so much gained too. He found it impossible to remember the person he had once been. All he knew was that in spite of the pride he felt at the changes wrought in Heliopolis and in spite of the love he felt for his world's panoramic beauty, the possibility, however slight, of true happiness dwelt in people not in places. Perhaps he would return to the citadel one day. But for now he had to forge a future elsewhere.

Reflecting on these things, he stayed out a while longer. Then, when the last shadows had brimmed up from troughs between the clouds and joined together to cover the whole expanse in darkness, he turned back toward the archway and allowed the soft glow and happy, murmurous chatter beyond to embrace him... for the time being at least.

The End

Printed in the United Kingdom by
Lightning Source UK Ltd., Milton Keynes
142034UK00001B/4/P